Castle Bravo

By

Karna Small Bodman

D0009498

Publisher Page
an Imprint of Headline Books, Inc.
Terra Alta, WV

Castle Bravo

By Karna Small Bodman

Publisher Page
P.O. Box 52, Terra Alta, WV 26764
www.PublisherPage.com
www.KarnaBodman.com

Tel/Fax: 800-570-5951
Email: mybook@headlinebooks.com
www.HeadlineBooks.com

Publisher Page is an imprint of Headline Books, Inc.

ISBN 978-0-938467-38-0 hard cover
ISBN 978-0-938467-45-8 paperback

Library of Congress Control Number: 2012936896

Bodman, Karna Small.
       Castle Bravo / Karna Small Bodman
       p. cm.
       ISBN 978-0-938467-38-0 hard cover
       ISBN 978-0-938467-45-8 paperback
       1. Communications—Fiction. 2. International Terrorism—Fiction. 3.
Washington (D.C.)—Fiction 4. Kazakhstan—Fiction.

PRINTED IN THE UNITED STATES OF AMERICA

For Taylor and Jim
...Who have a love of history...and international intrigue.

CASTLE BRAVO – CHARACTERS

The Principals

Tripp Adams, Vice President, GeoGlobal Oil & Gas
Pete Kalani, UCLA Student
Samantha Reid, Assistant to the President for Homeland Security
Dr. Cameron Talbot, Missile Defense Expert

White House Staff

Michael Benson, Chief of Staff
Ken Cosgrove, National Security Advisor
Hunt Daniels, Special Assistant to the President for Nuclear and
    Proliferation Issues
Max Federman, Assistant to the President for Political Affairs
Jayson Keller, Vice President of the United States
Angela Marconi, Special Assistant to the President for Public
    Liaison
Jim Shilling, Deputy Director, White House Office of Homeland
    Security
Joan Tillman, Administrative Assistant to Samantha Reid

Foreign Nationals

Sergei Baltiev, Opposition Leader in Kazakhstan
Nurlan Remizov, Exchange Student
Zhanar Remizov, Nurlan's Sister
Viktor Surleimenov, President of Kazakhstan

Others

William Ignatius, Secretary of Defense
Godfrey Nims, Lobbyist for GeoGlobal Oil & Gas
Jake Reid, Father of Samantha Reid

CASTLE BRAVO - The actual code name for a Top Secret U.S. Government project

ONE

The White House – Present Day

Could it happen here? Samantha Reid leaned over and studied the new classified report. It had been sitting on her desk in a special envelope when she arrived in the West Wing at 6:30 a.m.

The sun was just rising, creating wisps of light orange reflections on the Potomac River when she had pulled out of the garage below her Georgetown condo and headed toward The White House. She had been in a somber mood that morning as she mulled over the recent threats her Office of Homeland Security was investigating. *Why does every day feel like Monday?*

She had only been in the top job a few weeks and already it seemed that the tips, rumors and intel traffic were pouring in like some restless diluvial tide. There were concerns raised by the CDC about a biological attack using a new strain of virus. The Transportation Department had issued an alert about security on the Acela, the popular train that ran from Washington, D.C. to New York and then on to Boston. There were stories of bombs set to go off in the Lincoln Tunnel, threats of poisons in the food supply, and one particularly vocal group had distributed instructions all over the internet describing how easy it would be to blow up trains transporting hazardous chemicals.

Bad as they all were, each one was fairly localized. They could kill a lot of innocent people and do terrible damage to a certain section of the country, but this . . . this could be catastrophic. This new report eclipsed all the other memos in her In Box. She stared at the last paragraph. *This could change life as we know it and set us back to the year 1910.*

Samantha pushed a long strand of dark brown hair out of her eyes, shoved the report back inside the envelope, tossed it into her safe and slammed it shut.

Two

The White House

"Do you know where your money is?"

The six Deputy Directors of The White House Office of Homeland Security stared at their boss. Samantha often asked thought-provoking questions at their morning staff meetings, but what was she getting at this time?

"Do you mean what bank it's in?" the head of the section on Borders and Transportation asked.

"Is it really in a bank?" Samantha pressed.

"Well, sure it is. I get statements."

Samantha looked around the small conference table in her second floor West Wing office. "Anyone else know where his money is? Today? Any day?"

"Sorry. I don't get it," Jim Shilling said. "I wonder who's on her grassy knoll this time?" he murmured to the staffer next to him. Then glancing at his watch, he said to Samantha, "I thought we were going to review the latest on our Chemical and Biological Readiness Program this morning and talk about that CDC warning."

"I know that's your directorate, and we'll get to that in a minute," Samantha answered. "But first, I'd like to know if any of you has a clue what you'd do if you actually did *not* know where your money was? You didn't know, so you couldn't get it. Not for food, not for medical care. Not for anything."

Her question was met with a half dozen blank stares. She glanced down at a sheaf of notes she had in front of her and continued. "Let's say there was a massive power failure of some sort, and all the computers went down at once. None of the banks, the insurance companies, the hedge funds, nobody had any record of their deposits, their assets, their payment schedules, their debts. Then what?"

"Then they wait until the power comes back on," Jim said. "Besides, all the banks have back-up systems. We have power failures all the time after hurricanes, earthquakes, whatever. So what's the big deal?"

"Back-up systems? Some New York banks have back-up systems in Jersey City. Too close," Samantha said with a wave of her hand. "No. What I'm asking you to consider is a situation where all of the computers, the stock market, the ATM's, the railroads, the cars, the hospitals with all of our new electronic medical records, the telephone system, the electricity grid, refrigeration, water treatment, in fact everything using electronics, all of it is fried and won't work anymore. Not for a long while, maybe months, maybe as much as a year, until all the systems are repaired. No water, no food. Millions of Americans would die!"

"Hey, Samantha, that's never happened. What are you talking about?" one staffer asked.

"I'm talking about an electro-magnetic pulse," she said in a serious tone.

"EMP? You mean when a small nuke or one of those other E-weapons we've got is detonated way up in the atmosphere and it sends out those magnetic waves, kind of like massive micro-waves?" her Deputy for Energy and Nuclear Issues asked.

"Precisely," Samantha said.

"Okay, so the Pentagon has some of those new E-weapons," Jim volunteered. "In fact, remember back at the beginning of the Iraq war, we knocked out an entire TV center in Baghdad with a single small E-bomb. Well that's what they called it then. The Air Force dropped it to screw up their communications. But then we backed off." He stared at Samantha and pressed on. "So, why are you bringing it up now when we've got so many other things to deal with? And besides, it's never happened except for that one time. At least not any other time that I can remember."

"Actually, it did happen a long time ago," she replied.

"When?" A chorus of voices intoned all at once.

"Okay, I know it was before any of us were born," Samantha said. "But I'm sure you all know about, or have read about, the series of nuclear tests our government conducted back in the 40's and 50's."

"Sure. Weren't they out in the Pacific somewhere?" the head of the Executive Secretariat asked.

"Yeah, the Marshall Islands," Jim said. "We weren't the only ones, though. The Russians, well the Soviets, they tested weapons too in Central Asia. And a bunch of people were exposed to radiation, right?"

"Yes, they were," Samantha said. "But as I think back on it, we were trying to prove we had such powerful weapons, no one would ever attack us again."

"Sort of, 'You show me yours, I'll show you mine'," Jim said with a sly grin.

Samantha raised one eyebrow and replied, "Something like that. But my point is that we set off those bombs, out in places like Enewetok, Johnston Island, Bikini Atoll where some of the effects actually rained down on another island, and one of the results was that over two-thousand miles away in Hawaii the street lights dimmed, electrical systems were screwed up, circuit breakers were tripped, and there was permanent damage done to a telecommunications relay facility. And that was over half a century ago when we weren't relying on computers and networks like we are today."

"So why bring it up now? I haven't heard about any EMP threats out there." Jim said.

"Well, I just did. There are threats. They just haven't been carried out yet. "She glanced down at the papers in front of her. "This morning I got a classified memo from a contact at DOD about how both North Korea and Iran have been working on EMP weapons. We know that China has the technology. But now I figure they'd just get the North Koreans to test it. You know, use them as their proxy, and then China can just sit there and say, 'wasn't us.' And as for Iran, remember that high altitude Shahab III missile they tested a while back?" Her comment was met with silent nods. "Well, it turns out that they've also practiced launching a mobile ballistic missile from a ship in the Caspian Sea. What this means is that they could launch a small nuclear device high enough into space to trigger an EMP off one of our coasts if they wanted to. And I don't even want to think about some terrorist group getting their hands on one."

"So, bottom line, what are you suggesting?" Jim asked.

Samantha turned to face him. "What I'm saying is that since I read the latest intel, I've done more digging, and I believe this is a threat worth pursuing. Big time. We had a Commission that looked into these issues. It was appointed years ago, but nobody paid any attention to their reports. They came before the House Armed Services Committee every once in a while, but then it was disbanded. No more money. So, when was the last time you read anything about an EMP threat?"

"There have been a lot of TV shows about cyber-attacks and one I remember alluded to an EMP effect," Jim Shilling remarked. "But, hey, that's Hollywood hyping wild ideas. They always try to be edgy."

"Edgy?" Samantha echoed. "I'm talking about a serious threat, not a TV series."

"So what are we going to do?" Jim asked. "You know we've got a ton of other stuff on our plate right now. I mean, that WMD panel is telling everyone to focus on biological threats."

"And the DOT is about to put out new rules on train safety," another staffer added. "We're still trying to infiltrate that group that keeps threatening to blow up the Lincoln Tunnel. Well, the FBI is, I mean."

Samantha nodded as she assessed the anxious looks of her staff. "Look, I know we've got a ton of issues right now. Things we have to coordinate with the agencies. But our job isn't just to react to threats, but to anticipate them. And this EMP thing is really bugging me. What we need to do is rattle some cages. I'm going to bring this up on our inter-agency conference call this morning and ask for a threat assessment."

"Sounds like a full-employment act for our Missile Defense Agency," Jim remarked.

"They could be part of it," Samantha said. "The trouble is, the difference between us and the bad guys is that while they make plans, we just keep having meetings and appointing commissions. And that's not good enough. We've got to get this kind of threat on the President's radar screen before some group or some country decides it's time to set off a blast that could send this country back to the last century!"

THREE

Rongelap, The Marshall Islands – Early February, 1954

"Please take me with you!" the young girl pleaded with her lover as tears streamed down her face. "I'm so scared. I don't want to be here when the bomb goes off. Please!"

The Navy sailor cradled her in his arms, rocking her back and forth as he would a child while she sobbed. He wanted to take her. She was his treasure. She was the best thing he had found in his sorry life serving in the Seventh Fleet. But there was no way. He'd never get permission to take a woman with him. He couldn't marry her, even if he wanted to. He still had years to go on his enlistment. And she was so young. Hell, they were both young. But what does age have to do with it when you find a gorgeous girl swimming in a lagoon and you're deployed to build structures on some God-forsaken island? She had to be the best looking thing he had seen in years. Better than the ones back in Iowa, that's for sure. So they got involved. But what now?

"Maelynn, you know I can't take you with me now," he murmured as he stroked her hair. "It'll be okay. Don't worry. We've got a whole fleet of ships out here, thousands of people setting up these tests. Do you think we'd be here if it wasn't safe?"

She reached up and wiped her eyes with the back of her hand. "Our Chief says that many people have had to be moved off the other islands. It's been going on for years. And nobody knows when they can go back. If it's so safe, why can't they go back? I don't understand."

"We just want to be sure everything is okay before we let the people back on those islands. Sure we've been testing a bunch of stuff out here. Our mission has been to set up the tests and show the world what we've got so there will never be another war. You don't want another big war, do you?"

"No, I don't," she said, haltingly. "The Japanese were so bad, everyone was happy when the Americans came to our islands. But you dropped big bombs on Japan so the world already knows what you have. I don't understand why you have to show the world any more of them."

"It's called deterrence."

"I don't know that word."

"It means that if everybody knows we have these weapons, no other country will attack us again. There won't be a World War Three because we could fight back with bombs that are just too devastating."

"You keep using words I don't know. De-va-stating?"

"It means really bad."

"But you just said I would be okay when the next bomb goes off. How can I be safe if the weapons are so devas…devas…"

"Devastating?"

"Yes," she mumbled as she started to cry again.

"Honey, please don't cry. This next bomb will go off over a hundred miles away on Bikini Atoll. As I said, you'll be just fine." He reached into his backpack and pulled out a package. "But look. I brought this for you. It's my rations, all that I could carry this time. And here's my canteen. I want you to have them. And just…uh…just take care of yourself. Okay?"

She examined the package and the canister and looked up into his eyes. "Will you come back to me?"

"I hope so."

"But you have to. If you don't, my family….my people…."

He tipped her chin up and stared into her deep brown eyes. "Your family? Your people? What are you talking about?"

She turned away, refusing to meet his gaze. She hesitated for a long time.

"Maelynn, what is it? What's wrong? Something about your family? Are they sick? Are they all right?"

"No, it's not that. It's me. It's us. It's the…it's the…"

"It's the what?"

"It's the…the baby," she whispered.

He felt like he'd just been dealt a sucker punch. A baby? Maelynn was going to have a baby? His baby? He knew he didn't have to ask. Of course it was his baby. It had to be. It had only been a short time since he'd been coming to the island to work on the installation of weather stations and other monitoring devices, but whenever he could manage it, he stole away to spend time with her. And now she was going to be the mother of his child. When she mentioned her family, he knew that they were very proud. They had their own ways and as an unmarried and unclaimed mother, she would be shunned, possibly disowned. What the hell was he going to do?

He hesitated, thought for a moment and then said, "Maelynn, look at me. I have an idea."

She turned to him, her face anxious and still wet with tears. "What can we do?"

He reached over and pulled a ring off his finger and handed it to her. "This is my class ring. Here, take it. See? It has my initials on the inside of the band."

She peered at the ring as he held it up to the light and saw the initials PVC clearly marked for Peter Van Cleve.

"Tell your family that we were secretly married by my Captain. Tell them that the Captain of a ship has the right to perform marriages in my country. Tell them that you are my wife and that I will come back for you. Tell them now before they know about the baby."

She stared at the heavy gold ring and gingerly took it out of his hand. Then she wiped her eyes and paused for several seconds. Finally she said, "Yes. I pledge my life to you. You pledge to me?"

He nodded.

She fingered the ring and looked up with a hopeful gaze. "Yes," she said. "Now I will be wife and mother. I will care for your child until you come back for me."

Now what? He could hardly take her back to Maquoketa, Iowa. Not even after the war.

She could never live in the cold and the snow. Not after living among palm trees, eating coconuts and swimming in blue lagoons. Or could she? He took her in his arms, held her close and felt her warm breath on his neck. Maybe he could work it out. Maybe he could teach her his ways as she had taught him hers. Maybe after the government had exploded enough bombs and cleaned up the mess, maybe he could find a way to have her in his life. He said a silent prayer that he could figure out a way to pull it off.

He took a deep breath and said, "Maelynn, I will do everything in my power to come back for you. I give you my promise."

On board Joint Task Force-7 – February 28, 1954

"Captain, here are the readings from our weather station. They've been checking surface wind direction and barometric conditions every hour and upper-level conditions every two hours."

"What's the latest?"

"Remember, the earlier report said they expected no significant fallout for the populated Marshall Islands but…"

"But what?" the Captain barked impatiently.

"But the midnight briefing now says winds at 20,000 feet are blowing west from Bikini toward the inhabited islands. Looks like they're heading toward Rongelap."

"Heading west? I can't believe this!" The Captain looked down at his classified papers and said in a frustrated tone, "We've got over 42,000 military and civilian personnel working on this testing program, seven ships monitoring everything from blast elevation to electricity bursts and you're telling me that some guy at some weather station is concerned because the winds at some altitude are blowing a bit west? Is he suggesting we should stand down?"

"That's what it looks like…uh…sir."

"Get the command group together and we'll go over this one more time. This is our biggest test so far and even this one may not match the bomb the Soviets tested. And when was theirs?" The Captain stared off into space and then answered his own question. "It was two years ago. Two whole years and we're still trying to play catch up ball."

"I know, sir. But the islands…"

"Those nearby atolls were evacuated ages ago, and so I can't imagine any fallout…"

"But Rongelap, sir. We didn't tell the Chief to take any sort of precautions there."

"Precautions? It's over a hundred miles away. Besides, what precautions could they take? Hide behind a palm tree? Bury themselves in a sand dune? Get Serious."

"Maybe they should have been evacuated too."

"So now you're a radiation expert?" the Captain asked in an irritated tone.

"No, sir. Sorry, sir. It's just that we're all…"

The Captain softened his tone. "I know we're all over-worked, over-wrought, over-everything on this mission. But we have our orders and unless there are truly extenuating circumstances, our orders are to detonate at dawn."

Bikini Atoll – 6:45 a.m., March 1, 1954

The blinding flash of light was followed by a fireball of intense heat shooting up to the sky at the rate of 300 miles an hour. The earth shook and the ocean churned as water temperatures hit fifty-five thousand degrees. The largest hydrogen bomb ever detonated by the United States government measured fifteen mega-tons, one-thousand times as powerful as the bomb dropped on Hiroshima. Within minutes a monstrous cloud of nuclear debris formed twenty miles up in the air and then a white, snowy ash began to fall on twenty-two fisherman aboard a Japanese fishing boat named "Lucky Dragon." It was the unluckiest day of their lives.

The ash also rained down on Rongelap where the lagoons turned yellow and dead fish began to float to the surface. Maelynn was hiding inside her family's hut, clutching the rations with one hand and holding the gold ring in the other. What had happened? When she peered out at dawn, it was as if two bright suns were rising in the East. And when the ground began to shake, she was afraid that an earthquake had hit their precious island. She was scared. She wondered when her mother would come back from fishing. Maelynn was about to go out to look for her when suddenly, the older woman ran into the hut, her hair covered with white dust.

"Don't come near me," she cried out to her young daughter. "It came from the sky."

"It looks like fire ash," Maelynn said.

"I tried to wash it off but the sea is covered too."

Maelynn held out the canteen. "Here is water from my husband. You can wash your hair."

"No! No! We need it for drinking." She shook her head, reached for a piece of cloth and tried to brush off the white particles. "You stay there. I don't know what this is, but I am feeling strange. I think I may be sick."

The next day the children played in the ash that was now two inches deep. Then they too became sick to their stomachs. Maelynn's mother looked pale. Her hair started to fall out in large clumps as she lost her strength. She stared at her daughter and clutched her throat. "What is happening? The people are terrified. Everyone is getting sick. It must be from the bomb our Chief told us about. It must be the ash, the water."

"Here, mother. Drink from the canteen," Maelynn said, leaning over the woman who now was moaning in pain.

She took a small sip and pushed it away. "You save. Save for yourself and for the baby. And you stay here. Inside the hut. And you wait. We all will wait. We will wait for the Americans to come back. Surely, they will come back and save us all."

FOUR

UCLA Campus, Los Angeles – Present Day

"Is seat taken?" the young man asked in halting English.

"Nothin's reserved in this cafeteria." Pete Kalani said, looking up from his textbook. "You new around here?"

"Yes, I'm here on exchange program. I see you around, and want meet you when I see T-shirt," the young man said, pulling out a chair with one hand, and setting his tray of food on the long metal table with the other.

Pete glanced down at the writing on his black cotton shirt emblazoned with the letters S.A.I.N.T.S. across the front. Instead of a dot over the "i" there was a small mushroom cloud. "My T-shirt? What about it?"

"I've heard about group. It's anti-nuke group?"

"Sort of."

"That's what I think when I see. But what does S.A.I.N.T.S. mean?"

"It stands for the Society of American and International Nuclear Test Survivors," Pete said, taking a sip of his iced tea. "You've heard of us?"

"I saw video on YouTube."

"Which one? We put a ton of them out there," Pete said.

"The one showing people with radiation. It was like ours."

"Yours? Your what?"

"Oh, I explain. My name is Nurlan. Nurlan Remizov. I am foreign exchange student from Kazakhstan," he said as he grabbed his sandwich and took a bite.

"That's in Russia, right?"

"We were part of Russia. Old Soviet Union. No more. We independent now," he said with a hint of a smile on his broad face.

"That's cool," Pete said. "So what do you mean our video is like yours? You guys make videos about radiation?"

"Yes."

"You're kidding!"

"No. You see Soviets tested nuclear bombs in my country, and many of our people have bad times. Babies born wrong …it sad."

Pete stared at Nurlan. When he first saw the guy, he thought he might be an American Indian with his round face, slightly oriental eyes that were almost black, and straight inkjet hair. He had no idea what people from Kazakhstan looked like. Maybe they all looked like Indians. But what the heck. Here was a guy who knew about the S.A.I.N.T.S. A guy who seemed to have the same history he did. *Was this guy for real?* He wondered.

"Wait a minute," Pete said. "My family is from the Marshall Islands where the Americans set off tons of nuclear weapons a long time ago. A lot of my relatives got horrible diseases from the fall-out. Are you saying that you and your family are nuclear test survivors too?"

"Me? Some things." He pointed down at his leg. "Bones not so good. Radiation troubles last long time. Go through family. Tests done long time ago and my family suffered because they were in test places. They not told what happens. No warnings. Nothing.

Maybe Soviets thought no one there. I don't think that. They must know. They no care."

"I think the people in Washington knew too," Pete said with a scowl. "Bastards. I hate them. I hate the government. They make promises they don't keep. They set off bombs that killed people. And my own grandmother was on an island when radiation fall-out hit the place. She was pregnant with my mother at the time."

"But, she lived." Nurlan said.

"Yes. Just barely. After a while she and some of the others made their way to Hawaii. But right after my mother was born, my grandmother got polio."

"What happened to mother?"

"She was okay at first. I guess it takes a while for some things to go wrong. Anyway, she married my dad. He's Hawaiian. And she eventually got cancer and died when I was ten."

"I sorry for that," Nurlan said. "Same things happened my country."

Pete shook his head as he continued to stare at Nurlan. "I can't believe this. We have a group. We sometimes stage rallies or sit-ins when there's some sort of government hearing. But I had no idea there were people over in your part of the world with the same problems."

"Oh yes. We have meetings now too. We could not do them at first. But when we got independence, it was easier to do things. We have rallies now like you in West. We learned from your protests."

"Are they doing any good?"

"Maybe. We get press to come now."

"We don't get any press coverage now. I mean, there aren't any tests going on. This government has had a ban on atmospheric testing for a while. Though I wouldn't put it past them to do it again," Pete said. "Right now we're trying to get money for our people. We call it reparations."

"Can you get that? Soviets never give people anything."

"We've been trying for years. They keep appointing commissions, passing legislation, making promises, but then they forget to put up the money. It's getting so bad we want to find a way to really get their attention and fight back."

"Fight back?" Nurlan leaned across the metal table and said in a low tone, "We have to . . . as people say . . . compare notes."

FIVE

Washington, D.C.

Tripp Adams headed across Key Bridge toward Georgetown. He was used to gridlock on this particular span over the Potomac River but at eight o'clock at night, the commute traffic was over, and now he guessed that most of the folks leaving Arlington, Virginia were going into town for dinner. That's where he was headed, not to one of the trendy restaurants on M Street, but over to Samantha's condo where he figured she was putting together something simple. She usually said that with her crazy schedule, dinner ended up being whatever she could broil. That was fine with him. He didn't really care about the food, he just wanted an evening alone with her.

He remembered first seeing her many years ago on campus at Princeton when he was a senior and she was a freshman. How could he ignore the tall, gorgeous girl with the long brown wavy hair and striking green eyes? They both had classes in geology so he saw her in the halls on occasion. But back then, he was intent on graduating, getting out of New Jersey and joining the Navy, and he wasn't about to get involved with a nineteen year old even if she did have a body that would stop traffic.

As luck would have it, a dozen years later, he was now Vice President of GeoGlobal Oil & Gas and had been sent to head up their Washington, D.C. office. He had hired a top lobbyist, Godfrey Nims, to handle the Hill while Tripp had worked with The Departments of Energy, Commerce, Interior and The White House on a whole host of issues. He had met Samantha when a band of foreign agents from Venezuela had managed to cross the border and sabotage some of their natural gas pipelines. He and Samantha had collaborated, along with a number of government agencies, to find the culprits and put a stop to the havoc.

In the midst of all that turmoil, he had fallen for the brainy brunette, and that was quite a switch from his usual routine of playing the field. His buddy at the office, Godfrey Nims, had always given him a hard time about dating what he called "Fancies" or "FNC's." He said Tripp's dates all had long blond hair and great legs and looked like Fox News Clones. But as soon as Samantha came onto the scene, all that had changed. Not only was she great to look at, she was one smart lady. Washington was filled with bright women, but this one made him feel. . .what did she make him feel? Comfortable. Maybe that was it. They could be in the same room or driving somewhere, and they didn't have to talk all the time. Just being there was enough. Something else he liked was when she showed her rather off-beat sense of humor. Sometimes she had it. Lately, though, she had been so focused on her job and problems dealing with some of the egos in The White House, it was hard to get her to cool it and relax once in a while.

On the other hand, they did have a ton of things in common. She had been raised in Texas where her dad was in the oil and gas business. She had spent time out in the field with him, knew all about drilling rigs and pipelines, so in addition to the physical attraction, she was kind of like a soul mate when it came to his issues.

The trouble was, in addition to dealing with Washington, GeoGlobal kept sending him around the world to negotiate contracts with other governments. He had always enjoyed the travel, but now he found himself counting the days when he could land at Dulles Airport and head back to see Samantha. Then again, her job was getting so crazy, she didn't have as much time for him as she used to, even when he was in town. Since she had been promoted to lead that Homeland Security operation at The White House, her hours were brutal. She was on call 24/7 and it seemed that every time her cell phone rang, some city could be in danger. Talk about pressure.

He turned right on M Street and drove by a series of shops where students from Georgetown University were peering in windows featuring T-shirts, gold jewelry and ethnic food of one sort or another. He always wondered how they got enough customers in those stores since there was never any where to park on this stretch. He continued down to Wisconsin Avenue and turned right past the Shops at Georgetown Park. Down the hill, he turned right again on K Street under the Whitehurst Freeway and was amazed to find a guy pulling out of a place just a block down from Samantha's condo. *Rock Star Parking*, he mused as he took the spot. They always reserved the best parking space for the rock stars right in front of a stadium, and as he turned off the motor and grabbed the bottle of wine he had brought along for dinner, he felt a stab of the same sort of anticipation he sensed when he went to some of those concerts many years ago. The expectation of great music, camaraderie with friends and, hopefully, a chance to get lucky.

When she opened the door, Tripp set the bottle of wine down on a small table in the entrance, gathered Samantha in his arms, inhaled the faint scent of vanilla in her hair and lowered his mouth to hers. She wound her arms around his neck and pressed her body close. As he deepened the kiss, he heard a slight moan. *God, she tastes good, feels good, smells good.* He looked down into those jade green eyes and grinned. "Missed you, Samantha."

"Missed you too. I'm so glad you're back." She turned and picked up the wine. "Oh, it's a Pinot Noir. This is perfect. I've got veal chops and creamed spinach tonight. C'mon into the kitchen and tell me about your trip."

He followed her into a small galley style kitchen with maple cabinets and granite countertops. There was barely enough room for two people to be in the space, but he never minded bumping up against her body. And what a body it was. He tried to push those thoughts out of his mind, though he promised himself he'd get back to them later. He glanced around and reflected on how small her condo was. He knew she had given up space in return for proximity to The White House. People in Washington paid a ton to live in town and not fight the commutes on I-66, the Beltway, 270 or 395. And with her hours, it made sense to have this little place so near the action. At least it was across from a park where they sometimes went running together. And the restaurants at Washington Harbour were just across the street and down two blocks. So all in all, he could see why she picked this building. If they ever got serious enough to move in together though, they'd have to get bigger digs.

He watched as she reached into an overhead cabinet to retrieve two wine glasses. He liked the way her hips moved, and he began to wish that he could postpone the veal chops and move on to dessert. Her. That's what he wanted tonight. As if reading his mind, Samantha smiled at him. "Later," she said and pointed toward the bottle. "Would you open the wine while I toss the salad?" She grabbed bottles of oil and vinegar from a cupboard, sprinkled some bits of blue cheese on the lettuce, mixed the greens and spooned them onto two plates sitting on the counter.

Tripp pulled out the cork, poured a bit of wine into a goblet and handed it to Samantha. "Here. Try this. Tell me what you think."

She took a sip and closed her eyes. "Best thing I've tasted all day."

"Just wait till later," he murmured, pouring some for himself. "Well, let's see now. The trip was okay. Got a deal finalized in Norway. It's almost summer so you'd think it would warm up. No such luck up there. Glad to be back home. But enough of that. Tell me about things in your shop. That is if there's anything that's not classified," he said with a wry grin.

"Screwed up. Shifting. Changing," she said. "One minute I think we need to focus on train security, the next it's the ports, then it's a new type of weapon." She turned to face him. Holding her wine glass she asked, "Remember those kaleidoscopes we used to have when we were kids? You just move them a fraction and all the shapes change. Well, that's how I feel right now."

"Yeah. Kinda creates a new mosaic."

"Exactly. The trouble is, I feel like we have to be on top of all of them at once. I don't know how the President does it. Juggling things not only here but around the world."

"But he's got thousands of people in the government worrying about all that stuff. You've got people too, especially all of those bodies over at DHS. That department has, what? Hundreds of thousands of people, analysts, administrators, whatever. You just need to use them."

"I know," she said and gave a sigh. "I never was good at delegating. I'm always afraid somebody's going to drop the ball or overlook something. And we're talking about people's lives here."

"I know. Believe me, I know." He grabbed the wine and followed her into the small living room. There was a round walnut table and two ladder back chairs at one end of the room where Samantha had set their places. An arrangement of low candles had been set to the side. As they sat down, he saw that the reflections from the candlelight gave her face a rosy glow and made her hair kind of shine. Being with her again, after a long trip, made all the hours on all the flights drift away from his mind's eye.

But her mood was pretty somber tonight. He wanted to change that. "So, I wanted to tell you about a conversation I had with your dad today."

"Oh? What's the latest?"

"I'm really glad we took him on as a consultant. He's been great. Good man."

Samantha glanced over at the photo of her family perched on the glass coffee table in front of her sofa. It showed a rugged Jake Reid clad in blue jeans and a striped shirt with the sleeves rolled up, her mother who had died of cancer many years ago, Samantha as a teenager and her little brother clowning off to one side. Every time she looked at that picture, taken at their home down in Texas, she missed her Mom. But the look on her father's face made her smile. There he was. Big Jake as the wildcatters called him. One of the best in the business when it came to searching out and analyzing the most promising leases, the most likely places to find the precious oil and gas.

"He's pretty happy with the arrangement too" she said, "although I sometimes worry that he overdoes it. I mean, ever since he had that heart problem I keep asking him to slow down"

"That man is never going to slow down. You know that. In fact, he keeps bugging me about traveling to some of our overseas projects."

"Overseas? Where? Why?" Samantha asked in a concerned tone.

"Not sure yet. But you know we're negotiating exploration deals all over the place, especially in some of the former Soviet states."

"Way over there?"

"Gotta go where the oil is, my dear," Tripp said tasting the salad. "Hey, this is really good." He leaned over and poured some more wine into Samantha's glass.

"Well, I don't know," she said. "It worries me when he goes traipsing around the fields all the time."

"That's what he's good at. You can't ask a man to quit. Not at his age."

Samantha furrowed her brow. "I guess I can't. It's just that I love him, and I don't want to see anything happen to him. I want him to take care of himself."

Tripp reached over and took her hand. "Hey, hon, relax. Jake *can* take care of himself. You let me worry about him. You've got enough to worry about right now."

They finished their veal and creamed spinach and almost emptied the bottle of wine. Samantha was feeling a bit of a buzz, a much more pleasant sensation than anything she had felt all day in her chaotic West Wing office. She had missed Tripp when he was away on his latest business venture. She wished he could stay in town more. On the other hand, with her insane schedule, it was always frustrating to know that he was just across Key Bridge, and she was often too busy or too exhausted to be with him. She could look out her picture window and see his building, Turnberry Tower, across the Potomac. At least he didn't have far to go when he went home after one of their dinners. *Would he drive home tonight, or would he stay?*

She glanced over at the tall, muscular man she had idolized back in her college days. He had been on the crew back then, and even now he had the same physique she always associated with guys in that sport. She knew he worked out a lot, and she found herself berating the fact that she had skipped her usual morning runs along the Potomac ever since she got this new job. There just wasn't enough time in the day. At least tonight she had carved out a few extra hours to concentrate on Tripp, and she gave a silent prayer that her cell phone wouldn't ring for a good long while.

She started to clear the dishes when he pushed back his chair. "Here, let me help you with these," he said, picking up his plate and walking to the kitchen. She blew out the candles and took the glasses and wine bottle off the table.

"Coffee tonight?" she asked as she put the plates in the dishwasher. "Or how about dessert. I've got some sorbet in the fridge."

He leaned against the counter and grinned at her. "Guess it's not made with green tea and lime mousse."

"What in the world are you talking about? Green tea and lime mousse? Where did you hear about that?"

"Just some stuff they were serving on this last trip. It looked kind of weird, so I asked the waiter how they made it. Get this. I wanted to remember so I could tell you about it. Anyway, he said they take essences, now there's a word for you, essences of tea and lime and pump it out of siphons into a bowl of liquid nitrogen."

She burst out laughing. "And you ate that stuff?"

"No. I took a pass."

"Good choice," she said, rinsing off her hands and turning to face him. "Next time you're in Texas you should go to our State Fair. They've got better things there like Fried Milky Way Bars."

He chuckled and shook his head. *Enough chatter.* He flicked off the kitchen light and pulled Samantha into his arms, lifted her up and carried her down the short hallway to her bedroom. She started to giggle as he somewhat unceremoniously plopped her down on top of the white comforter, sat down beside her and started to unbutton her blouse. "Thanks for the great dinner, but now it's time for the dessert I've been thinking about for weeks."

SIX

Southern California

"Great beach weather, right?" Pete asked his new friend.

"Sure is," Nurlan replied. "Good you borrow car for day."

"Yeah. One of my buddies lets me use it once in a while, and with exams coming up and studying all the time, I figured we could use a break."

Pete drove off the UCLA campus on Westwood Boulevard and turned right onto Wilshire. "Ever play volleyball in your country?"

"Sure. Is Olympic sport. We have television, you know," he said with a laugh.

"I just wondered. I mean, I have no clue what you do over there. Well, I did see that dumb Borat movie a while ago."

"That movie so bad," Nurlan said. "We no happy with that one. My country very civilized. We have quarter of world's oil."

"That much? You guys must be rich."

"We try. My government bring in good companies to get oil out of ground. People make lots money. Government people make money. Oil people make money. Lots money some places, at least when price is up. But even when price is down, people want oil. So they drill."

"So your government is okay?" Pete asked.

Nurlan laughed. "Is okay some times. We have many bad governments for years, is all . . . how do you say it? Is all relative. That's right. My people go all back to Genghis Khan. He started in Kazakhstan."

"I didn't know that. I read about him in history classes but I had no clue he was in your country. I guess I didn't know where he was. Pretty bad guy though, right."

"Bad guy? Sure. He killed many people. But then he had big empire, and he only taxed people half a percent, so after while they think it no such bad deal."

"Half a percent? I never heard of that," Pete said.

"Compare to what Soviets did when they came. They killed million people when they took over all land and all animals. So you look and Genghis Khan no look so bad. Now we don't have Soviets running things any more, but our government takes forty-five percent taxes. And I no like President. He no good guy."

"I don't like ours either. In fact, I don't like anything about Washington. They make promises they don't keep," Pete said with a scowl. "They're all a bunch of liars."

"You mean when they promise help your people? You told me that," Nurlan said.

"Yeah. That and a lot of things. I've been sending messages to The White House, to Congress, to everybody. But nobody even bothers to answer."

"What you tell them?"

"I remind them that they're supposed to vote money for reparations. For health care for our people who were hurt. For everything we need. But they never do. The S.A.I.N.T.S. don't have the money to get a big lawsuit together or anything like that. But a lot of our people are so fed up that we're trying to figure out some other ways to get their attention."

"Like what?"

"Make some threats maybe. I'm not sure yet. I'm working on that," Pete said as he turned right on San Vincente Boulevard and began to wind through Brentwood. He drove past office buildings and restaurants and finally through a lovely residential neighborhood. A few joggers ran past rows of trees that lined the median, and a pair of bikers rode along the curb.

"This nice area," Nurlan said, gazing at a fancy house partially blocked by a stone wall.

"Yeah. Some people have made it big around here. I'm still trying to live on my swimming scholarship and the few bucks I saved from a job last summer. Until I got laid off, that is. The economy was so bad, the store where I worked had to close."

"About summer jobs, I have idea I want tell you about."

"Yeah? What's that?" Pete asked, winding to the end of San Vincente and turning right on Seventh Street.

"I have good summer job back home. It not in Almaty, that best city. It is way west, over by Caspian. That's okay because it pays good."

"What kind of a job?"

"It's with company I try for long time to get into. They making nuclear energy and some people say maybe they make some kind weapons. I watch them, and I think if I get job there I see what they do. If bad, maybe our protest group can find way to shut it down."

"So you're gonna be a spy?" Pete asked, turning onto Pacific Coast Highway.

"Yes. Good idea, you think?

"Why would they give you a job? Don't they check people out?"

"I am expert with computers. My major here. You know that. They need people like me. So why not take job and watch things while I there?" Nurlan asked.

Pete thought about that for a while. "So you've got this job lined up, and you're going to spy on them and make money at the same time. Sweet deal."

They drove through a tunnel, and on the other side they saw the crowds on State beach. Pete circled around and finally found a parking place with a broken meter. "C'mon. Let's get our stuff. There are some guys over there by the volleyball net. I've got a ball in the trunk. Maybe we can get a pick-up game. Your legs okay for that?"

"Sure," Nurlan said with a shrug. "Maybe not for long time, but I want to play."

Pete's serve just skimmed the net. One of the others spiked the ball back over and Nurlan set it up. They ran, dove, hit and served again for the next half hour and just barely eked out twenty-five points in the first round. "You want to go another round?" Pete asked, swiping beads of sweat off his forehead.

The sun was high over head now and gentle waves were lapping at the shore. It was almost noon. "Nah. It's getting pretty hot. I wanna hit the water. Maybe we can play again later. Okay with you both?" one of their opponents asked.

"Sure thing," Pete said with a wave of his hand. "Thanks. Good game." He retrieved the ball, grabbed their towels and duffel bags stacked at the side of the net and sauntered down the beach in search of some good scenery. "Hey, check out the girls over there," he motioned to where a half dozen young women clad in skimpy two-piece bathing suits were sunning themselves. How about we hang out right here?"

"Looks good." Nurlan spread out his towel and reached inside his bag for a couple bottles of water. He offered one to Pete.

"Thanks." Pete was still focused on the women. "See what they're wearing?"

"You mean bathing suits?"

"Yeah. Bikinis. Remember we talked one time about how my grandmother was on an island when a huge bomb was tested? It was the one hydrogen bomb they exploded. A thousand times bigger than the one they dropped on Hiroshima, and radio-active ash fell all over her village?"

"Sure. You told me all that."

"Well, the place they destroyed with that bomb was called Bikini Atoll. That's where they got the name for the bathing suits."

"Not much left of it now, right?"

"It was pulverized," Pete said. "Not much left of the bathing suits on those girls either. But they're a damn sight better to look at."

Nurlan stopped looking at the girls and turned to Pete. "I want talk about summer."

"Yeah. Your job. Sounds cool," Pete said.

"Not just my job. I have idea about job for you. Why don't you come with me?"

Pete was astonished by the suggestion. What in the world did this guy have in mind? "Come with you? To Kazakhstan? Get a job there? You've gotta be kidding."

"Why kidding? There's big reunions of Nevada Semipalatinsk in summer, and we could go together."

"Oh, is that the name of the anti-war group you've been telling me about?"

"That's it. We have offices all over country. You know Greenpeace group? It like that but we work only nuclear things. We very organized. We even have museum."

"A museum? What for?"

"It shows radiation poisoning. We have pictures. People born wrong, some sheep with two heads."

"Jesus! That's awful," Pete said. "I told you a lot of our people got polio and cancer and a lot of other bad stuff from all the tests. I never saw an animal with two heads though."

"We had them. Soviets set off bombs and told sheep herders leave area, but some could no move sheep. They try hide. And then bombs go off. And other people farther away were told government predicting earthquake. That was when they did underground tests, and they knew everything shakes up. At time people surprised that government could predict earthquakes. What crazy things. Now we know what they do, but then, people not know."

"So wait a minute," Pete said. "You want me to come to your country over the summer to go to a reunion of this anti-nuke group?"

"Sure. We have good time. You see how we get people together and maybe get ideas how you run S.A.I.N.T.S. same like we run Semipalatinsk people. We name it because that is where tests go off. We not go that place. We go near Caspian. Marches will be many cities. Where we go, maybe I get you job too."

"I'm not a computer expert, I don't have any money, and I don't speak your language," Pete protested.

"No matter. We get cheap plane tickets. I loan you money. You pay back when you get job. You no speak Kazakh. No matter. Many people speak English. Maybe if my company have no other jobs, you could get job other place. Maybe down at docks. Lots ships there. My sister works boat cruises. Other companies there too. " Nurlan said. "We could have great summer. I'll send emails."

"I gotta think about all this." Pete turned and stared again at the girls sunbathing nearby and wondered what the women in Kazakhstan looked like. He didn't really have many plans for the summer. He was going to look for a job near the campus since he couldn't afford to go home to Hawaii. But he hadn't noticed many job openings lately. Now this guy was talking about traveling half way around the world. What a crazy idea. Or was it crazy?

"I serious about summer," Nurlan said. "We should stay together. As you said, think on it. We both want help our people. We both want stop nuclear weapons. And we both hate governments. Maybe we work together, Nevada Semipalatinsk and S.A.I.N.T.S. If we put all together, think what we do."

Seven

The White House

"Good afternoon, Miss Marconi. Miss Reid is waiting for you at her table," the Maitre 'd of the White House Mess said as he led the Assistant to the President for Public Liaison into one of the most exclusive eateries in the world. The tall young woman with dark hair and violet eyes nodded to a friend sitting at the large round staff table in front of the room. If you didn't have a guest, you could usually find a seat at this table for twelve where no reservation was required. It was often the best place to pick up the latest gossip circulating through the West Wing. But today, she was having lunch with her closest friend, and they had reserved their own table on one side of the richly paneled room.

"Here we are," he said, pulling out the wooden chair and handing her a navy blue menu with a piece of gold braid down the center.

"Hi, Angela," Samantha said, glancing at her watch.

"Sorry I'm a little late. I just had a rash of phone calls, and I raced over here as fast as I could. If I had an office here in the West Wing, I'd probably be more punctual. But running back and forth to the EEOB all day slows me down a little bit," she said, referring to the Eisenhower Executive Office Building across a short driveway where most of the White House staff was housed.

"No problem. I wish you had an office here too. Of course, it wouldn't be nearly as big as the one you've got across West Exec.

"Are you kidding? I'd take a room the size of a confessional to be in the West Wing. Anybody would."

"I know. I just wish there was more space here. Anyway, let's order, and then I want to hear what's going on in your shop."

A Filipino waiter clad in a navy blue blazer hovered nearby and quickly moved up to their table. "May I take your order?"

"Sure," Angela said. "How about the chef's salad and some iced tea?"

"And for you, Miss Reid?"

Samantha always marveled at how the waiters all seemed to memorize the names of everyone who worked in The White House. "Let's see. I think I'd like a tuna sandwich with some fruit on the side. No fries or chips. Oh, and a diet coke please." He nodded and walked back to the kitchen

"You should eat the chips," Angela said. "You look so thin these days."

"I know. I feel like the Botswana Poster Child. But I just don't seem to have much of an appetite."

"Why? What's the matter? I thought Tripp was back in town."

"He is," Samantha said, the hint of a smile crossing her face. "That's the one good thing in my life right now."

"A pretty darn good thing, my friend, if you ask me. My Mom fixed me up with another Italian guy the other night."

"Again? What does this one do?"

"He owns a poppy seed farm."

Samantha chuckled. "She never gives up, does she?"

"Not on your life. And speaking of lives, have you saved any today?" Angela asked with a wide smile.

"Afraid not. In fact, with so much going on, it's getting harder and harder to get anyone to focus on threats we're seeing right now."

"So who's not focusing?"

"Max Federman for one."

"Max? That's because he's the Political Director. All he ever wants to talk about is how he's going to get Jayson Keller elected President next year. And actually Keller is way ahead in the polls. Remember when he was chosen as VP, people called it the Kangaroo ticket. More power in the hind legs."

"I know. But if this country is attacked again, there goes his precious election," Samantha said with a sigh.

"So you'd think Max would pay careful attention to everything that's going on with Homeland Security. I don't get it," Angela said as the waiter brought their drinks.

"You'd think. But when I went through our priorities at this morning's senior staff meeting, he tried to shut me up saying that we had to be careful not to *unduly* scare the American people. It's like he wants it to appear that this administration has everything under complete control all the time so Keller can coast in on our coat tails or something."

"Nobody ever coasts into the Oval Office. He, of all people, knows that," Angela countered, stirring some sugar into her tea and taking a sip.

"All I know is that when I try to bring up some truly scary scenarios, he's the first one to try and shut me up."

"Can't you just keep working with the agencies like you always do and shrug it off?"

"It's hard to shrug it off when you feel like you've got the weight of the world on your shoulders."

"Wait a minute," Angela said, "Aren't you being a little bit dramatic?"

Samantha leaned forward and said in a low voice, "Look, if you had information that pointed to a possible threat to our entire economy, wouldn't you want the senior staff to focus on it?"

"What are you talking about?"

"I can't say too much about it because I got it from a classified report."

"Everything you do is classified," Angela said.

"Well, almost everything. But let me ask you this. If there were a threat, or, say, a type of weapon that could shut down communications, shut down the banking system, shut down the internet, where would we be?"

"Back to Dixie cups and string?"

"Get serious!" Samantha said. "I read somewhere that Bill Gates said that while aviation was the key to the twentieth century because it moved people and things around the world, the internet is the key to the twenty-first century because it moves ideas around the world. So it's just about as important as you can get."

"Well, sure there have been a bunch of cyber attacks. But those usually mean they're stealing identities or injecting viruses and messing some things up. Not closing the whole system down. Sorry, I just don't see how some terrorist group could pull that off. I mean we've had blackouts and stuff like that, but nobody has figured out how to shut everything down."

"Let's just say that there *is* a way, and it scares me to death." The waiter brought their entrees and Samantha started to pick at the fruit on her plate. "Sorry. I didn't mean to get all maudlin today. Tell me what you're working on these days."

"Well, let's see. We've got so many groups trying to get the President's attention, it's ridiculous. Just this morning I got a request from the city of Stockton. They want to President to attend their Asparagus Festival."

"Oh geez! What did you tell them?"

"Nothing yet. But maybe he could hit that one after he stops by the Garlic Festival in Gilroy," Angela said with a grin.

"He's not going to go to those things, is he?"

"Probably not. But they send in a request year after year."

"Those are pretty silly. What else is going on?" Samantha asked as she finally took a bite of her tuna sandwich.

"I get a slew of e-mails from every group you could imagine asking for money for weird things. There's one guy who's sent maybe a dozen messages. Says he's got some group called the S.A.I.N.T.S."

"Sounds like a basketball team or maybe a jazz group."

"Don't I wish! At least there might be some entertainment value there. With this guy, all he does is complain. It's gotten so bad, I wouldn't dream of sending an answer."

EIGHT

Astana, Kazakhstan

The blue turrets and blue dome on top of the Presidential Palace gleamed in the bright sunshine. Roses in the surrounding gardens created a carpet of fragrant red and pink hues as the block long building welcomed government workers, ambassadors and visitors from around the world. President Viktor Suleimenov marched through the ornate receiving room on the second floor, past large paintings of Kazakh mountains and nomads riding horses across the steppe . He entered his special cabinet room and pushed his bulky frame into the heavy chair at the head of the long blond wood table. The chair was upholstered in red that matched the tie he was wearing to this meeting of his most trusted advisers. Prisms of light from the crystal chandeliers shown down on their notes for the gathering. The President shuffled his papers, adjusted his glasses and began with no preamble at all.

"I don't like it! I don't like their meddling, their threats, their army training programs. It sounds like they're gearing up for another onslaught on their former territories. Look at Georgia. Look at Ukraine. We thought we would be safe. After all, we were the last of the Soviet Republics to declare independence. And do you think they would be grateful for our support all these years? No. They are not grateful. They talk only about restoring the glory days of the Soviet Union."

The ministers laughed nervously at their President's outburst. They were used to this new president making snide remarks about the current Russian leaders, but in recent meetings he had become more and more belligerent. Where was this going? They all leaned in to hang on his next sentence.

"I have word that there are going to be massive demonstrations over the summer. The Semipalatinsk people are going to be staging protests all around the country commemorating the terrible acts inflicted on our people during the Soviet nuclear tests years ago. You all know they had hundreds of explosions over our lands and they didn't stop until 1989. This is going to be a reminder of the callousness of the Soviet military from those days. And I for one don't see much change in their attitude today. They never did compensate any of our people who are still suffering from radiation sickness today.

"So here's what we're going to do. We're going to support those protests or rallies or whatever they turn out to be. We will see to it that they are covered by our radio and TV stations for all the world to see. I want everyone to remember what the Soviets did to us."

"If I may ask a question, Mr. President," one minister asked hesitantly.

"Yes. Go ahead."

"You will pardon my questioning of anything you have said, sir. I simply ask how will this keep the Russians from showing more muscle when it comes to their dealings with us? Won't this just make them mad and perhaps strengthen their resolve to make a move?"

There was a murmur around the table as other ministers nodded and raised their eyebrows in anticipation of the President's answer.

"I have more plans. Big plans. We have all seen what happens when nations announce programs to develop nuclear power, especially Moslem nations."

The ministers nodded and several spoke at once. "They are condemned by the Americans, the Europeans, others. . ."

"There are demands that they sign the nuclear non-proliferation treaties. . ."

"There are threats to bring in inspectors. . ."

"The Israelis bomb them . . ."

The President raised his hands to quiet the room. "Of course, we already have four nuclear reactors. No one can criticize those. They have been running for years. But if we announce . . . one day . . . that we are starting a larger program to develop more nuclear power *and* develop our own nuclear weapons, what do you think the reaction will be?"

"Nuclear weapons?"

"Outrage."

"Fear."

"Demands that we stand down."

"Yes. Yes. All of that will happen, I am sure," the President said. "But let me also ask you this. What could we possibly do to protect ourselves any better, to inoculate ourselves so to speak against the Russian fever of conquest and intimidation?"

The room erupted in questions and cries of protest. "You can't possibly mean. . ."

"The Americans would come down . . ."

"Our own people would protest . . ."

"The European Union . . . "

"NATO might . . ."

"All right! Enough!" the President bellowed. "What have the Americans been able to do about India and Pakistan's nuclear weapons? What has Europe done about Israel's arsenal? Come now, we all know they have the weapons. Thirty years ago there were about eight countries that had missiles and technology that could be a threat to their neighbors. Today it's more like thirty countries that have that capacity. Why shouldn't Kazakhstan be one of them . . . again?"

For a moment there was silence in the room as they all processed this information. Finally, one minister spoke up. "But, Mr. President, your predecessor met with the American Secretary of State and made an agreement. What was his name?"

"Baker. James Baker," another ministered answered.

"Yes, him. And then those other senators got involved."

"Sam Nunn and Dick Lugar," the Vice President said. "I met with them when I was appointed to that non-proliferation task force back in the 90's. That was when everybody was worried about the Iranians."

"Yes. Remember, their agents from Tehran were running all over the country trying to make deals to get some of our uranium," one minister volunteered. "Just because we're a Moslem country doesn't mean we want to do a weapons business with Iran though."

"Maybe not then," the President said. "But now, well, they have been good partners when it comes to trade." He looked around the table at the anxious faces and added. "Yes, I know all about those old agreements. I know about the Nunn-Lugar program. I remember when that other media man with all the money, Ted Turner, was financing some of it. And then all those American scientists came over here, and we let them take our weapons grade uranium back to their country and remake it into nuclear fuel for their reactors. That whole operation was called Project Sapphire, and it was Top Secret. We have declassified it now as many of you know."

Several ministers nodded.

President Suleimenov looked down at his notes and shook his head as if he was disgusted with what he was reading. "Back then do you all realize that we had the fourth largest nuclear arsenal in the world? Bigger than that of Great Britain, France and China combined? We had the uranium. We had the weapons. 1400 of them. And with multiple warheads. And what did we do? We gave them up." He sighed and then raised his eyes and his fleshy lips curved up into a slight smile. "However, did you think we gave them *all* up?"

"What do you mean?"

"We kept some of them?

"Where are they?"

"Are they safe?"

The President glanced over at his military aide guarding the door. No one else could spy on this meeting. He decided he had to trust these men. After all, they were his hand-picked team. He felt fairly confident that these ministers would ratify his plan once he took them into his confidence. They would have to or they would be out of office and out of favor. Everyone in the room knew that, and so he continued. "You see, I have already begun a secret program. Not to develop a huge stockpile of nuclear weapons. No, that would not be wise. We are simply utilizing a small amount of enriched uranium that we saved to develop a few small nuclear devices. It's all underway now. The program has already begun."

"Already?"

"Where?"

"When?"

Again, he raised his hands to quiet the room. "A select group of our scientists at the plant near the Caspian has been working on a brand new nuclear weapon for quite some time. I did not want to announce any of this until I learned if they were going to be successful. I have just received their report. They say they are ready for a test."

"A test?"

"In the atmosphere?"

"No one has done an atmospheric test since…"

"Quiet!" the President shouted. "It will be a small test southeast of the Caspian. Down toward the Turkmenistan border. There are no people there. As you all know, it is a very desolate area."

"But on the way down there, isn't that where some of the new oil and gas is being drilled?" The Minister of Energy asked, giving the president a puzzled look.

"That's hundreds and hundreds of miles away," the President said with a wave of his hand.

"What about the protesters? They are against *any* type of testing. Anywhere," the minister pressed.

"They will be too busy organizing their reunions and rallies all around the country. Besides, they won't know about it. There will be no announcement. Let me repeat that." He stared at the ministers and said again, "There will be *no* announcement beforehand. Do you all understand? No announcement until we know for sure that our new weapon works just as it should. And once we know, then and only then, will we say to the world, and especially to the Russians, that we have our own deterrent. Is that clear?"

There were mumbles of "Yes, sir," and, "Certainly, Mr. President."

As President Suleimenov began to gather his papers together, signaling the end of the meeting, his Vice President, sitting to his right, spoke up again. "Mr. President, just to understand the situation as you see it, are you saying that you have information that the Russians really do have designs on our country? Information that moves might be imminent?"

"Let me answer you this way," the President said. "If you were the leader of Russia and you wanted to expand your empire, as they have tried to do throughout history, would you do it now when you have over 140 million people? Or would you wait until 2050 when your population is expected to drop to 110 million and China and India had populations that would have increased exponentially? I believe we can all figure out the answer to that question."

NINE

Arlington, Virginia

Samantha pulled up to the entrance of the modern building where a uniformed valet opened her door. "Good evening, Madam. Welcome to Turnberry Tower."

She was used to this routine now. When she had first visited Tripp's contemporary condo, she had been amazed at the tall steel and glass structure with a doorman who had an English accent, a concierge in the lobby and condos so large, any one of them could hold three or four the size of her little place in Georgetown. Even though she had a number of reports to review tonight and an early morning meeting, Tripp had insisted she come by for what he said would be a special dinner. She had no idea what he was talking about. It wasn't her birthday. Not his. Not an anniversary of anything she could remember. Not of the day they met or of the first time. . .*what a night that had been*, she reflected as she headed for the elevator.

He had simply said he had a surprise for her, and he really wanted her to come. Since he wasn't in town much of late, she did want to see him again, so she had worked hard to finish a number of projects. She then spent the afternoon chairing an inter-agency meeting on the Lincoln Tunnel situation, listening to a conference call with CDC, HHS and FBI officials about that virus problem and reviewing some proposed talking points for the President to use in a meeting he had tomorrow with a business group worried about added security measures he wanted installed at major ports. Whenever the President had meetings with outsiders on his schedule, the speechwriters prepared talking points which then were sent around to various offices to be cleared. Now that she headed up his Homeland Security operation, it was just one more pile of paperwork she had to deal with on a daily basis. Then just before she had left her office, the Chief of Staff's secretary had called to ask if she would stop by his office first thing in the morning, before the Senior Staff meeting. She had no idea why he wanted to see her. He hadn't sent an email or sent around any questions. But any summons to his first floor West Wing office could never be ignored. After all, he basically ran the place. So she had added it to a long list of commitments for the following day.

She stepped off the elevator and knocked on Tripp's door. When it door opened, she gave a little cry of joy. "Dad!" She threw herself into his arms as he gave her a hug.

"Hi Pumpkin," Jake Reid said with a big grin.

Samantha loved the way her dad called her "Pumpkin." He had done that for as long as she could remember, saying that you find pumpkins out in the field just as he often found her – out in the fields tagging along with him when he was prospecting, checking oil rigs or inspecting the gauges on gas lines. "What are you doing here?" she asked as she stared up at the burly man she loved so much.

"Tripp and I will explain it all to you over dinner. Come on in. He just opened some wine for you. I've got my scotch and soda here."

They walked into a cavernous living room with sliding glass doors that led out onto a balcony with a great view of Key Bridge,

Georgetown and some of Washington's monuments off in the distance. Tripp came in from the kitchen carrying a glass of merlot in one hand and a can of Budweiser in the other. He handed the wineglass to Samantha. "Here you go sweetheart. Pretty surprised, huh?"

Samantha leaned over and gave Tripp a quick kiss, tossed her shoulder bag on the side of the black leather couch and took the wine glass. "Surprised? I'm amazed." She sat down and motioned to her father to sit beside her. You didn't tell me you were coming to town. What's going on here?" She glanced over at Tripp and then grinned at her dad. "Okay, you two, come clean."

"Guess we can't let it wait till dinner," Jake said.

"Guess not," Tripp said, pulling up a side chair. "Remember how I told you that Jake had been bugging me to take him on some of our trips overseas?"

"Yes," Samantha said warily. "But remember *I* said that he should take care of his health."

Jake reached out and took her hand, "I do take care of my health, sweetheart. I'm in great shape"

"But Dad, you've got a pacemaker now," Samantha said with a note of concern in her voice.

"Honey, I've got a pacemaker, not a wheelchair. Look at me. I'm fine," he said, taking a sip of his cocktail.

She turned to Tripp. "Does this mean you've come up with some overseas assignment for him?"

"Yep! I've got a big trip coming up myself that involves a government negotiation, well, sort of a renegotiation. And since we took Jake on as a consultant, he's been analyzing the data on this deal, and now headquarters thinks it would be good to have him along. He could be a real help to us on this one, along with all the lawyers we always have to drag to these meetings." He held up his beer in a toast to her father. "And after we re-do some of the terms of the leases, we're going to head out to the field because they've run into a few problems, and Jake might be able to iron them out. I mean, since we're over there, we can call it a two-fer."

"But where? Where are you going?"

"To one of the stans."

"The stans? You mean Uzbekistan? Turkmenistan? I hope you don't mean Afghanistan? What stans?" she asked.

"To Kazakhstan," Jake replied. "The biggest of them all. Isn't that great?"

"Kazakhstan?" she asked. "But that's so far away. I mean, it goes from what? The Caspian all the way to China?"

"Girl knows her geography," Jake said with an approving nod.

"Okay, I know they have oil and gas," she said. "But aren't we already developing those fields? Why do *you* have to go over there?"

"Their government is trying to pry some more bucks out of us. Not that that's so unusual. But it kind of complicated, so we've got to go talk to their Oil Minister and a few others and figure out a way to sweeten the deal without, well, without breaking any laws," Tripp explained.

"You mean the Foreign Corrupt Practices Act?" Samantha asked.

"Oh yeah. Of course, we're just about the only country playing by those rules. You know that." Samantha nodded as Tripp took a swig of his beer and went on. "You should see the kinds of bribes, payoffs, deals the other countries cut when they put together their energy contracts."

"Kind of makes you wonder how we ever win that game," Jake observed.

"Our sense is that they're trying to get more of our guys in there and wean themselves off the Russians and some of the others. They know we've got the best technology, and at least we're honest about it all. Besides, they get a pretty hefty payout once the wells come in."

"Of course, it takes years," Jake said. "But still those guys have been doing okay since we all started drilling over there. The way they divvy up the payments, they're developing their own set of oligarchs. Some of the Russians may have bought up a bunch of villas on the French Riviera, but the Kazakhs are no slouches when it comes to Rolexes and off-shore real estate."

Samantha took a sip of her wine and put her hand on her father's arm. "So you're really going all the way over to Kazakhstan. How long will you be gone?"

"They haven't told me yet." He glanced over at Tripp who shrugged his shoulders. "But look at it this way," Jake said. "I've never been to that country. It'll be a great adventure. Besides, this time of year the weather is still pretty nice. We need to get going, though, because over the summer the temperatures can really get up there. Up to 120 or more, or so I've heard."

Samantha sat back and thought about all of this. The two men who mean the most to her in life are about to go traipsing off to the other side of the world, and one of them has a pacemaker. What if something happens to him? What if his heart acts up? Where would they find medical care in a place like that? She didn't really know anything about Kazakhstan, but she couldn't imagine that there would be any good doctors, especially heart doctors, out near some new oil fields. No. there wouldn't be any, and that meant her father's health could be at risk. She felt like the moment had come when the child becomes the parent, and she was now very worried about his welfare.

But what could she do about it? It sounded like he really wanted to go. Of course, Tripp probably made it sound too exciting to pass up. Could she trust Tripp's judgment on this one? Was there any way she could dissuade her dad from making the trip? She doubted it. It sounded like a done deal, and she hadn't even been told about it until they finalized their plans. Now that she thought about it, her dad always made his own decisions. He was a tough guy who ran his crews with a pretty iron hand. The men liked him though. Liked his forcefulness, his determination, his way of encouraging them even when a well looked like it might end up as a dry hole. Some of them did, but he was always able to put a good face on it and push on to the next one. His record had been amazingly good, considering the odds in the business. She took another sip of her wine, leaned back on the couch and crossed her legs.

"I guess there isn't much I can do to persuade you to skip this one, is there?" she said, facing her father.

"Honey, I want you to be happy for me. Don't be a pessimist. Wasn't it Churchill who said, 'A pessimist sees the difficulty in every opportunity? An optimist sees the opportunity in every difficulty?' Look, this is going to be great fun." He motioned to Tripp, "Besides, it gives me a chance to get to know this man of yours a little better."

Samantha felt herself blushing. Was he *her* man? She knew that she was the only woman he was seeing now. That is, whenever he was in town. But with his travel schedule and her new job, they hadn't carved out as much time to be together as they used to. She thought she was falling in love with Tripp. Was he in love with her as well? He had never quite said as much, so she kept trying to hold back a little.

She had been married once before to a great guy. She had thrown herself into that relationship. They skied together, biked together, hiked together. But it was on one of those grueling hikes up in the Tetons that a sudden storm had come up. He lost his footing and fell over a sharp cliff. She had leaned over screaming his name, powerless to get down there to help him. She had called for the medics on her cell, but by the time the rescue team arrived, it was too late. He had died from the fall.

After that horrible experience, she had developed an awful fear of heights. Every time she had looked down from an airplane or even one of those glass elevators, she felt queasy, light-headed and short of breath. She had tried to fight it and sometimes when she was with Tripp, she felt a bit more secure. Looking back, after her husband died she had spent some two years grieving and not getting involved with any other man. Until Tripp. Now as she looked over the rim of her wineglass at the handsome man with the great build, short brown hair and eyes the color of dark chocolate, she wondered if she could go through it all over again. Or, if he would ever ask her to.

Tripp got up from his chair and said, "I've got some dinner warming up. It's take-out, but we've got a pretty good set-up here." He turned to Jake. "There's a great deli around the corner, and they deliver some good pasta" then to Samantha, he said, "I've even got salad for you, my lady. Let's get things on the table and we can talk some more about the trip."

As Samantha took her wine glass to the dining room table, she took a long look at her dad and wondered why she didn't feel happy for him. The trouble was — a trip like this was just what he'd been angling for. He knew the business, and he was tough as nails. So why was she worrying? Why was she picturing an hourglass and wondering how much more sand would slip through in her father's lifetime now that he had a heart condition? As Tripp poured more wine into her glass, why did she have a feeling in the pit of her stomach that this whole thing just wasn't something to celebrate?

TEN

UCLA Campus

Powerful arms tore through the water with a vengeance. When he got close to the edge, he gasped for breath, made the turn and kicked hard, propelling him out from the wall. He raced to the other end, and as he touched the tile and surfaced he saw the scowl on his coach's face when he read the stop watch.

"59.45! You're never going to catch the Michael Phelps's of the world with that kind of time. What's the matter with you?"

Pete gulped some air and hoisted himself out of the pool. Grabbing a towel, he threw it around his shoulders. "I thought I was smoking it this time."

"Looks like you've been smoking something all right," the coach said derisively. "And what's with your form? That turn back there wasn't tight. Not nearly fast enough." Then glancing down at his clip board he said, "What's going on with you anyway? Looks to me like you should be spending more time training and less time with that nutty group of yours I heard about. The S.A.I.N.T.S.? I'll tell you something, Kalani, either you train harder and shape up, or this scholarship of yours could be pulled next season. And there won't be any saints on the selection committee to save your ass. You got that?"

Pete stared at the man. Lose his scholarship? That couldn't happen. He had to finish college. It was his only ticket to a good job, to a decent future. He knew he could swim and he thought he was getting better. Okay, maybe he had skipped a few workouts. Maybe he was too focused on the S.A.I.N.T.S. and the rest of his studies. His calculus course was a bitch. And so was the English Lit class he had to take. He couldn't afford any of the student tutors, and if he lost his scholarship he had no idea where he'd get enough money to graduate.

He had less than seven hundred dollars to his name. He had nailed a part time job at a shoe store over in the Mall at the beginning of the semester. He had wanted to work there because it was the only place he could find size 14 shoes and get them at a discount. But right after Christmas, their sales had been so bad, they laid off all the new guys, just like what happened last summer. He looked down at the floor and took a deep breath. "You're right. I need this scholarship, and I need to work harder. I'll try to fit in some extra time over the weekend"

"You do that. You've got to shave several seconds off that hundred meter butterfly or you won't even qualify for the finals." The coach turned toward another swimmer who was hanging on the side of the pool and added, "And all that talk about the Olympics? Forget it. The only thing you seem to have in common with Phelps is big feet."

Pete headed to the locker room and glanced at the tile walls. He always thought they were the color of Crest toothpaste, and right now the whole scene left a bad taste in his mouth. It wasn't just the chlorine either. It was the pressure. The incessant carping of the damn coach. The time he'd have to spend in the pool when he needed to concentrate on final exams. He turned on the shower and thought about the offer to go to Kazakhstan with Nurlan. He did like the guy, even if he was a bit of a nerd. Then again, it seemed like the nerds were getting all the good grades and good jobs these days. He wondered how much money he could make over the summer. They had talked about a lot of possibilities. Nurlan said he would be going to a place called Atyrau, a town on the Caspian. He had looked it up on the internet and found out that there were a bunch of oil companies around there. He knew that the guys who worked the rigs down in Texas and Oklahoma were cleaning up when it came to hourly wages. But he knew jobs were tight down there. Sure it was tough work, but he could handle it. If there were any American companies with crews over there by the Caspian, maybe they could use him. After all, there wouldn't be too many U.S citizens around so maybe they'd give him some preference. He'd have to think about that. Maybe he could ask Nurlan how to contact one of those outfits. Then if he could nail down a good job, he could make enough to pay back the air fare, handle his expenses and have some bucks left over for next semester.

He got out of the shower, dried off and pulled on a pair of sweat pants and a T-shirt. The more he thought about it, the more he wanted to jog over to Nurlan's dorm and talk about the trip some more. He knew Nurlan would be leaving right after final exams, and he had been bugging Pete to make up his mind. He had said it would be a great adventure and not to worry about money too much because Nurlan had lined up a place to stay in the same building where his sister had a small apartment. She had a friend who wanted to sub lease a place, and they could have it for a good price. Pete wondered about the sister. All Nurlan had said was that she was pretty involved in the Nevada Semipalatinsk protest movement because he had been affected by the tests. He knew that Nurlan walked with a slight limp, but he never complained or talked much about it, so Pete hadn't pressed him. At least the guy had been able to play a fairly good game of beach volleyball. But had he suffered too? Were there other things wrong with him? Pete knew that sometimes the effects of radiation skipped a generation. He knew that somehow it got into the genes and screwed them up and then even grandchildren could get leukemia, thyroid cancer, kidney and liver problems, and some young people were diagnosed with schizophrenia. He hadn't seen any of those symptoms in Nurlan. And he hadn't seen too much of that in Hawaii with the survivors he knew there, though the cancer rates were out of sight. But over in Kazakhstan where there were over a million people exposed to excess radiation from the Soviet tests, Nurlan had said that the effects were much worse.

Pete had thought a lot about things Nurlan had told him concerning the effects of the Soviet tests. While the U.S. Government had been callous and seemed unaware of some of the dangers of radiation back in the 40's and 50's, it sounded like the Soviets didn't really give a damn. Nurlan said they even herded groups of people close to the test sites to examine them later and see the effects of radiation. They had literally been human guinea pigs. It was monstrous.

Then again, he had said that the Soviets used Kazakhstan not only to test nuclear bombs, but they used the country as one of their main gulags. They sent all sorts of prisoners there to do hard labor just for being a so-called "Enemy of the People." Whatever the hell that was. Even Alexander Solzhenitsyn was kept there for years, forced to work in below freezing temperatures with little clothing and scarce food. A bit of black bread was a delicacy, and most of the prisoners quickly died of starvation and extreme cold. He said that there were miles and miles of hills that were really mass graves.

He thought about that for a while and figured that while what had happened in Kazakhstan was a testament to Soviet brutality, the American government had also let people, his people, starve when they were moved to different islands and left to fend for themselves. Then he thought about the time when Roosevelt had rounded up all the Japanese people living in the states and put them into camps during World War II. That was another group that should be getting better reparations for what the government did to them.

Pete left the sports complex and headed out into the bright California sunshine. The balmy air was quite a contrast to the images he had about gulags and people freezing to death. Of course, in the summer the people of Kazakhstan had the opposite problem. It could be brutally hot. Did he really want to go way over there and work in that heat? The more he thought about it, the more he figured it was okay as long as he could get a good job, save some money and hook up with the big protest group.

As for his own protest group, he had sent several more messages to that White House e-mail address he had been using. Something called Public Liaison. But no one had ever answered him. The more his messages were ignored, the more determined he was to exact some sort of revenge on the government. The unfeeling, uncaring government that had caused so much death and destruction with their god-awful nuclear test program. It wasn't right. It had never been right. And now if he could get international support, he just might figure out a way to make The White House and Congress pay attention and grant reparations. And if they didn't, it just might be pay-back time.

ELEVEN

The White House

"You wanted to see me, sir?" Samantha said, pushing open the door to the first floor corner office of the Chief of Staff. Through the back windows she saw that a gentle breeze was ruffling the leaves on the trees bordering the South Lawn. She wondered if she had ruffled some feathers and whether that was why she had been summoned to this early morning chat. Her boss was the National Security Advisor. She reported to him. But the Chief of staff was closest to the President, so when he summoned a member of the staff, you always complied.

Michael Benson glanced up from a print-out of the President's schedule that was lying on top of a stack of papers on his mahogany desk and motioned her to sit down. "Yes. We need to talk about this latest dust-up you seem to be having with Max Federman."

As a member of Congress, Mike Benson had been a staunch supporter of the President in his first term and had developed a take-no-prisoners reputation when it came to pushing through the President's programs. When the President was re-elected, he decided he needed some muscle in the front office. The first Chief of Staff was a friendly Hispanic governor, but the President thought he might be a bit too friendly. He needed someone to knock heads and play the bad cop to the President's good cop image. So he had sent the Governor to be his Ambassador to Spain and brought in Benson. Now Samantha faced him with a slight sense of trepidation.

"Yes, he heard me bring up the subject of a new threat at the Senior Staff meeting. This whole EMP idea has been bugging me, and I think it deserves a threat assessment. Evidently Max has a different view."

"This EMP idea has been bugging you? Who exactly is doing the bugging, if I may ask?" Mike asked in a rather imperious tone.

"It isn't exactly some *one*, it's the whole issue."

"It's the whole issue," he mimicked. "And just what makes you think that this is something the entire federal government should suddenly start studying?"

Samantha shifted in her chair. She knew that the intelligence agencies were all working overtime gathering information from agents around the world, sifting through intel from allies, placing people in dangerous situations to try and infiltrate any number of terrorist organizations and give us warning of plans and plots being hatched in all kinds of places. As they got advance word, they had been able to prevent dozens of attacks over the past several years. They also had teams of people, mainly from the cabinet Department of Homeland Security assessing the safety of entry points, ports and border areas while other groups were working on more amorphous issues such as biological and chemical threats. But so far no one was paying any attention to the threat of an electro-magnetic pulse. No one except for a few scientists who had served on the old EMP Commission. But as she had told her staff, Congress dutifully held hearings every few years without any spotlight ever being shown on their reports. And now that commission had been disbanded.

So why was she getting so exercised over such an esoteric idea? And why now? Just because she had read a report about some meetings and missile tests that took place overseas? No, it was more than that. She had read that report, and it had almost made her hair stand up when she thought about the possible effects of such an attack on any part of the United States. It wouldn't take much. Just a small nuclear device. Just a small delivery vehicle. Just a small ship with a small crew could wreak so much damage that they'd all be living like the Amish . . . if they were living at all.

She leaned forward in her chair, brushed a strand of hair back behind her ear and made eye contact with the Chief of Staff. "Look, I know we've got a lot going on right now what with the Lincoln Tunnel plot, the food supply issues, CDC worries and all the rest. . ."

"That's putting it mildly," Mike said.

"It's just that I read a classified report from a contact at the Pentagon about how both the Russians and the Chinese have considered using EMP type weapons at various times. And you know about the Iranian missile tests."

"So the Russians and Chinese considered an EMP weapon. But they never did anything with them," he countered. "You know that. Obviously, cooler heads prevailed. Both of those countries know that if they ever attacked us with *any* type of weapon, we'd retaliate against Moscow or Beijing in a heartbeat. Of course, they wouldn't use them. And as for Iran, they've been testing for years."

"But what if a weapon were set off in our atmosphere and it had no return address?" Samantha pressed.

"What if? I could give you dozens of what if's right now. We have red team/blue team exercises going on all the time. Is that what you think we should do? Add EMP to one of the exercises?" he asked.

"It wouldn't be a bad idea," Samantha said. "We could get some of the former EMP Commission people on one side and a few analysts from the Pentagon, DHS and maybe Energy on the other. And I could assemble an inter-agency task force to look into sources for this type of weapon. I mean, double check the dismantling that's going on of existing nuclear materials. Work more closely with the Nuclear Threat Initiative people. That sort of thing. What do you think?"

"I think your whole idea would be wasting valuable resources when we really can't afford the personnel right now."

"But . . ."

He raised his hand to quiet her. "Samantha, I appreciate you've been handed a tough job heading up that directorate. But it's my job to balance interests here. We can't take on every idea, every group, every threat. We just don't have the people or the budgets to cover every cockamamie idea that comes out of a thriller novel these days."

"But this isn't . . ."

"Listen to me. The reason I wanted to talk to you in private, not in front of the whole senior staff at one of our morning meetings, is because I want you to quiet this down, not rev it up. Max Federman did come to me after you raised the issue in the meeting. He pointed out that he's trying, we're all trying, to help in the Vice President's election bid."

"I know that, but how . . ."

"And what we're all trying to do is to project an image of control, strength, power if you will. You know that the first job of a President is to protect the country. It's not arranging doctor's visits for everyone who has the flu or finding jobs for people who don't bother to finish school or figuring out who should marry whom. The other candidates can argue those issues all they want, but what *our* candidate will be arguing is the continuation of a government that has and will protect its people. We're doing a fairly decent job of that right now, and Jayson Keller is going to keep those policies in place. In other words, we need to *reassure* the people that we're on top of things, not create a lot of noise about threats to the country that have no real foundation and no purpose other than to scare a lot of folks into thinking they're in constant danger. We don't need that. And we don't need your "Cry Wolf" tactics right now. You can investigate all you want. On your own or with your buddies at DOD if you need to. But right now I want no publicity on this crazy notion of yours. No inter-agency meetings. No play acting and no more fights with Max? Is that clear?"

Samantha sat there stunned. Since she had been named head of the White House Office of Homeland Security, she thought she would have the support of the higher-ups. Obviously, she thought wrong. What now? Would she just have to take the Pentagon report and file it away in her safe and forget about the whole issue? That's what Mike was really asking her to do. Maybe he was right. Maybe she had over-reacted. Lord knows she and her small staff had enough problems to work on right now.

She sighed and said the only thing she felt was appropriate at a moment like this, "I understand your point. And Max's position. Of course, I do. And I respect your position."

The Chief softened his gaze and stood up, effectively ending the meeting. "Thanks for coming in early." He glanced at his watch and added, "See you in a little while at the Senior Staff Meeting. We have a lot on the President's schedule to talk about today, including that state visit coming up."

"Yes, I know," Samantha said, getting up from her chair. She walked out of the office, nodded to the secretary, went into the hall, turned right and started up the stairs to her second floor office. Her words *Yes I know* echoed in her mind. Yes, she knows what? That she serves at the pleasure of the President and that really means at the pleasure of his Chief of Staff? Sure. That part was obvious. So if she wanted to keep her job and focus on the many actual threats facing the nation right now she'd have to prioritize her time. Okay, she knew she'd have to do that. But how was she going to stop *thinking* about an attack that could be absolutely devastating?

TWELVE

Washington, D.C.

"So when do you leave for Kazakhstan?" Godfrey Nims, the company lobbyist asked, leaning against the door jamb of Tripp's K Street office.

"Late tomorrow night," Tripp replied.

"Before you leave, do you think we could snag a golf game?"

"Sure. We'll go out to Burning Tree. Don't have to worry about tee times out there." Tripp swiveled around to glance out the picture window behind his desk. Weather looks good. Maybe we could take a break and head out after lunch," he said, taking a sip of his ever present Starbucks coffee.

"What about Jake?" Godfrey asked. "If he's still in town, maybe he could come along."

"No, Jake flew back to Houston to get things organized at his place and pack up the right clothes. We'll meet up at the airport for the first leg to Frankfurt."

"Gonna be a long flight this time, huh?"

"Yeah. It's about eight hours to Germany. Then we get another flight that takes about four hours over to Almaty."

"I wonder what that place is like."

"It's actually a pretty neat city," Tripp replied. "Word is that everyone wants to live there. Nobody really wants to live in Astana, the capital."

"So why not have the capital in Almaty?"

"It got too crowded, and the government was trying to develop some other areas. Kind of like what Brazil did, I guess. You know, everyone wanted to live in Rio but they wanted to get things going farther inland, so they built their capital in the middle of nowhere."

"Yeah. Brasilia. Been there," Godfrey said. "Weird place. Kind of looks like something out of a sci-fi flick. Strange round buildings, up-side-down structures. When I was there years ago I heard about how all the government types couldn't wait for the weekend so they could fly back to Rio and hit the beaches and clubs. Of course they built that place a while back so at least they've got a few decent restaurants and apartment buildings now. But still."

"Well, I guess it must be sort of like that in Astana. There was another reason though."

"Yeah? What?"

"Almaty is pretty close to the Chinese border but Astana is way north, away from China and also away from Russia. So I figure it was a strategic move in case either of those countries decided to make a move on them."

"Oh, you mean with the capital so far inland, they'd have plenty of warning before any tanks rolled in?"

"Something like that."

"But Russia isn't going to go in like they invaded Afghanistan," Godfrey said.

"Don't be too sure. There have been rumblings about Russia's designs on that country ever since it broke away. I mean, look what they did to Georgia. They always use the excuse that they're simply protecting ethnic Russians who happen to live in one place or another. And there are a ton of Russians living in Kazakhstan."

"Oh great. So you're going over there and Russia might invade?" Godfrey asked.

"No, I didn't say that. I don't think anybody has picked up troop movements. The State Department hasn't put out any travel restrictions. I was just giving you the lay of the land."

"Well, let's just hope the Kazakhs can fend them off if anything does happen."

"They probably can," Tripp said. "Anyway, I think it's going to be a good trip. We'll nail down some final payment schedules, head over to Atyrau on the Caspian and then go see our teams out in those fields that seem a bit screwed up right now."

"Seems strange that *you're* going into the field."

"With Jake on this one, he's the expert, so I figure we'll go together. It shouldn't take too long. Besides, it gives me a chance to see another part of the country."

"Kind of interesting that you've hired a man who could be your future father-in-law," Godfrey said, raising an eyebrow.

Would Jake be his father-in-law? Would he and Samantha ever get their act together and make it permanent? He sat back in his leather desk chair, put his feet up on the desk and pondered the idea. It wasn't that he hadn't thought about it. In fact, he thought about *her* all the time, especially when he was on the road and hadn't seen her in a while. He missed her on the long trips. Then when he was in town they tried to coordinate their schedules, but it didn't always work out. He knew his job wasn't going to change much in the near future. But hers might. If Jayson Keller were elected the next President, she might decide that it was time to leave and go back to the private sector. After all, even when a new President was from the same party, everyone in The White House tendered their resignations as a matter of custom. They had all served the previous President, and the new one had to have the freedom to appoint whomever he wanted. Sometimes he kept people on, especially the ones who weren't political like some of the secretaries at the NSC. A couple of them had worked for four or five presidents, knew how the world worked and had contacts in every major capital. They were too valuable to let go. But almost all of the Assistants to the President, Deputies and others usually left.

As he thought about it, Tripp realized he'd be damn glad when the next election was over and Samantha could get out of that rat race. Maybe then he could talk her into slowing down a bit and even consider moving in with him. As for marrying her, he'd think about that later.

"Uh, father-in-law?" Tripp said in an offhand way. "Not sure if I'm ready to call him that. We brought him on board because he's one of the best in the business. You know that."

"Sure," Godfrey said. "Just seems it won't hurt to really get to know the guy, and you'll be spending a whole lot of time with him on this one. You could learn a lot."

"I guess," Tripp answered. "Gotta be careful though talking about this father-in-law stuff. Samantha's great. But she's so damned busy all the time, and worried all the time . . ."

"You'd be worried too if you had her job. I know I would be."

"Maybe. It's kind of a drag though with her being on call 24/7, having to work late almost every night and never having a life."

"And you think your life is much better?" Godfrey asked.

"At least I get out for dinner. And even golf sometimes." Tripp checked his watch and reached over to pick up his phone. "And that reminds me, I've got to give her a call and see if she can break free tonight. I promised I'd let her know when we had our travel plans lined up."

"So you *only* want to see her to talk about an itinerary?" Godfrey said. "Fat chance."

"Mr. Princeton is on line two," Joan said. The efficient administrative assistant had worked for Samantha since coming to The White House and she was glad to have the young woman on board. She not only managed Samantha's calendar, arranged inter-agency meetings, coordinated sensitive documents and was able to make sense out of the hordes of paperwork that circulated through the office, she had turned out to be a very loyal friend as well. And in a competitive place like The White House where the old adage, "If you want loyalty, get a dog" usually applies, she was a god-send.

Samantha picked up the phone. "Hi Tripp. How's it going?"

"Usual routine over here and I know, I know, I don't even have to ask how your day is going, now do I?" he said with a chuckle.

She sat back in her chair and wound the cord around her finger. She loved to hear his deep voice whenever he called. She conjured up his image and could picture him leaning back in his leather chair with his feet propped up on the desk, drinking cup after cup of Starbucks. "You're right. It's been non-stop over here," she said. "I talked to Dad this morning. He said he's arranging for his neighbor to take the dog while he's gone and for the housekeeper to come in twice a week and water the plants. It sounds like you guys are talking about a pretty long trip. He said he didn't know yet how long he'd be gone. So what's the plan?"

"He's right. We're not sure yet because we don't know exactly how long these negotiations will take. Sometimes the government types want to wine and dine you and do the whole show-and-tell thing about how great their country is before they get down to signing anything. But this time, I figure it could go much quicker than that because we already have one team over there, and this will be kind of an add-on to that contract. Anyway, I'm thinking a couple of days for the formalities and then we're going to take some of our people out into the field and do some investigating."

"Will they let you do that? I mean, just wander around on their land?"

"Why not?" Tripp asked nonchalantly. "We've drilled in one particular area. Now we're starting a whole new field, and if we extend some leases and have the talent on board, I see no reason why we can't go check them out."

"That all sounds a little fast to me," she said. "I mean, I thought you had to sign leases, finish all kinds of paperwork, have it go through their various energy committees and all that bureaucratic nonsense. Even here it takes an age for leases to get the okay. And then, there's usually some environmental group filing lawsuits that delay everything."

"I know, sweetheart. Boy, do I know! But we're not dealing with the U.S. Department of Energy or Interior or Bureau of Land Management or any of them. We're going to Kazakhstan where there are only a few guys in charge. Of course, they've made a fortune by being in charge. Talk about the Russian oligarchs. These guys learned from the best. I hear that some of them have followed the Russians to the French Riviera to buy up a few mansions."

"So how do you handle that? We talked a bit about the Foreign Corrupt Practices Act, but you must have to work awfully hard to compete for the best leases, especially against the Chinese and Indians, right?"

"Not to worry, my dear. We get local partners and we work it out. Tell you what. Can you get away tonight for dinner? I wanted to tell you some more about the trip, the schedule and all of that."

Samantha looked down at her computer and clicked on her calendar. She still had two more meetings that afternoon and the last one could go long. "Uh, let me think." She paused for a moment. She really did want to see him. She always wanted to see him. And she certainly wanted to find out more about this Kazakhstan place he was taking her father. "I've got a late meeting, but what about

7:30? I may not get home in time to cook much of anything. Could we go out somewhere?"

"No problem. I didn't mean for *you* to fix dinner. I'll swing by, and we'll hit someplace casual." He added almost in a whisper. "And then . . . let's plan on some private time."

THIRTEEN

Almaty, Kazakhstan

The crowd gathered around their President on the edge of the Green Bazaar in the central city. The usually raucous atmosphere was interrupted by calls to quiet down from a dozen aides fanning out into the throngs of well-wishers. President Surleimenov stepped up onto a makeshift stage and held up his dombra, the traditional two-stringed lute. He began to strum an old folk tune describing the Golden Steppe. A well-dressed woman carrying a shopping bag stopped to listen. A small boy, his black hair ruffled by the warm breeze stared as reporters flocked around and photographers took pictures of the performing candidate.

These are my people, the President thought to himself as he finished the song and accepted their applause. He gave a slight bow and then reached out to grab the microphone offered by his chief assistant. "Patriots. I stand before you today not only as your president, but as your candidate in the upcoming election." He paused while several men in front clapped loudly. *Must be members of my re-election committee.* "I come here to this city of shimmering buildings in the foothills of the Zhailiskii Alatau

Mountains, home to one and a half million hard working people to tell you how hard I am working on your behalf….how we are continuing to grow our economy, invest our oil riches, and build the new Silk Road that runs through our great country connecting China to Western Europe. Yes, with all of this, we are developing new sources of income for all Kazakh citizens.

"Now you know our history. A history of brutal Soviet oppression." He heard mumblings of ascent in the group and continued. "Yes, we all know that many of you are descendants of the thousands of Chechens the Soviets sent here during World War II. One quarter of those poor people died of starvation and freezing temperatures within five years. Others, the ones who were too old to travel, what happened to them?" More grumbling from the back rows of onlookers. "Yes, you remember. If you were too old, you were simply shot! And years before that, well you know the story of how the famous Dostoyevsky was exiled to this country after being thrown into a Russian prison. And for what? I'll tell you. For being a member of a fellowship club that the Czar didn't like. But we know that compared to the Russian prison, he preferred our country. Even back in those days.

"We all prefer our country now, don't we?" The comment elicited a roar of approval. The crowd was warming up to him now. He could feel it. "We prefer it because it is independent. We are the masters of our own fate. Never again will we allow the Russians to rule our country, will we?" Shouts of "No, Never" permeated the late afternoon rally. "And yet there is a candidate who might allow just that." He paused for effect. "An opposition candidate who is cozying up to our former Russian masters. A candidate so corrupt he has amassed millions that he has stashed in a bank far away in San Francisco. A candidate who has bought a penthouse in that city in a most appropriate place called Russian Hill. A candidate who has also bought a villa on the French Riviera where seventeen of the twenty most expensive villas are owned by Russians. It's obvious he likes his neighbors over there better than his neighbors right here. Right here in Kazakhstan! Now he may like the Russians, but many of our compatriots do not.

"This weekend, this very weekend, there will be a series of demonstrations by the brave Semipalatinsk survivors and their families. They will be highlighting the atrocities committed by the Soviets during their devastating nuclear testing program some years ago—a program that still affects our people and their children today. I want to welcome them to all of our cities and encourage you to give them your support as they publicize their plight to the world.

"So, finally, my message to you today is just this: I am working for you! I am fighting for you! I will keep the Russian imperialists away from you! And on that note, I will have a special announcement soon, very soon, about a new project that will serve to protect us not only from Russian expansion, but from any others who would wish harm to this great nation. Now I ask you for your vote so I can keep working. Working for YOU!"

The crowd erupted with shouts of "Viktor! Victory! Viktor! Victory!" The President waved, took a slight bow and stepped off the platform. He motioned to his chief aide to walk toward his limousine, climbed inside and barked to the driver, "Take us to the corner of Satpaev and Furmanov."

His aide grinned. "Sounds like you want to stop at the Vogue Bar over there. Do we have time?"

"Absolutely. I need a Snow Queen."

"Ah yes," the aide said, gazing out of the window at the crowds returning to the Bazaar. "Purest vodka in all of Kazakhstan!" He leaned forward to close the window between them and the driver, then shifted on the leather seat to face his boss. "Mr. President, you referred to a special announcement. Do you mean the new nuclear testing program by the Caspian?"

"Of course that's what I mean. The head of our nuclear facility informs me that they have hired several new computer experts along with additional scientists. They believe they'll be ready for a test soon, very soon indeed."

FOURTEEN

Bethesda, Maryland

"That's a 420 yard par four with a slight dog-leg to the right," the Caddy said to Tripp as he handed over the driver. Tripp looked out and saw the small pond called Loch Lemon, named for a former member of the prestigious Burning Tree Club, a male bastion since the 1920's. He was hitting from the back tees and knew he needed to aim for that pond on the left side of the fairway, about 275 yards away. There were trees to the right and left and a dry creek extending from the pond across the fairway.

Tripp took his time with his backswing, hit the ball and followed through, but he pulled it slightly to the left into the rough, leaving him about 190 yards to the pin. "Damn. Thought I had that one aimed perfectly," he said to his partner.

"Let's see if I can do better than that," Godfrey said, teeing up his own ball. He took a strong swing and sent the ball 240 yards straight down the fairway toward the pond. "Now how come your handicap is eight and mine's a fourteen?" Godfrey asked with a grin.

"Tough game," Tripp said as he started to walk to where his ball was lying in the rough. The caddy pulled out his five iron and handed it to him. As Tripp gazed out at the pond, the trees and the dry creek, he said, "You know, this is as pretty as anything you'll see at Augusta."

"You got that one right," the caddy said.

Tripp hit his ball but it rolled into the bunker to the left of the green. Godfrey hit a great five iron to the lower left of the green. "Guess this just isn't my day," Tripp said. "I feel a little off-kilter."

"I always wondered, what's a kilter?" Godfrey chuckled. "But just wait until you get to the green. You can putt better than anyone else around here."

Tripp then hit with his sixty degree wedge from the bunker to the mound on the right side of the green, hoping his ball would roll back toward the hole. It actually went in.

"Nice work! You got a birdie after all," Godfrey said with a tip of his hat.

"I'm amazed I made that one," Tripp said.

Godfrey finished the hole with a par and they started to walk. "I've been thinking a lot about this trip with Jake," Tripp said. "There's so much riding on this one, I have to admit it's kind of hard to concentrate."

"You think the Kazakhs will stiff you on these negotiations?" Godfrey asked as they walked to the next hole.

"Not sure. It's getting more complicated by the day. Kind of like commercial jujitsu. I got an email just before we left the office saying that their authorities want a bigger slice of the pie. We keep telling them how much we're all going to have to invest in this project. I mean this Kashagan field is *in* the Caspian Sea. That sucker ices over in the winter and the oil is under a ton of pressure. It's much more complicated than the wells we've got in the Middle East. Well, you know all about that."

"Yeah, sure. So is there any chance you'll walk away from this one?"

"No way. We've got a whole consortium going in there. Besides, once we get that field up and running, we figure it could be the world's biggest producer after Ghawar in Saudi Arabia. So I've *got* to get this deal together."

"Wish our Congress would let us drill more on our own continental shelf. We've got a ton of new safety measures in place since that BP spill and at least we wouldn't be sharing all that oil with a bunch of foreigners," Godfrey said. "You heard that Russia is getting ready to drill off Cuba?"

"Sure. But that's your bailiwick. Keep the pressure on."

They continued the game and when they got to the 14th hole, Tripp remarked, "You know, this is where I had that hole-in-one last year."

"It's a 150 yard par 3," the caddy said handing Tripp his 8 iron.

Tripp knew it was a pretty narrow outlook off the tee with a large bank of trees all along the right side. That would force him to drive from the left side of the tee. He had seen a lot of his buddies hit it into the trees. Tripp swung and his ball hit the green but rolled six feet over the back edge into the rough. Godfrey's ball went into the back right bunker. Tripp chipped back onto the green and then made the short putt for his par. Godfrey used his sand wedge to get out of the bunker and onto the green, but it rolled down twenty feet past the hole and he two-putted for a bogey.

"Guess that's what separates the men from the boys," Godfrey muttered. "Trying to beat you is always a quixotic move, to sort of coin a phrase."

They finished the game, tipped the caddy and sauntered into the locker room to change their shoes and clean up. The flags hanging from the ceiling always gave Tripp a feeling that he was in some State Department briefing room. There were state flags, military flags, even weird flags that various members had donated.

They ambled into the so-called 19th Hole, the bar and card room, and stood at the long classic wooden bar that extended across one end of the room. They ordered their drinks and took them to one of the square card tables with a green felt cover. Over in the northwest corner of the room, they saw a couple of men playing gin rummy, an Ambassador and former Congressman. Tripp waved and thought about how it didn't make a hill of beans what your title was. Not here anyway. In fact, this was one of the few places in Washington where nobody gave a damn about your job description or what your resume said about you. As the inscription painted in gold on the lintel over the entrance between the locker room and the 19th Hole declared, "Here the robes of office are set aside and every man is king." A quote from Justice Samuel Whitaker. Here it was just golf. Well, golf and the latest political gossip. Couldn't get away from that.

He glanced at the caricature drawings of long time members lining the wood paneled walls. His picture wasn't up there yet. He figured he'd have to be a member for at least ten years to be granted that honor. Maybe some day.

As they sat down, Tripp said, "You know, I really love this place."

"Even though the women bitch about it a lot?"

"Yes, well Samantha says she doesn't care if I play here. In fact, she says that she'd rather have me out here than at some family club where a lot of other attractive women are floating around." Tripp sipped his martini and then added with a grin, "She did ask me once if the word golf really stands for *Gentlemen Only, Ladies Forbidden.*"

Godfrey burst out laughing. "You're seeing her tonight, right?"

"A little later. She usually works late. But you know, this will be the last time I'll see her before heading out, and I'm afraid she's going to complain again about my taking Jake overseas."

"But I thought he asked you to take him."

"He did, but she's worried about his heart, the pacemaker, the long flight. She's pretty protective of the guy. Always has been."

"You mentioned that. But Jake's a pretty tough guy. He can take care of himself, don't you think?"

"Ever since he had that heart operation, she's been kinda freaked out, it seems."

"Guess they're pretty close"

"Sure are. All I can do is try to convince her that we'll be fine."

"Can you do that?" Godfrey asked raising his eyebrows.

"I have no idea."

FIFTEEN

The White House

Samantha glanced at the President's schedule and flipped through a set of talking points for one of his meetings with a citizen who had called in a threat. It was actually a 12-year-old boy who thought a guy's behavior at a Metro station was rather strange, and he had used his cell phone to alert the police. They had raced down and found the guy had some poisons in a suitcase. The President was going to give a special award to the kid in the Rose Garden. Nice touch.

When she had driven in at dawn, it looked like it would be a lovely summer day. She caught herself wishing she could play hooky, just once, and go running. Or better yet, go swim some laps at the health club. Since being promoted to the top job after the previous occupant had flamed out and been arrested for a hit and run, among other transgressions, she'd had precious little time to think about staying in shape. Then again, she ran up and down the stairs in the West Wing and darted back and forth to meetings in the EEOB all day long, so at least she was keeping her heart rate up.

She checked her watch and saw that it was time for the daily call that often sent her heart rate rising even more while she was just listening on the phone.

Samantha dialed up the daily inter-agency conference call on her secure phone. "Samantha Reid here."

"Morning Samantha," the CIA contact said. "I've got DHS, State and FBI on. We're just waiting for DOD and we'll get started." He paused, and Samantha could hear him rustling some papers in the background. Then she heard the Pentagon Assistant Secretary click on. "Guess we're all here now," the moderator said. "Full plate today, and I'd like to start with the exercises planned for Washington's Puget Sound. As you all know, DHS and DOT are coordinating this one. They'll have emergency boats out there with new radiation detectors to be sure we can prevent a terrorist group from smuggling any kind of nuclear material in through that harbor."

"Why'd we pick Puget Sound? I mean, we've got, what? 95,000 miles of coastline in this country? Why there?" the FBI agent asked.

The DHS rep answered. "It's as good a place as any to test the equipment. They've got two commercial ports, biggest ferry system, pleasure boats, the whole gamilla. Anyway, we're on track with that one. I'll report back in a couple of days whether our stuff works or not."

"Next item," the FBI agent said. "Border patrol has been picking up a ton of illegals coming into Texas who speak Chinese, Arabic, and Farsi. Forget the Mexicans looking for work. We've got a huge problem tracking these other guys. DHS, are you coordinating those searches?"

"You bet. Trouble is Congress has cut funding for the fences, especially the virtual fence. As for what's left of the original fence, there's a gang that's taking down the connecting posts and putting up cardboard look-alikes which they can mow down when their groups are ready to cross. We need more manpower, and we've got a request ready to go to the Hill. Oh, and one other item. Guess this could go into the comic relief category. Just figured out that the uniforms for our Border Patrol guys are made in…you guessed it…Mexico. We're looking for a new supplier."

"Samantha, what've you got in your shop today?"

"NSA picked up some chatter about a possible cyanide attack on the DC Metro system. DOT is all over it. Jim's trying to get traction on some biological components that may be missing. I could have more on that tomorrow. Samatha paused a moment remembering the Chief of Staff's warning. He did say she could "investigate with her buddies." He just didn't want any publicity. She plowed ahead. But meanwhile, I want to talk about another issue I brought up the other day about preparing for an EMP attack."

"Uh, Samantha," the moderator interrupted. "Have you seen any actionable intelligence that anything like that is even remotely on anybody's radar screen?"

"Yes, well in a way. And I said before, the Iranians have been testing certain types of missiles out in the Caspian that they could use to stage such an attack. It almost looks like a rehearsal. And even if they're not planning to use them, we have no idea who they're selling them to."

"But wait," the CIA agent said, "They may have the missiles, but we have no intel to indicate they've figured out how to miniaturize a nuke so it could be used as a warhead. You know that. So why all of this anxiety on your part?"

"Okay," Samantha replied. "Let's just say that I *do* see a big threat out there, if not from Iran, then possibly from others. I don't want us to be the French at Agincourt."

"Aren't you being a little overly dramatic? This isn't exactly the 15ᵗʰ century," the DHS rep said.

"No, but if a bunch of terrorists were able to stage that kind of attack, it'll seem like it. I want to get a threat assessment going very privately, of course. I want to see proposals made to harden our electricity grid. I want to see a budget for safeguarding more of our military communications."

"We've already hardened a lot of ours," the Assistant Secretary from the Pentagon said.

"All of them?" Samantha asked.

"Well, not all," he conceded. "Besides, with these deficits, we've had our budget trimmed so much we had to cancel a bunch of tests of our missile defense system."

"Which is exactly the system we'll need to stop an EMP attack!" Samantha interjected. "When will Congress ever learn?"

"Time's up, folks," the moderator said. "Samantha, if you get the go-ahead from higher-ups at The White House, for an assessment or anything else on your list, keep us posted. But meanwhile, we all have more than enough to keep our staffs busy. Anything new develops before tomorrow's call, you all know the drill. CC me and the others in a classified email. Talk to you later." And with that everyone promptly hung up while Samantha gripped the phone, stared at it and just sighed.

Sixteen

Washington, D.C.

"What's this?" Samantha asked as Tripp handed her two print-outs.

"Trying to decide where to take you to dinner tonight," he replied, stepping inside her Georgetown condo. When my folks are in town, they always like to go to the Four Seasons down the street, so I printed out their menu. But Godfrey likes to hang out at The Palm, so I printed that one out too. I haven't taken you to either one, so I figured we should check them out. What do you think?"

Samantha perused the first page from the Four Seasons. "Hamachi Salad, Scallops, Octopus, Striped Bass." Then she switched to the one from The Palm and read out loud, "Wedge of iceberg with blue cheese dressing, New York Strip Steak with Hand-cut French Fries and Creamed Spinach. Hmmmm," she said as she glanced up him and grinned. "Guess it's rather obvious. We're going to The Palm."

"Hoped you'd say that." He gathered her in his arms as the menus fluttered to the floor. "Good choice, but my first choice is to taste you, sweetheart." He lowered his mouth to hers and pulled her tightly against his chest. He savored the feel of this woman and, once again sensed the hint of vanilla in her hair. He loved the masses of dark brown hair that framed her face. He liked that little widow's peak thing on her forehead too. He liked the way her great bod molded into his. The fact that she was about 5'8" and he was 6'1" meant he didn't have to bend way over to make it work. He cradled her head and kissed her once more. When she finally broke free, she whispered, "Do we need a reservation?"

"I made them at both places, just covering my bases. I'll call the hotel and cancel." He pulled out his cell phone and made the call while Samantha went into her tiny living room past the beige couch and coffee table, flanked by dark green side chairs, and two floor lamps. She turned out the lights, grabbed her purse and, with Tripp pocketing his cell, they closed and locked her door.

Tripp drove over to 19th Street and was about to turn right toward the restaurant when he pointed to a sign in a store window. "Hey, would you look at that? Don't see too many of those around D.C." Samantha peered at a sign that read, LAND OF THE FREE . . . BECAUSE OF THE BRAVE.

"I can see why you like it. Do you ever miss the Navy?"

"Not really. Did my time, had a lot of adventures. Well, I've told you about most of them. Seems like the stuff I'm doing now gets me to more places than the Navy ever did."

"I know," Samantha said in a plaintive tone. "And now you're leaving again. When?"

"Late tomorrow."

Samantha thought about all the times she had said goodbye to Tripp as he went jetting off to yet another negotiation or assignment for GeoGlobal. The last time she had been on an airplane was when she had flown down to Venezuela to arrange a rescue operation when Tripp had gotten into trouble down there. He had been kidnapped by a street gang and held for ransom. She had arranged for his company to pay a fee to a private contractor Tripp had once worked for after his stint in the Navy. It was an outfit that did security work for clients all over the world. They had mounted a very clever operation, found him, drugged the bad guys and high-tailed it out of town. It had taken all her courage to get on that plane since her fear of heights hadn't improved much over the years. Except now that she thought about it, maybe it was getting a little better because every time she went over to Tripp's apartment up on the 18th floor and they stepped out on his balcony, she didn't shake as much anymore. Maybe it was Tripp's proximity that calmed he down. And now with her crazy White House hours, she hadn't traveled or stayed in a hotel in months. When she thought about that, it occurred to her that it had been a long time since anybody had put a mint on her pillow.

"Here we are," Tripp said, pulling up in front of the long awning in front of The Palm. The valet opened his door, handed him a chit and then ran around to help Samantha. Once inside, Samantha pointed to a wall of drawings. "Looks like they've got a caricature of just about every politician in town."

"Yeah. Kind of like the walls over at Burning Tree. We've got caricatures up there too. But just of the members."

"Is yours up there?" She asked, waiting in line for the Maitre'd.

"Not yet. I'm not that important. But speaking of important, tell me the latest. Since knowledge is power in this town, what knowledge have you amassed since I last saw you?" he asked with a sly smile.

"A lot," she whispered. "But it doesn't make me feel powerful. In fact, when I get on our conference calls, I feel like I've been relegated to the role of spear carrier in some dreadful opera."

He laughed quietly and replied, "From your descriptions of that White House, sounds more like a soap opera to me."

"May I help you sir?" The Maitre d' asked.

"Yes, reservation under the name of Adams. I reserved a booth."

He consulted his roster, checked off the name, pulled two menus from behind his stand and handed them to a young man hovering nearby who showed them to their table.

"Now what's this about not having any power?" Tripp asked as he smiled across at her.

"Well, I don't mean absolutely *no* power. It's just that I'm working on a particular issue and nobody else seems to think it's important."

"I know what you mean about being ignored. Yesterday I had lunch over at the Metropolitan Club with another member of our Kazakhstan consortium."

"You mean somebody else is going with you besides Daddy?"

"No. I've got their proxy. That's not the point. I was just thinking about all the guys I see over at that Club all the time who are usually ignored by the current administration."

"What kind of guys? I hardly ever have time to go out to lunch. And if I do go, it's really quick and not to some private club."

"Well, over there you always see the used-to-be's."

"Used-to-be's?"

"Sure. You know. The guy who used to be Secretary of State, the one who used to be Director of the CIA, former Ambassadors, former Senators. You rarely see the people who are *in* power. They're too busy exercising it to go there for lunch. Just like you, my dear. And as for the formers, well you know how it is. Once you have an important job in this town, you never leave. You hang around, try to get some position as a lobbyist, join a law firm or if you can't line up one, you just call yourself a consultant. You don't have power any more, but you do have time to have lunch at the Metropolitan Club."

Samantha laughed in spite of her mood. "Guess you have a point there."

A waiter appeared. Tripp scanned the wine list. "Bring us a bottle of Carneros Pinot Noir if you would, please." He looked at Samantha, "I think you'll like that one." The waiter scurried off as Tripp continued. "Now then, what's this issue that nobody wants to pay attention to? Oh wait, isn't that Max Federman over there?" Tripp nodded to a table across the room.

Samantha turned to look over her shoulder. "Sure is. I think the other guy is one of the major contributors to Jayson Keller's election campaign."

"They both look like they eat here a lot," Tripp said.

Samantha chuckled. "What's that in front of them?"

"Looks like huge plates of fried onions. Guess that's why they both could use a membership in Weight Watchers."

"On the subject of Max, he's been watching me at The White House lately."

"What do you mean?"

"He's trying to muzzle me when it comes to some of my issues. My job is to analyze threats and work with all sorts of organizations to figure out ways to deal with them. Well, you know that. But he says *his* job is to get Keller elected and he doesn't want me calling attention to any of our vulnerabilities. He's trying to paint a picture of an administration where everything is hunky-dory so they can tell voters to keep it that way."

"So what if something happens on their watch? They'll get blamed big-time."

"That's the whole point and I am really getting worried about a new threat. I guess I can tell you. I mean it's been out there for years, but now I've seen some reports that make me very nervous." She went on to tell him about the effects of an EMP attack, how all computers, electronics, everything would be fried, how people would starve because trains, trucks and cars couldn't move.

"Guess we shouldn't have had that 'Cash for Clunkers' program a while back," Tripp observed.

"What do you mean?"

"Well, think about it. We got rid of all the old cars. But they're the only ones that don't run on fancy electronic systems. We should try to keep a few Chevies from the 1950's around, right?"

Samantha shook her head. "Get serious. This is really important."

"I know, honey." Tripp reached across the table and took her hand. "I don't mean to make light of any of your issues. Just trying to lighten the mood here. After all, this is our last night. For a while anyway."

He gazed into her eyes. Those dark green eyes that always kept him mesmerized. It was times like this that he wished he had a simple desk job in the city. Not one where he had to go traveling all over the world, visiting everything from dictators to dachas. Maybe after this trip he could cool it for a while. Spend more time with Samantha. Maybe. With him and Samantha, it was always maybe.

"Here you are sir, a nice vintage," the waiter said, expertly pulling out the cork and pouring a bit of wine in Tripp's glass. He took a sip, nodded to the waiter who filled Samantha's wine glass about a third full and then did the same for Tripp. "Have you decided on dinner yet, sir?"

Tripp had already checked out the menu online but looked to Samantha. She said, "Sure. A small Caesar salad and a strip steak medium rare with a side of creamed spinach."

"Same for me, except I'll start with the iceberg and blue cheese." The waiter hurried off. And Tripp said, "Now then, before I leave I just wanted to mention that last season we talked about going down to Naples to visit my folks. We never made it. But they keep bugging me about bringing you down there sometime. They have a ton of friends who always want to come to their place there in Port Royal. Dad says that when all these people make the trek south to stay at his place, he calls it the Mooch March."

Samantha burst out laughing. "So everybody mooches on your parents. When you have a gorgeous place, what do you expect? But you really think they want us down there too?"

"Of course they do. I know you never know when you can get away. Just keep it in mind. We can always head out sort of spur-of-the-moment. Anyway, about my own trip, I wanted to let you know that we've got it all scoped out. I'm meeting Jake tomorrow night at JFK. Then we're taking a flight to Frankfurt, changing planes and heading over to Almaty. Used to be their capital. But that's been moved. Almaty is still the financial center of the country. Kind of like our New York, I guess. Anyway, that's where we're having our meetings because given a choice, all the business types, even the government types, look for excuses to spend time there."

"It's just that it's all so far away," Samantha said, sipping her wine.

"I know. But once we get a new contract settled, Jake and I are heading over to Atyrau. That's on the Caspian. A lot of exploration is going on in that area. Well, south and west of there anyway. There's a port there for the oil tankers. Not as neat as Almaty by a long shot, but we've got a bunch of guys out there scouting locations, and that's where Jake is going to come in real handy."

The waiter sidled up to the table carrying two plates. "And here is your salad, madam. And one for you, sir. Anything else I can get for you. More bread perhaps?"

Samantha shook her head and the waiter disappeared into the din of conversation.

"That's what worries me," she said, taking a bite of the lettuce.

"Stop worrying. We've been all over this. He'll be with our guys. He'll be with me. We've got our tickets lined up, going business class, and we'll be in the best hotels. It's not a Third World country, you know. With all of their oil wells, these guys are richer than Croesus. We just want to nail down a piece of the action. And Jake's gonna help us do it."

Tripp poured more wine and was glad when the waiter reappeared with their steaks. "I hope the Caesar was to your liking," he said, exchanging the plates.

"Actually, the croutons were so crisp, I couldn't hear the conversation," Samantha quipped.

At least she can still maintain a sense of humor, Tripp thought. A good sign since he wanted to get her off the subject of Jake's travel and onto something a bit more pleasant. But just then he saw that Samantha switched back and was looking up at him with pleading eyes. "So you promise you'll look after Dad? Even if he doesn't always look after himself?"

Tripped stared at her, nodded his head and said, "I promise."

Back at the condo, Tripp felt it was time to keep a promise to himself. Tonight of all nights, he wanted to stay. Stay with this woman, calm her fears, reassure her that the trip would come off without a hitch. But who was he kidding? That wasn't the only reason he wanted to stay. No, he wanted to take her clothes off. Very slowly. One piece at a time. He wanted to stare at her great body, lie down on her crisp white sheets and make love to her. He wanted to feel her hair slide through his fingers, smell her scent, stroke her thighs and hear her catch her breath and call out his name as she said, "Please now." She always said, "Please now." He loved when she did that. And he could hardly wait to comply.

Seventeen

Frankfurt, Germany

"Passports, boarding passes out," the security agent shouted to the long line of passengers waiting to board the flight from Frankfurt to Almaty. Pete and Nurlan shuffled along, shifting their back packs as they juggled an armful of newspapers and paperback books. They had been waiting over an hour in a line that snaked around the terminal.

"As soon as we through line, we go buy sandwiches take on board. They only give pretzels, peanuts on plane." Nurlan said

"This whole travel bit is a total drag these days," Pete said as stared at two teenage girls being wanded by an agent next to the X-ray machine. "Those girls don't exactly look like a security threat to me."

"I wonder why they shake down like that," Nurlan asked.

Pete took a closer look. "Probably set off the alarm with all those pierced body parts."

"But they no terrorists," Nurlan said. "Good thing machines can't know what we think about. Right?"

"Shhhh. Careful what you say around here. We came up with a bunch of cool ideas about dealing with our own governments on the way over, but we've gotta be quiet right now." Nurlan nodded. Pete glanced around the modern airport and said, "I thought it was kind of weird that we flew from LA to Frankfurt and then have to backtrack to Almaty. Then again, I know you said they had that non-stop flight and it was cheapest way to go."

"That right," Nurlan said, motioning to a separate line of well-dressed people headed to Business Class. "See people there? They pay three times what we pay and just get some food."

"Yeah. Seems stupid to me. We all get there at the same time."

"Glad I didn't have to bring a computer along on this trip," Jake said, handing his passport to the agent at the head of the Business Class line. "Just one less thing to worry about."

"Yeah, well, I've got to have mine for the background research, the talking points, the meetings, and then sending all the results back to the home office. I also promised Samantha I'd be in touch every day. Course I could email her from my blackberry, but this way it's easier to send a longer message. Gotta keep the woman happy, you know?"

They moved ahead, quickly passed through the metal detector, retrieved their carry-ons and sauntered over to the waiting area for their flight to Almaty. "That little girl of mine is turning into a worry-wart," Jake said. "You'd think that her job would keep her busy enough without spending time wondering if I've taken my vitamins and done my exercise."

"Hey, she just wants to keep you around for a while. You know that."

"I know you're right. It's just that she took a whole year off from college back when my wife got cancer. Samantha was the 24/7 caregiver back then. Worked like a trooper. Wouldn't even let me hire a private nurse. I just don't want to see her thinking about a repeat performance. I mean, look at me, I'm in great shape."

"That you are." Tripp glanced around at the hordes of passengers waiting to board their flight. "Wish I could say that for all these other people. With all the weight they're packing, it's a wonder a plane can take off."

"You know, the airlines are charging for heavy baggage. Why don't they charge for heavy people?" Jake asked.

"Now, there's an idea. Maybe they should have people stand on a scale along with their bags. If you weigh too much, pack a lighter bag or vice versa. Otherwise, pay a fee for the extra weight. Think that would work?"

"Nah. Some group would probably bring a lawsuit," Jake said. "On the other hand, look at all the students on this flight. Guys with backpacks. At least they're in better shape. Must be going over there for summer break, although in my day the kids usually stayed here in Europe."

"Now a days there are lot more options," Tripp said. "Ever since the Soviet Union broke up and the countries got a bit of freedom, they built all sorts of hotels to attract the tourists. Wait until you see where we're staying in Almaty. It's the new Marriott. Just opened. It's got a tower that's the tallest building in town. There's a movie theater, not that we'll take time to go there. But it also has the usual fitness center that we can check out and it's got tennis courts and a swimming pool."

"Well, you should tell Samantha about that. Maybe it'll calm her down a bit."

"There's the boarding call. Let's get going," Tripp said, glancing around at a couple of young guys, one who was walking with a slight limp and another one wearing a T-shirt with the words S.A.I.N.T.S. across the front. "At least we can get on ahead of the basketball players, or whatever they are."

"We can hang here for a few more minutes," Pete said. "Gotta wait for all the rich guys to board first." He looked up at a TV monitor. "Maybe we can catch some news. Even here in Germany, they've got CNN on. Look."

Nurlan watched the screen as the announcer said, "Welcome to our international viewers. There are some new developments on Wall Street as the Dow has dropped again today. Traders are concerned about the falling dollar and high inflation due to predictions of much higher deficits. Here to sort it out is the new Assistant Secretary of the Treasury. Do you have a prediction for our viewers about the outcome of the next FOMC meeting?" He turned to a middle aged man who was somewhat hunched over the desk, adjusting his glasses.

"We have to assess the impact of asset allocation on monetary velocity. And to the extent it increases inflationary pressures on M1, the Fed may decide to raise rates by 50 basis points or more."

"What he say?" Nurlan asked, looking perplexed.

"I haven't got a clue," Pete replied. "But I'll tell you this. If our groups can pull off any of the plans we've been kicking around, America is going to have a helluva lot more to worry about than inflation and basis points. Come on, looks like it's our turn to board."

Eighteen

Washington, D.C.

"A turkey wrap and an ice tea, please," Samantha said, pushing her tray along the rail at the front of Cosi. At 17th and G Streets, the popular sandwich shop was right across the street from the EEOB. It was jammed, as usual, this lunch hour.

"I'll just have a fruit salad and some yogurt," Angela said to the clerk.

"Are you on another diet or something?" Samantha asked her friend.

"Sort of. I mean, I think my weight's perfect. I'm just too short."

Samantha laughed and replied, "Don't be silly. You're taller than I am."

"But you're a size eight and I'm a twelve. So it'll have to be fruit for a while."

They took their trays and drinks outside to wait for their orders to be delivered and were happy to find a couple of young men from the Legislative Affairs Office finishing up. "Can we snag your table?" Samantha asked.

"It's all yours," one of the fellows said as he pushed back his chair and tossed a cup in the trash can.

"I wonder what those guys are pushing on the Hill these days? Congress hasn't passed a budget yet. They haven't figured out a reconciliation bill, but they seem to find time to work on all sorts of nutty resolutions," Angela said, sitting down at the small round table facing 17th Street.

"Which ones this time?" Samantha asked.

"Well, let's see. Somebody submitted the Great Cats and Rare Canids Act."

"What's a canid?"

"You know. Wolves, coyotes, foxes, jackals Stuff like that."

"Are we protecting them or targeting them?" Samantha asked with a grin.

"Beats the heck out of me. They've saluted the 70th anniversary of the Idaho Potato Commission, designated July as National Watermelon Month, and a Congressman from Ohio sponsored a National Funeral Director and Mortician Recognition Day."

Samantha almost choked on her tea. "How do you keep track of all this nonsense?"

"I usually get contacted by interest groups pushing these things, but I put them off to their respective Congressmen who always want to please their constituents. I even got a request this morning from some scientists who said that a group in Australia discovered the DNA of kangaroos, and they want White House backing to do a study here to see how closely they relate to human beings. Maybe they heard about our Kangaroo ticket."

"I'm probably related. My favorite toy as a kid was a pogo stick," Cammy said still chuckling. "Dealing with all these groups, it sounds like you're kind of ambivalent about your job, right?"

"Well, yes and no," Angela said with a smile. "Oh, and I meant to tell you. Remember the guy who emails me all the time. The S.A.I.N.T.S. guy?"

"Sure. You said you had a dozen or so emails, right?"

"At least. It's just that now he's getting a little more belligerent. Maybe I should turn him over to the Secret Service."

"Maybe you should. Of course, they're pretty busy with all the nut cases out there."

"Guess you're right. He hasn't actually threatened the President. I'll wait a while and see if he just goes away."

"Ladies, here's your order," a young waiter said as he put two plates down on their table. "Anything else you need right now?"

"I think we're fine, thanks," Samantha said. "Let's get away from shop talk for a minute. Tell me about your date last night. Didn't you have some new guy lined up?"

Angela dawdled with her fruit, picking up one raspberry at a time. "Well yes. He wasn't exactly what I was hoping for though. I met him on line and he sounded smart, but turns out he spends his days pouring over SEC documents, investigating derivative schemes."

"Sounds fascinating," Samantha deadpanned. "But was he at least cute?"

"Let's just say he's got a great face for blogging. At least he was better than the last guy. Remember the one whose hobby was carving gourds? He always smelled like hand freshener. Seems like it's been a cavalcade of losers. But what about you? Heard from Tripp?"

Samantha brightened at the sound of his name. "Yes, he's been great. He promised to email me every day and he's kept his word. They're over in Almaty negotiating with the Kazakh energy minister, and he says it's going really well. They'll be heading over to another city, name starts with an A. Seems all their major cities start with A. I don't know why. Anyway, I love hearing from him.

He says Dad's doing great and is excited about going out to the field to check on the new exploration area." She took a bite of her sandwich and continued. "I really miss him, you know." Angela nodded sympathetically. "The only trouble is that after that disastrous trip down to Venezuela when he got in trouble and we lost touch, well, now it seems that every time I get an email, it feels like a Cinderella moment."

"You mean you're afraid he'll disappear at midnight?"

"Something like that."

"Hey, lighten up. He'll be back soon and you can relax. Now, tell me what's happening in your shop. How did that meeting go the other day with Benson. You said he called you in."

"Right. He and Max Federman are so focused on getting Jayson Keller elected, I'm afraid they're ignoring a lot of important issues."

"Your issues."

"Well, sure, my issues. They're important issues. When I was in his office, I happened to look over at his phone system and saw that my office was number seventeen on his speed dial."

"Well, he does have a direct line to the President, to Keller, to DOD, State and a lot of other folks. Just be glad that you're on his directory at all. But what issues is he avoiding?" Angela asked, finishing her fruit and reaching for the yogurt.

"The one I'm most worked up about right now is this EMP threat. I told you about that, well not the classified parts, but the idea in general. It's not that we have intel about a specific threat right now. It's just that this is something that could have such devastating effects on our whole country, I think we should be doing more to protect ourselves."

"We don't have the money," Angela said.

Samantha sighed and sat back in her chair. "I know. With the deficits we inherited, to say nothing of the entitlements that keep ratcheting up year after year I don't know how we're ever going to deal with half the situations that come across my desk. It's just that I can't get this one out of my mind."

"But you said yourself that no one is actually predicting this kind of attack, right?"

"No one predicted Pearl Harbor or 9/11 either. Unfortunately it seems that our intelligence community uses the past to predict the future. But now we've got to think about these Black Swan types of events and get our act together.

"So what are you proposing?" Angela asked.

"Well, for one thing, take our electricity grid. We should harden it. All of it. If one point fails, now we work around it. We can re-route the power even though it can take some time. Back in 2003 when power on the East Coast went down, there was a domino effect. But nothing was permanently damaged. Eventually they got it going again. With an EMP effect, all the safety devices would fail and be damaged themselves. Nothing would be re-routed. It would all be totally fried, and could take months or years to get back online."

"Why would it take that long? I don't get that."

"The big transformers we have could take a year or two to manufacture and replace. We stopped making those things and all their parts years ago. We have to go overseas to get them from places like Japan. It could take ages. And even then, we'd have transportation problems to move them around."

"Geez," Angela said, staring at Samantha. "I had no idea. We're that vulnerable, huh?"

"And that's only a small part of it. There would be no communications. No 9-1-1. No GPS. No computers. No food or water cause you couldn't get it here. Remember the old Boy Scout song?"

"You mean, 'Be Prepared'?"

"And we're not!"

NINETEEN

Almaty, Kazakhstan

"My God! That baby only has one eye." Pete exclaimed, staring at the large picture of a deformed child pasted on a placard. Thousands of demonstrators were marching quietly, almost reverently, down the large thoroughfare in the heart of the city.

"I tell you before," Nurlan said as they stepped into the street and joined the crowd. "Many born wrong. Not just ones near nuclear tests in Semipalatinsk, but their children and then their children. Look over there," he instructed, pointing to a young couple dragging a wagon carrying two little kids, one with a tiny face but a huge forehead. The other looked like a little soap bubble."

"What's the matter with that one?" Pete asked, wide-eyed. "That boy. Where are his arms and legs?"

"Some babies born with bones too soft. Call them jelly babies. And see other ones back of them?"

Pete craned his neck to see a gaggle of youngsters, struggling to keep up with the march. "They've got what we call cleft palates," Pete said.

"See lot of that here," Nurlan confirmed. "My sister has few problems. Not this bad. She just not so strong. She beautiful though. You will see," he said with a grin. Then as he scanned the crowd again, he frowned. "But many people from test sites have things you not see now. They get cancer of kidney, liver, lungs."

"I know," Pete said somberly. "That's what happened to Maelynn, my grandmother. I told you about her. How she died of polio. And then my mother got cancer." He looked down at the road, trying to hold back the memories and the tears. He was only a teenager when it happened, and he was torn apart watching her fight the effects of the drugs, endure the pain, and try to be brave. She was better than he was, and he was ashamed. He should have been more upbeat, more cheerful, a better son in her last days as her body, wracked with pain, finally gave up. He brushed his eyes with the back of his sleeve and murmured, "Do you have any idea what it's like to watch your mother die of something that could have been prevented? I mean, prevented if the damned government hadn't exposed the family to that radiation? Or maybe cured if she could have gotten enough money from them to get better treatment?"

Nurlan put his hand on Pete's shoulder and nodded. "Yes. I know. And these people know. He made a sweeping gesture toward the crowd. "They all know. There were over million people exposed to Soviet radiation back in sixties. Even famous scientist Sakharov."

"Andrei Sakharov?" Pete asked, moving aside to make room for an old man and woman, walking hand in hand.

"Yes. They bring Sakharov to watch test of hydrogen bomb. He then go back to Moscow. Treat him like hero. But later he got radiation sickness too."

"I never knew that. But I did know about hydrogen bombs. It was one of those bombs that my government," he paused and muttered, "bastards," and then continued, "it was the American Navy that set off that kind of bomb on Bikini Atoll but then the radiation floated over onto Rongelap where my grandparents lived."

"Same bomb?" Nurlan asked. "As you say, small world. But now with marches, we get attention of world." He looked around and pointed to several cameramen lined up along the side of the street. "See? Maybe CNN comes today. You think?"

"Sure, why not?" Pete answered. "Actually, this is a huge crowd but very well organized, I have to say. The signs are good. Most look home-made so they can't say it was some orchestrated thing. I mean, it looks grass roots."

"Grass roots?" Nurlan asked, raising his eyebrows. "What means grass roots?"

"It's just a term we use to mean that the people all believe in this. They're all involved. It's not phony. They're not paid to come here or anything like that."

Nurlan shook his head and chuckled. "Nobody paid to come here. Costs us all money to come here. It is money we want from Russians to help us get better medicine. Things like that."

"They didn't pay anything?" Pete asked.

"No. Nothing. Oh, Kazakhstan finally pay a little to some people who live right by tests. But it only about sixty dollars a month."

"That won't buy anything today, would it?"

"No. So we arrange protests. You saw how we do this at meeting this morning."

"I know. I was really impressed with the way your group communicates. I already sent a bunch of emails to our guys back in the states. We already use Facebook, Twitter, YouTube and all of that. But there are a bunch of new sites your guys have. We'll get on those too. You were right about comparing notes. I think we may be able to get some big protests going. Maybe not as big as yours, but the pictures here are incredible. And the kids. My God. The kids. It's so sad. You said we could share pictures and show some of these in the States. That would shock a lot of folks. Not sure if it would be enough to shock The White House, or upset enough members of Congress to vote for more reparations for us, but I could send some pictures and add some threats that we talked about."

"You talk about threats. We must see what we can learn when we get to Atyrau tomorrow and my job at nuclear place." Nurlan pointed to a side street. "Let's stop here. My legs hurt from marching. There's place here called Coffeedelia."

"A coffee house?"

"Sure. Has American coffee. We go there. Then later we go to Da Freak."

"Da Freak?" Pete asked. "Sounds weird. What kind of place is that?"

"It's club. Play good music. But we change clothes. Get dressed nice."

"Why? You don't like my S.A.I.N.T.S. T-shirt?"

"Not that. But here people dress up." He pointed to two men watching the protesters from the sidewalk. One looked like he was in his late 30's, about 6'1" tall with dark hair, wearing a dark suit and carrying a briefcase. The other one was in his sixties, a bit rougher looking, but also wearing a coat and tie. "See those guys?"

"Yeah, looks like they just came from a business meeting or something," Pete said.

"Maybe. Here people look better than in states. Women in clubs wear nice dresses like for what you call cocktail parties."

"Cocktail dresses? I haven't seen one of those since I watched an old movie on TCM."

"You will see. Maybe first we go Central Public Baths. Then we go to Club. And tomorrow we fly to Atyrau and begin new jobs."

Pete took one last look at the marchers and said, "This protest is your revenge on the Russians. Pretty soon, I'll plan mine on The White House."

TWENTY

The White House

Samantha scanned the list of emails on her computer screen and scrolled down to the one she waited for each day.

"Hi Hon. Almaty is a neat city, pretty warm — 90 today. Met with oil guys. Finalized the contract – had to give up some % but we can live with it. City is crowded though. Stood by and watched a huge protest march. Poor people were victims of Soviet nuclear tests years ago. I feel for them. Heading over to Atyrau tomorrow. That's the city on the Caspian where we'll be operating. Already have explorations south of there that Jake will check out. Then we'll head home. Keep in touch. Miss you, T."

She smiled as she read it again. Tripp had been true to his word and emailed her every single day. She really missed him and was finding herself day dreaming about when he and Jake would arrive back at Dulles. She planned to go out and surprise them both. She wondered how many more days it would be. It sounded like it could be at least three or four in the field and then a day or two to travel back to that city with the strange name and then another day to fly home through Frankfurt. Maybe it would be a week or a little more.

She glanced down at her schedule and realized she'd be chock-a-block with work all week anyway. Besides the meetings, she had a bunch of invitations. The most impressive one was for the State Dinner the President was giving for the President of Poland. That was a must-go. The others were for charities, dinners, receptions, and embassy events. She sifted through the stack and wondered if she would find the time to make a drop-by at any of them this week or next. She knew that she wasn't being invited because the host or hostess was that fond of her personally. In fact, she hardly knew any of them. No. They were inviting titles, especially White House titles. Those and Members of Congress along with the usual sprinkling of cave-dwellers — members of Washington's old guard, the elite who had lived here for generations. They owned the newspapers, the top law firms, the best real estate. They often had an initial before their name or a III or IV after it. All were listed in The Green Book, the "Social List of Washington," and their wives were chairmen of all the charity balls. They usually lived in Georgetown, Kalorama, McLean, or maybe Potomac, and Samantha didn't know any of them, except for Tripp. She figured he fit right in since his family had been fixtures in this town for years, although now they split their time between D.C. and Naples.

It seemed that whatever subject was at hand, whether a meeting or an invitation, her thoughts always seemed to turn back to Tripp. She was really falling for this guy. Fast and hard. But with their crazy schedules, she wondered whether they could find a way to be together. Really together. She was falling in love with him, and when he was away like this, it just made her all the more determined to make what time they did have together all the more precious. As soon as he got back, she promised herself that she'd get him to talk about it. Somehow.

She pushed the thought from her mind, checked her watch and realized she'd better leave for her meeting with the NSC Advisor. She had requested a few minutes with Ken Cosgrove to brief him on the latest EMP intel with the hope of soliciting an ally. With all that he had on his plate, though, she worried that her chances were pretty slim.

Twenty-one

Atyrau, Kazakhstan

Pete was astounded! "I thought this was some sort of back-water jerk town."

"What you mean 'back-water jerk town?'" Nurlan asked as they gathered their bags and back packs.

"When we flew in here, I thought it was just going to be a little town on the edge of that big lake with a few refineries and some run-down hotels or something. But they've got big buildings, roads everywhere, churches, those things with the onion domes on the top, and a ton of water."

"So not so back-water? Yes?" Nurlan said, flinging his backpack over his shoulder and pointing to the exit door. "I told you check internet."

"I never got the time. I just figured you'd tell me about it. But I never thought it would be this big, this modern, this . . . I don't know . . . just this much of a place. This could be fun."

They pushed through the swinging doors to the vast airport lobby where a throng of men and women, children clutching their mother's hands, and a bevy of taxi drivers had gathered to welcome the flight. Nurlan scanned the crowd and shouted, "There she is."

Pete craned his neck and spotted a very pretty young girl with long, straight black hair and huge round eyes waving at Nurlan. "*That's* your sister?"

"Yes, that's Zhanar. She say she meet us."

The young woman clad in black slacks and a light blue shirt tied at the waist rushed forward and threw her arms around Nurlan. "Welcome home!" she exclaimed with a wide smile. When she pulled away, she extended her hand to Pete. "And you are Pete Kalani. Nurlan has told me all about his friend. So glad you could come to our city. You will like it here. I promise. I have a car outside. Come. We go to the apartment."

Pete followed behind the brother and sister team and couldn't take his eyes off Zhanar. *What a knock-out,* he thought. *And those eyes. Looks like a fawn or something. If Nurlan had shown me a picture I would have signed up for this gig from the get-go.*

They drove through the city, past a Renaissance Hotel with an impressive curved entrance, another high-rise hotel called AK ZHAIK and a stone monument of what looked like two warriors on horseback. Instead of a weapon, one was carrying an instrument like a banjo or something.

Zhanar kept up a running commentary as they passed a stadium and then drove closer to the water. "First this place was a fortress. Then it was a city called Giuryev. But a while ago, they changed it to Atyrau. That means the place where the river flows into the sea."

"Cool!" Pete said, staring out the window of the back seat.

They drove through an industrial area where Zhanar pointed to a fish cannery and a meat-packing plant. "And over there, see? Those are the ship-repair yards. I have a job on a boat, you know."

"That's what Nurlan told me. He said you did something with the tourists. Do you have a lot of them here?"

"Oh sure. They come in the summer. We give them boat rides. I'm like a tour guide. And I have good news," she stopped at a street light and turned around to face Pete. "I know of a job for you. On our boat. The Captain needs a helper. I told him you were coming and when he heard that you speak English, he said okay, he could use you."

Pete broke into a big grin. It seemed that where Zhanar was concerned, all he was doing was grinning. "Hey, that's great. So a lot of people speak English here."

"Yes, all the educated people do, and you can help with the boat and with the tourists and we can take the bus together from the apartment to go there. The money isn't a lot, but it's enough," she added.

They arrived at the modest apartment building, and Pete was happy to find that their sub-let had two small bedrooms, a decent if tiny kitchen with a table and several chairs, and a bathroom with a shower. Not much of a view, but when he thought of it, he didn't intend to spend much time in the place. When he wasn't working and saving his money and communicating with his S.A.I.N.T.S. group, he wanted to spend as much time as he could with Zhanar. He had no idea if she had a boyfriend. She wasn't wearing a ring. He figured Nurlan would fill him in on her life once they settled in. He'd have to take it easy, though. Wouldn't want to get the brother riled up by making a pass at the sister too quickly. But what the heck, he had the whole summer.

TWENTY-TWO

The White House

Samantha opened the door to Ken Cosgrove's corner office on the first floor of the West Wing just as he was closing the door to his safe in the white bookcase and spinning the dial. He stood up and motioned to the oval table in the other corner. "Hello, Samantha. Have a seat. You know Hunt Daniels, of course. Since he deals with nuclear proliferation issues here, I thought it would be good to bring him up to speed on your new issue."

"Sure. Hi Hunt," she said, nodding to the lanky guy with sandy hair and brilliant blue eyes. She knew he was a Lieutenant Colonel in the Air Force and was detailed from the Pentagon to the NSC staff. In this job he didn't wear a uniform. He was a neat looking guy. Prety tall. Very fit. But he was just a colleague, not someone she'd be attracted to. She wasn't attracted to anyone but Tripp. Seems like he occupied her entire space-available in the warm feeling department. She refocused on Hunt and the task at hand. "Glad you're here. There's a lot we can talk about."

"That's what Ken said."

The NSC Advisor joined them at the table, opened his ever-present leather notebook and grabbed a pen. "Now then, Samantha,

I hear you've been riling up a few people on the political side these days."

"Well, uh, yes. I guess you could call it that," she said somewhat defensively. "But, Ken, you've seen the intel about those Iranian missile tests, the new ones along with the others using the Shahab-III. Then there are the notes on Russia and North Korea. I mean if any of those countries developed some sort of EMP weapon, we could be toast."

"I've read the reports," Ken said, "but what makes you think that there's an imminent threat? I agreed to this meeting because you've been sounding like there's an urgent need here."

Samantha glanced down at her notes. She never came into any sort of meeting without notes. "It isn't that I've seen actionable intelligence that an operation is underway. No. Nothing like that. But these latest reports look like a great big wake-up call to me. And that's our job. Trying to look ahead."

"She's got a point," Hunt said. "Wasn't it Wayne Gretsky who said something to the effect that you don't skate to the puck, you have to learn to skate to where you think the puck is going to be?"

"Okay, you two. Let's review the bidding here. We know that Iran has been testing missiles capable of carrying a nuclear warhead into space. We don't know if they've perfected that warhead yet, and even if they did, there's no consensus that they'd aim it at us," Ken said. "Israel would be the most likely target."

"Right," Samantha agreed. "But *if* they develop such a weapon, and maybe they already have, they could easily sell it to God knows who, and we already *know* that the Russians, the Chinese and the North Koreas *do* have the capability." She shuffled her papers and added, "

Ever since Congress disbanded the EMP Commission…"

"Lack of funds. The usual excuse," Ken said.

"Yes, the funding issue," Samantha continued. "But ever since they did that, nobody, and I mean nobody has paid any attention at all to preparing for any sort of EMP attack. I went back and read their last report, and it was positively chilling. If some country or some group were able to set off a pretty big nuclear explosion in the atmosphere over, say, Kansas, it could destroy the infrastructure of much of our economy since we're so dependent on electronic systems. You know it could destroy all electronics in its line of sight. Millions would die of starvation. There would be no medical care except rudimentary first-aid and then we'd have no refrigeration for drugs. Think about it, Ken, a dirty bomb in New York would kill thousands. Maybe more. A chemical or biological attack would hit thousands as well. But an electro-magnetic pulse would absolutely wipe us out. No electricity, no water filtration, no food, no transportation. There would be a complete breakdown of society. I mean, talk about gun control. There wouldn't be any. Guys with the weapons would be protecting their families, scavenging for what food was available. The cities would go first. The average city has about a five-day supply of food before trucks and trains bring in the next shipment. Well, there wouldn't be any trucks or trains." She sat back and crossed her arms.

"She's right about all of that," Hunt said. "Trouble is, in order to harden our grid and protect the internet and phone lines and all the rest, well, can you imagine what that would cost?"

"At least our military has hardened some of their communications facilities," Ken said.

"Not enough, if you ask me," Hunt said.

"And you are proposing what, Samantha?"

She had her answers prepared. Samantha knew that you never presented your boss with a problem. You presented him with solutions, preferably a list of solutions. He could agree or pick and choose or take nothing, but at least you had done your job. She handed Ken a memo with a copy for Hunt. It was a list of options. At the bottom were the lines AGREE _____ and DISAGREE _____ along with a place for his signature. "Okay, here's the way I see it now. First, we go for an appropriation to work with the utilities at least to protect our electricity grid. We need to harden what we've got and get replacements ordered. You know the big turbines, generators, high-voltage transformers, even the switching systems for the phone companies, all of that, and have them in a protected area. If we did need that stuff in an emergency, and we didn't have it stored somewhere, it could take years to get it. Sure, it'll take bucks. Sure. We all know that, but at a minimum, we start there. Point two. Call in the major banks and ask them to review their own back-up systems."

"We're already doing that for cyber-attacks," Ken volunteered.

"I know that. But a cyber-attack wouldn't fry *all* of their components. We need more protection." She referred to the memo and went on. Then we go to the House Armed Services Committee..."

"Betty Barton's committee," Ken said. "She's the toughest bean-counter on the Hill. You both know that."

"Yes, I realize that," Samantha said. "But I think that with enough facts we can go up there and paint a pretty scary scenario for her, and maybe we can get her to protect the grid and then maybe restore funds for an expanded missile defense system."

"You mean the funds she knocked out of the last budget in order to pay for those new tankers and Marine One helicopters?" Hunt said.

"Exactly," Samantha replied. "Obviously, we've got more testing to do, but I really think that missile defense is our best weapon against this sort of thing. We've now had, what, 30 or 40 successful tests against ballistic missile targets?"

"Thirty-eight," Hunt volunteered. "I guess you could make a case for not only stationing interceptors on our coasts like the ones at Vandenberg in Santa Barbara, but having some looking inward toward the possibility of something getting through to the heartland and being launched from there. Your whole Kansas scenario."

"Good thought," Samantha said. "Now I have another idea. With the head of Poland coming over next week, let's try to get some points into the President's remarks about the importance of missile defense and how we've changed our position after the previous administration stiffed them on those promised interceptors. I know we're trying to get things back on track."

"Another good point," Ken said, making a note. "I know the issue is on the agenda, but maybe we can highlight it in some of the public remarks." He turned to Hunt. "Put a memo together for my signature on that one." Hunt nodded. "Now what else?"

"Well, while I know that the Pentagon is working on all of our current MDA programs, I still think we need something new. Some new ways to intercept an attack that could take place high up in our atmosphere."

"I may have a two-word answer for that one," Hunt said.

"And what is that?" Ken asked, shifting his gaze from his note-taking.

"Cameron Talbot!" Hunt said.

"You mean that brainy scientist who helped us in India and did some laser thing after that?" Samantha asked. Then she raised her eyebrows and looked straight at Hunt. "Oh yes. Didn't I hear that you know her rather well?" In fact, she had heard that Hunt and this Cameron person were quite an item and had been for some time.

Hunt shifted in his chair and held both hands up. "Guilty as charged. But here's the thing. She works for Bandaq Technologies, one of our top defense contractors and yes, she's always working on the edge, coming up with new gimmicks. She had that new laser and she's perfecting some other ideas that all have to do with disabling enemy missiles. Well, you both know that."

Samantha nodded and Ken murmured, "Go on."

"Well, one thing we could do is to talk to the Bandaq people and let them know about our focus here and sign her on as a special White House consultant" Hunt suggested. "That way we stay in close touch, share intelligence. She's got all the right clearances, and we keep track of where she is on her latest projects."

"I like it," Ken said. "We've used her before. Sounds like a good time to get her on board again. I'll coordinate with the SecDef and let you know."

Hunt nodded again. "Once you give me the word, I'll talk to her and her people right away and keep you posted."

"As for the Hill, I'm afraid we've got a real challenge there," Ken said. "But I take your point about hardening the grid as a first step."

"And added money for the missile defense budget?"

"I'll take it up with Legislative Affairs, but don't hold your breath."

Hunt interjected, "Do you think there's any leeway in the DHS budget? I mean that Department of Homeland Security does have a forty billion dollar budget.

"And some 200,000 employees," Samantha added.

"I'll have someone take a look at that," Ken said, adding to his notes. "Meanwhile, we'll all keep up with the intel and, Samantha. . ."

"Yes, sir?"

"Let's keep our little confab inside this room for now. I'll have to run it by Benson, of course. And I hope he agrees to keep it quiet for now. The last thing we need is for Max Federman and the Vice President to get all hot and bothered again."

Samantha almost let out a sigh of relief. Finally she had an ally in Ken Cosgrove. Finally there was someone who recognized the risks and was willing to pay attention. And as for Hunt, he would be a great addition to the team. Now, if she could just stop worrying about some type of attack and get the images of vigilantes marauding through the streets of our cities waving guns and searching for food and water out of her head, she'd be in better shape.

TWENTY-THREE

South of Atyrau, Kazakhstan

"Pretty desolate country out here," Tripp said as their company driver drove the Jeep Cherokee south along the Caspian shoreline.

"Well, they wouldn't be drilling close to the city," Jake commented. "I have to say that Atyrau was better than I expected. Renaissance Hotel was pretty good. I wonder what kind of set-up they'll have when we get to the fields?"

The driver answered, "Pretty basic. Our guys have put up some Quonset Huts, that sort of thing. And we've got a few trailers. Some are good size – double-wides. And since we plan to be there for a while, we've got most of the good stuff in place. Extra bunks, food supply, machine shop, trucks, fuel depot, the usual."

"Sounds good to me," Jake said. "But I doubt if you're used to roughing it on most of your travels for the company, right, Tripp?"

"I have to admit they usually put me up in places like the Four Seasons. But this will be an adventure. Remember, I served in the Navy. You should see some of the places I've had to sleep." With the mere mention of the word sleep, Tripp conjured up the image of Samantha and the last night he had spent with her. He could just see her now right after taking her usual warm bath, wrapped in that big white towel of hers, with her hair damp along the edges. She usually pinned it up, but she had such a mass of silky hair, a few tendrils always slipped out. Her skin was always glowing and her smile was. . . well, the only word he could think of at the moment was enticing. She sure was that. Enticing, exciting, whatever. He had walked over and picked her up, towel and all, and carried her to the bed. He was already undressed and he couldn't wait to rip the towel off and plunder that body of hers. But he never did that. He forced himself to take his time. He knew she liked to savor the moment, so he took her in his arms, kissed her while he wound his fingers in that mass of hair, pulled her close to him and stroked her neck and back. She had responded by pressing her breasts to his chest, and it was all he could do not to take her right then and there.

"Uh, Tripp, you okay over there?" Jake asked. "You look a million miles away."

"Tripp jerked his head up. "I guess you could say that. I was thinking about Samantha. You've got quite a girl there, you know."

"Best woman on the planet. Next to her mother, of course," Jake said.

"I remember the first time I met her, well, not the first time. The first time was back at Princeton, but we weren't involved back then." Jake nodded knowingly as Tripp went on. "I mean, after my first meeting with her in The White House, I came back to my office and told our lobbyist that I had met this gorgeous woman with high cheek bones. And he just laughed and asked me if I had ever known a woman with low cheek bones."

Jake chuckled. "Still sending her those emails?"

"Oh yeah. I wonder if I'll be able to get through from the field, though."

"Sure you can," the driver said, pointing straight ahead. "See, there's a cell tower up on that ridge. They've installed them all over the place. We're in touch with headquarters all the time. Have to be."

After several hours, they finally pulled into a complex of huts, trailers, storage facilities and garages. "Can't wait to get out with the crews," Jake remarked, checking out his surroundings.

"I hear they're really anxious to meet you too, Mr. Reid," the driver said. "I expect they'll want you out there first thing in the morning. We'll have a truck convoy heading out at around six. Like to get going before the sun gets too high around here."

"No problem," Jake said. "I'll be ready." He turned to Tripp. "You know I don't think I've properly thanked you for taking me along on this trip. We've had a great time so far, and if I can help these guys for a few days out here, it'll top it all off. Makes me feel young again, kind of like one of the wild-catters."

They unloaded their gear and Tripp said, "Looks like an office over there. I'll go see if I can set up my computer."

Jake called out, "You send another email to Samantha and tell her we're doing great out here. Having the time of my life!"

TWENTY-FOUR

Atyrau, Kazakhstan

"They're going to do test. Nuclear test!" Nurlan said, wide-eyed. "I knew they were doing things with nuclear energy at plant but when I signed on, I didn't know they already had weapons." He stared down at his plate of food at the small table in their kitchen. "I've got to do something."

"What can you do?" Pete asked, sampling the lamb shish kabob that Nurlan brought home. At least it wasn't horse meat this time. They ate a lot of that here but Pete couldn't get used to it. He didn't mind the flat noodles that came with the lamb though. They called it "Plot," and it had a bunch of rice, carrots and onions all mixed together. It was kind of sticky but that was okay. It tasted pretty good.

"I have idea," Nurlan said reaching for his glass of green tea. "They put me on computers, and I'm best computer guy they have."

"That figures," Pete said. "But still, what can you do about a test? Do you think you can stop it somehow? If you did, they'd just reschedule it or something, right?"

Nurlan paused for a moment, chewing on the lamb. "I have idea. They already set up missile site down south. But we have controls from here. Complicated you say. But I'm in control room. I'm on computer and maybe I can keep it from going off on ground."

"How would you do that?"

"Not sure. I try to, what is it you say all time? I try screw it up. Somehow."

Pete shook his head. "You better be careful. What if you're caught? What would they do to you?"

Nurlan looked up at the ceiling, stared at the cracked plaster and finally replied, "I won't get caught. I cover things. They not know computers like I do. That why I am put there. They been showing me all systems, how they work, how missile is set off, what is count down, all things. I been thinking this ever since I start work. I not tell you until I know. Now I know. So want you know too. But you can't tell anybody. All big secret."

"Who is in charge of all of this? Is it the government? Is it the President? Are they involved in this test? I figure they have to be but this could cause all sorts of trouble with other countries, couldn't it?"

"Don't know about trouble. But I hear talking about how President wants test. So we do test. We do it tomorrow."

"Tomorrow? I'm glad it's a long way away from here," Pete said, taking another sip of the tea. He would rather have had a Coke, but he decided he had to go with the flow here.

"I come home tomorrow and if plan works, we celebrate."

Twenty-five

The White House

"Who does she think she is? Saul on the road to Damascus getting revelations?" Max Federman muttered to the Chief of Staff. He had settled his paunchy frame into a chair in Mike Benson's expansive office across the West Wing from the NSC Advisor's enclave. Mike's was just a few steps away from the Oval Office, the ultimate sign of power and access. Through the windows, protected from spying microwaves by special glass, grey storm clouds were gathering over the South Lawn, while on the North Lawn, members of the White House press corps were scrambling to do their constant stand-ups before the storm hit. Mike leaned back in his leather chair, steepled his fingers and felt like the dark scene outside really mirrored his mood right now.

"I know. The lady certainly can be persistent. Cosgrove told me that she's still working this EMP threat because she's been studying military intelligence."

"Military intelligence? Isn't that sort of an oxy-moron?"

"Sometimes," Mike admitted. "Kind of like Civil War. Anyway, Cosgrove says they're working quietly."

"Quietly? How can you raise an issue that she says could involve terrorists, rogue states, wild weapons and all the rest and say that it'll be done quietly?"

"For now, what they're doing is bringing Dr. Cameron Talbot on board as a consultant and studying the defense budget along with the numbers at DHS looking for money to protect some of our infrastructure."

"Looks to me like she's getting protection money to shore up her own position here. Good God, Mike. Can't we shut the woman up?"

Just then a loud clap of thunder echoed through the corridors. Mike glanced out the window as wind driven rain drops began to pelt the glass. "At least we're not under attack here yet. As for shutting her up, I did speak to her about raising the issue at the Senior Staff meeting. At least she hasn't done any more of that."

"Well, that's damning with faint praise," Max said. "Seems like you tell her 'No' and she goes running to Cosgrove. Either she didn't get your message or English is her second language."

"Trouble is," Mike said, "she's damned effective in her job. Besides, the President likes her."

"So we can't fire her?"

"I'll keep watching her performance. You can be sure of that. And by the way, speaking of performance, how are the Veep's numbers right now?"

"Campaign is looking pretty good, so far. Not quite time for the balloon drop though. There are a ton of events and rallies on his schedule, and we're always looking for ways to appeal to the various groups. You know, the women's groups, the Hispanic groups, the ethnic groups, the black groups. You got a group, he wants to do your convention."

"As for ethnic groups, we're making sure he's involved in all the meetings and photo ops with the President of Poland on his State visit next week," Mike said.

"Yes. Glad we could get that wired with the Scheduling Office."

"What about the Hispanics? What happened to that Rose Garden event the other day? I heard there was some confusion with your media people."

Max shifted in his chair and shrugged. "Yeah, well, we kind of dropped the ball on that one. There was this kid, Juan Santos, local kid, who won a Science Fair over in Maryland. He had some sort of model airplane that does the loop-de-loops or something like that. So we figure it could be a great photo op to invite him in, have him fly the plane, have the President and the Veep give him another award and be in all the pictures. Then we'd distribute them to our Hispanic data base of newspapers, internet sites, the whole bit."

"So what happened? I was on the Hill that day and missed that one," Mike said.

Max hesitated and took a deep breath. "Well, after bringing in the kid, inviting in every Hispanic and Mexican photographer in town and doing the whole stunt, we got press releases and photos all ready to send out and guess what?"

"What?"

"We find out that the damn kid is a Filipino."

Mike burst out laughing. "Can't win 'em all, Max. Just keep at it. We need Jay to win in November and be in Oval next January. Too much riding on this one to mess up."

"I know, boss. I know."

"Okay, keep me posted. And meanwhile, I'll be keeping a close eye on our lady Samantha. It's just that you know she's never been the kick-the-can-down-the-road type. She always wants to fix it. Now!"

"Yeah, well if you can't get her to pivot on this one, we may have to find some other miss-step we can use to fire her ass."

TWENTY-SIX

South of Atyrau, Kazakhstan

At 6:30 a.m., Jake and Tripp were tromping through an oil field, led by the GeoGlobal on-site supervisor. Even at that early hour the air was warm. Just a precursor to the scorching heat that would move into the area during the summer months. They walked past several storage tanks and Jake saw that the tall, cylindrical one was a gunbarrell tank used to separate oil from salt water. There was a frenzy of activity as crews worked on installing an oil rig pulling unit very similar to the ones Jake had used in West Texas. It was about double the height of a tall telephone pole.

"Come on over and help us check out one of our pump jack well heads," the supervisor said to Jake. "We've been having some trouble with this one, and it's the same type we're planning to use on our next set of wells. May need to trouble shoot these suckers, though. Tell me what you think. Then later I'd like to get your take on our plans for the new field. Sure is great to have you out here with us."

Jake beamed at the praise and set to work with the crews for the next several hours while Tripp watched the action, chatted with the supervisor, and thought about sending another email to Samantha. He checked his watch and decided it could wait a while.

With the time difference, she probably wouldn't even have a chance to read it for several hours. He had tried to give her a flavor of the trip so far, the places they had seen, the tenor of the negotiations, and especially Jake's excitement at being out here as a top-flight consultant. She had answered his emails, but never said anything about her work. He knew she couldn't send much over the internet. It would be like posting your agenda on Facebook for the whole world to see. She had told him she was invited to a bunch of social stuff, dinners and the usual DC events. He didn't care much for the Embassy circuit, but he did try to hit some of the receptions on the Hill, if only to keep up his contacts with members of the energy and resource committees. He was thinking about Samantha a lot these days. It was always this way when he was away from her. Even though he felt good about the deal they had struck back in Almaty, he was anxious to wrap up this field trip and get on the plane to Frankfurt.

He leaned into the Jeep to check out one of their maps when suddenly he felt the ground begin to shake. "What the hell?" he shouted to Jake and the crew. "You guys have earthquakes over here?"

Tripp jerked his head up when he saw what looked like a blinding fireball miles up in the sky. An explosion of some sort. A big one. But why is it way up there. Seems almost like a space shuttle is exploding, but that didn't make any sense. He hadn't heard of any space activities around here. Sure, the Russians still had a rocket company in Baikanor, but that's nowhere near here. What could it be? He raced to the wellhead where a dozen crew members were shouting and pointing toward the horizon.

"What's that?"

"Something exploded."

"Helluva fire."

"Did you feel it?"

"Damnation!"

Just as Tripp got to the cluster of men, he saw Jake grab his chest and collapse on the ground. He raced over and kneeled down. "Jake, what is it? Your heart? What?" He shouted to the others, "Help me. Jake's hurt or something. Anybody see anything? Did something hit him? Kick back or something?" They gathered around as Tripp leaned down and shouted, "Jake! Jake! What is it? Can you hear me?"

Jake's eyes were open but they had a dull stare. They weren't moving. Tripp was frantic. "Heart attack? Could it be a heart attack? But he's got a pacemaker. Wonder if it's screwed up or something. Maybe he needs CPR." Tripp stretched Jake out on his back, tore open the man's shirt and began to put pressure on his chest. Continuous chest compression. That's what they called it. He pushed down, over and over and over again. Had to get the blood flowing to the brain. Had to force it. If he let up, the blood flow would stop. If he could just get it going, keep it going, maybe he could revive the man. He kept up the pressure, up, down, up, down. After several minutes, he called out to the Supervisor, "See what I'm doing here? Can you spell me for just a minute? Watch. Like this. We can't stop. Can't break the cycle."

The supervisor knelt down and repeated the routine while Tripp shouted to the other men who had gathered around. "Need help. Any medical help around here? Anyone? Anything?" He reached into his pocket for his cell and saw several other men doing the same thing. But they were all shaking their heads.

"No bars."

"No signal."

"Mine's cut off."

"I know I charged this sucker."

"What's the matter anyway?"

"Don't know. Must be a power failure or something."

"Yeah. Wait a minute. Listen. Motors are off. Look at the equipment. Everything's stopped. What the hell?"

Tripp looked over at rigs. They had all quit. He stared down at his cell phone. Nothing. Then he knelt beside Jake again. "Okay, I'll take over again. Gotta keep up the pressure. It might take a while, but we can do this. We've *got* to do this." Tripp kept up the CPR routine. His own breath was now coming in ragged gulps. How in hell could this have happened? Jake was fine yesterday. He was fine this morning. Ate a good breakfast. Jumped in the Jeep. Anxious to get out here with the men. Happy that they wanted his help. Said he couldn't wait to be involved. And now this.

He leaned closer. No breath. He tried again. Several more agonizing minutes ticked by as he kept up the motion. Again. Again. More time, more tries. It wasn't working Nothing was working. He'd been trained in the Navy. He could do this. He had seen some of his buddies shot up, in bad shape, they had pulled through. Jake would pull through too. He had to. "Breathe, Jake. Breathe." He commanded. The other men were mumbling, shaking their heads. Tripp leaned down again, checked for a breath, a reaction, something. But there was . . . nothing!

Now a few of the men were shouting orders as the driver raced over to the Jeep. He tore open the door and jumped inside. He inserted the key but he couldn't get it started. Then as Tripp briefly looked up, the driver cried out, "Car won't start? What the hell is going on here?"

The supervisor leaned down and said, "Never seen anything like this." He tried to take over the CPR routinne again, but Tripp pushed him aside and felt for a pulse in Jake's neck. He waited, counted and screamed, "Jake is dead!"

Twenty-seven

Atyrau, Kazakhstan

"They're falling overboard. My God! They can't hold on!" Pete shouted to the Captain as he tried to regain control of the boat. It was listing badly and the wheel wasn't responding. The engine had sputtered and stopped. Wind whipped waves crashed against the side, shifting the trajectory once more.

Pete grabbed a guard rail and raced to a box holding the life preservers. He shouted to a handful of men trying to crawl to the starboard side. "Come help me! Have to throw these out. People overboard. Maybe some can't swim. Hurry. Now. Here, take these." They grabbed and shoved and tossed the jackets overboard. Pete saw that two of the men were trying to put on the life vests themselves rather than throwing them to the tourists screaming in the water. "Help them for God's sake."

Others rushed up, grabbing the side of the box, pushing, shoving. It was chaos. Complete chaos with the Captain trying in vain to restart the engine and failing once again. Pete saw dozens of people bobbing in the water, one woman was desperately clinging to a life vest while propping up a small child's head above the water. Pete tore off his sneakers and dove over the side. He used powerful strokes to reach the hysterical woman. He treaded water while trying to get the vest on her. But the little one was crying and clinging to his mother's neck. She went under, and Pete reached out, pulled her to the surface, snatched the child and finally managed to get her arms through the vest. He shouted to her to hold on. She grabbed frantically at his shirt. "My baby. My baby," she screamed.

Pete had a grip on the child and shouted to her to hold onto his belt. Now, with the mother grasping and coughing, he frog-kicked while he held the baby's head above the churning water. He glanced back and saw more people slide into the water amid more shouts and screams. He kept up his pace. *Only another couple hundred yards to the dock,* he thought. He took a deep breath and pushed on. The woman was breathing heavily, but she was holding on. The baby was still shrieking when he reached the planks at the boarding area. He pushed the woman toward a set of stairs that extended down into the water. She let go of his belt and grabbed the stair. She looked back, "My baby."

"I've got him. He's okay," Pete said. "I'll hand him to you."

"Aren't you coming up too?" she called.

"Can't. Gotta go back for others." He pushed the baby up and into the grateful arms of the young woman. She was crying again. But this time, they were tears of relief. She tore off the jacket and tossed it down to him.

"You take it. For you. Or for somebody else. Thank you. Thank God for you." She twisted some water out of her sodden skirt, held the baby close and ran toward the street.

Pete put on the jacket, and with its buoyancy he was able to race back to the startling scene. He scanned the area where now a small convoy of row boats had gathered to try and pull some of the tourists out of the churning water. The main boat was now leaning at a perilous angle. Nobody could hang on. It was going down. Any minute now. He swam closer and saw a young girl thrashing in the water near the bow of the boat. *My God! It's Zhanar. Maybe she can't swim. Gotta get her outta there. Away from the boat. It'll go down and take her with it.* He called her name, but in the din and cacophony, he knew she couldn't hear him. He swam faster. He had to get to her. Had to save her. He saw her go down. He did a surface dive and grabbed her hair. Then he got hold of her arm and quickly pulled her to surface. She was coughing and sputtering. *Good. Coughing is good. She's alive.* He pulled her to him and cried out, "I've got you. It's going to be okay. Stay with me now. I'll get you out of here."

She opened her eyes, shook the water off her face and stared at him. She still couldn't talk. But her eyes said it all. They said she was terrified. He held her tight while beginning his frog kick once again. "Don't worry. You're going to be all right. Try to relax. I've got a good hold on you."

She coughed some more and gasped. "I can't swim very well. Just a little. People are drowning. Have to help."

"Let me get you away from here first. More boats are coming. People are helping. But you're the one I want to help now. Try to float on your back. I'll hold you up and get you to the shore."

She tried to float but her legs kept sinking. "Can't do it," she cried out.

He turned her around, got a good hold under her shoulder and used a sidestroke to propel them both away from the sinking ship. He saw dozens of others swimming in front of them and more off to the side. They were sharing life preservers and vests and clawing their way to the armada of small boats. Some were clinging to oars as fishermen hauled them on board. Pete kept a tight grip on Zhanar and kicked hard toward the dock.

When they finally were able to crawl up a ramp, she coughed a few more times and blurted out, "You saved my life."

Pete took her in his arms and held her. She was still shaking but she started to calm down when he stroked her hair. "You're okay now. And look, others are coming in on the little boats. It's going to be all right."

"But what happened?" she asked. "All I know is that all of a sudden, the boat seemed to lean over or something, and the Captain was shouting and people were scrambling, and when I tried to help some of them, I fell overboard. It was awful. I was so scared. I tried to stay near the boat. Tried to find something to hang onto."

"You don't stay near a sinking ship, Zhanar. It'll go down and take you with it."

"I didn't know that," she whimpered.

"I have no idea what happened. The engine failed and the wind picked up and . . .wait, look over there, all the lights in those buildings are out. Must be a big black-out or something. Does that happen a lot here?"

"No. Not really," she said looking perplexed. "And look. There are people running over on that road."

He glanced out to the street again and said, "Wait. The buses aren't moving. The cars look like they're stalled. How could that be?"

Zhanar stared in astonishment at the scene playing out in front of them. It was as if a video of a car chase had been put on PAUSE. "What's happening?" She said with growing panic in her voice.

Pete squinted into the sun, then turned toward her again and shook his head. "I have absolutely no idea, but this has to be the strangest thing I have ever seen."

Twenty-eight

The White House

Ken Cosgrove dropped his Blackberry into the lead-lined cabinet at the entrance to the Situation Room, walked back to the conference room and took his seat at the long polished table as Hunt Daniels, Samantha Reid and Mike Benson rushed in. The room, with its cream colored fabric walls and cherry cabinetry always reminded Samantha of a law office rather than a unique underground facility carved out of the space underneath the old White House swimming pool. Down in this environment, they couldn't hear the driving rain that had enveloped the District for the last two days.

Samantha didn't know why she'd been summoned to this meeting in the Sit Room. She hadn't heard about any new threat to America's national security. In any event, she was always happy to comply when her boss included her in high-level meetings. After all, around this White House, everyone knew that knowledge is power.

"Staff is getting the SecDef, DNI and JCS on teleconference. Secretary of State is traveling today." Ken swiveled his chair to check out the six screens positioned around the room and saw that the other officers were coming on line on a screen on the far wall. They all turned to watch as first the Director of National Intelligence and then both the Secretary of Defense and the Chairman of the Joint Chiefs of Staff announced their presence. Members of the Sit Room staff were assembled in the Surge Room just beyond, analyzing a continuous flow of data coming in from satellite images, internet updates, and other sources. One of them came in and handed the most recent satellite image to the quartet at the table.

"Here's the latest photo from our AF XSS-11 satellite," Ken announced. It's obviously a nuclear explosion in southwestern Kazakhstan. Not a large blast by any means, but definitely nuclear. You've got the same pictures. What do you make of this, Will?" He asked the SecDef.

"A test of some sort, of course. It was conducted out in a very remote area just east of the Caspian. Nothing there. Nearest activity might be in some oil fields, as far as we can tell. No cities or towns. But that weapon was not detonated on the ground. It was up in the atmosphere. Looks like it could be fifty miles up or more."

Samantha almost cried out. *The oil fiends. Tripp. Dad. Were they anywhere near this blast? They said they would be somewhere near the Caspian.* She grabbed the photo and tried to study the image, but she couldn't focus. She was holding her breath. *Could they have been affected? Would there be radiation? No, not if it was 50 miles up. But could they be hurt in some way? How close were they? Oh my God! If it was 50 miles up, there could have been an EMP effect. What if there really has been an EMP? All of my nightmares could be playing out right there!! Is that why Ken invited me to this meeting?*

She had to know. "Ken, do you think . . . I mean could it have created an EMP? Just like we've discussed? There may be people in that area. My family. My father."

The NSC Advisor turned his head in her direction. "Your father? What are you talking about?" The other men stared at Samantha as her voice quivered, and she took a moment to try and control herself. "My Dad is doing consulting work for GeoGlobal. They've got contracts with the government of Kazakhstan. He's over there helping out in a test area along with..." Her voice faltered.

"Go on," Ken said.

She took a deep breath and tried again. "Along with Tripp Adams. He's a Vice President of GeoGlobal and a good friend of mine. They left last week and said they were going to southwestern Kazakhstan to check on some wells, and I'm afraid they may be out there." She pointed to the satellite photo. "Right out there!"

"But I can't imagine the government staging a test in any area where crews would be working," Hunt said. "That's insane."

"Is it?" the Secretary of Defense asked. "Soviets did that all the time. Then again, maybe in Almaty or Astana, they didn't know exactly what was going on way west by the Caspian, although that's kind of hard to believe."

Samantha was valiantly trying to concentrate. She asked, "I wonder where their control room was? Who was in charge? Has their government made any statement yet?" The questions were blurted out in quick succession. After thinking and fretting and planning what to do in the event of a macro attack involving an electro-magnetic pulse, which she realized was a bit far-fetched, but still presented a definite national security threat, now the whole concept had morphed from theoretical to reality.

The JCS Chairman answered, "We're just getting word that President Surleimenov made a brief statement about a small test of their new nuclear capabilities, but he said there had been a mistake. Something about human error. We don't know yet what he means by that, but I see that State has already sent over a formal protest. Got that a minute ago. You must have copies there."

Ken shuffled some papers and pulled out a sheet. "Yes, we have that one. But still, this atmospheric test doesn't make any sense. How could they do this? Do your people have any intel on a nuclear facility producing weapons like this anywhere in Kazakhstan?"

"Not yet, we don't," the DNI replied. "They must have been working in secret for quite some time to pull this off. We had agreements with the Kazakhs beginning back in the 90's, to dismantle their nuclear weapons and facilities. You remember 'Project Saffire' all negotiated by Jim Baker and the Nunn-Lugar boys back then. We paid the Kazakhs a ton of money, took out the material and reprocessed it here for our own use. At the time our people thought we got it all. That was the deal."

"The trouble with these nuclear proliferation agreements is that we can negotiate to remove the stuff, pay them for the stuff and even destroy the stuff," Hunt Daniels said. "But you can't destroy the intelligence that was used to developed the weapons in the first place."

"And . . . it sure looks like they kept some uranium anyway," Ken replied. "Could be an insurance policy against the Russians."

"But Kazakhstan was just about the last of the republics to break away," Mike Benson interjected. "They've been trying to get along with Moscow. At least that's been my understanding."

"After Georgia, who can blame them for being worried?" Hunt Daniels said, studying the photo in front of him. "But the real question is, why was this bomb detonated so many miles up? If it was just a test, just a show of strength, why not explode it over water or even underground?"

"That's what we have to find out," Ken said. "We're not getting any information from the region, and we all know why. Samantha is absolutely right. This damned explosion must have set off an EMP and ruined all of the communications for miles around. It looks like a fairly small device, so it'll be hard to tell how far its line of sight extended. How large an area was affected. But if there are any people within range, it's got to be causing havoc, that's for sure."

Samantha broke in, "How can we find out? Can our ambassador do anything? Do we have any people anywhere near that area? We *have* to figure this out."

"I have to admit, Samantha, that you were the canary in the coal mine on this issue," Ken said, pointing his remark more at Benson than at Samantha. "You all know that Samantha has been talking about making an effort to protect ourselves from an EMP attack, and it's absolutely ironic that we're now looking at one."

Samantha felt the Chief of Staff's eyes on her. Though she felt some measure of vindication for waving the EMP flag, she was too upset with her own worries to even meet his gaze.

"But there's no reason to believe that Kazakhstan, of all places, would be planning to attack us, or anybody else for that matter, even if they did have an effective EMP weapon," Benson said. "I'll admit that this is the first time we've seen an actual atmospheric test that has caused such a thing. Well, for 60 years anyway. But it doesn't mean that the United States is in any danger."

The Secretary of Homeland Security spoke up. "I believe you're right, Mike. But on the other hand, if they have perfected such a weapon, and we'll have to get more intel on all of this to see exactly what the effects were, but *if* they do have it, we have to be prepared for the possibility that they might sell it. After all, they're right across the water from Iran. Across the Caspian, I mean. I believe this calls for immediate action on our part. It's good that State has already sent a protest, but I would recommend an urgent session with the IAEA, a demand for immediate inspections, a notification to our allies and a possible call for a UN meeting. And from that memo sent by the Secretary of State, I believe he would concur."

"I, for one, agree with all of those moves," Ken said. "We learned our lessons dallying around with Iran, to say nothing of the Six-Party Talks with North Korea which always remind me of the 'Hokey Pokey' – you put your right foot in, you put your right foot out – what's the point? I see this as a major destabilizing development, and we need to act fast. Will? What's your take?"

The Secretary of Defense looked particularly grim as he paused for a moment, reached for a glass of water and then said, "I agree on the demand for inspections and getting the IAEA in there ASAP. We need to raise the provisions of the Non-Proliferation Treaty which Kazakhstan acceded to back in 1994. Looks like they've violated the provisions, and we have every right to come down hard on that regime. As for the UN, well, you all know my views on the effectiveness of that place. The word feckless comes to mind."

"Right on!" Hunt said. "But about inspections, if they won't allow immediate access and try to fall back on their 'this was a mistake' line, then what's *our* fall-back?" Hunt asked.

"Then we get really tough. The President can order Treasury to freeze assets of certain banks and particular individuals. Assets in our country, of course. And since we've been doing a lot of energy business with that regime, we have a certain degree of leverage. We'll get a quick study done of what they've got here. As for getting other countries on board, I figure Russia would be the first to sign up," Ken said.

The Defense Secretary nodded and added, "Now, about the government in Kazakhstan, they're not on our CPC list. Only ones on the Countries of Particular Concern list right now are Burma, Eritrea, Iran and North Korea. It never occurred to me that we'd have to consider Kazakhstan for that list." He shrugged and added almost as an afterthought, "I mean, who woudda thunk?"

It never occurred to most of the people around here that an EMP could be set off either, Samantha thought. *The IAEA, NPT, UN, allies, I can't even think about any of that until I find out about Dad and Tripp. This is a national security issue, one that could have world-wide implications, but all I can do is picture the two men I love stranded out in some god-forsaken oil field. Are they still alive? How will I know?* As the others began to gather their photos and notes and wind up the meeting, she realized that she had spent the last several months analyzing and working to prevent terrorist attacks, ideas and plans that often kept her up at night. But now the political had become personal. And suddenly she felt powerless and absolutely petrified.

Twenty-nine

South of Atyrau, Kazakhstan

"Let's wrap him up, get him into the Jeep."

"Jeep won't start."

"Nothin's working."

"I've got to get him out of here. Out of the sun," Tripp called out to the supervisor. "I can't believe this happened to Jake. We knew he had a bad heart. Had a pacemaker. But how could it have failed him? I just don't get it. Now, what the hell are we going to do? I've got to get him back. Back home. Back to . . .God! What can I tell Samantha? This is the worst thing I could ever imagine."

"Samantha?" the supervisor said. "Who's Samantha?"

"She's his daughter. Works at The White House. Didn't want him to make this trip. Begged him not to go."

"Oh Jesus!" He shook his head and looked down at his cell phone again. "Don't know how to get help. None of our phones are working. Cell towers must be down. Might be some reception back in Atyrau, but who the hell knows? Question is, why isn't anything working? Could that thing, whatever it was, have knocked out all the power or somethin'?"

Tripp stared at the man and suddenly blurted, "That's it. That's what Samantha's been talking about." He pointed at the clouds of smoke still visible on the horizon. "She said that if a nuclear weapon of some kind were detonated high enough in the air, it could set off a bunch of pulses. Kind of like microwaves, I guess. And if that happened, it could fry all the electronics anywhere around it. But have you heard anything about Kazakhstan having nuclear weapons? And even if they did, why in God's name would they shoot one off?"

"Beats hell outta me," the super replied. "But wait, if there're these microwave things, how long do they last? When can we get our phones back and get our trucks started?"

"I have no idea," Tripp said, his blood pressure rising with every phrase. "Isn't there anything around here we can use? I mean, an old truck or anything that doesn't have a lot of fancy electronics?"

"Not that I can see," the man replied. He scratched his head and gazed around the drilling area. We'll check everything back at the base, but nothin' here can move us out. We're gonna have to fashion some sort of gismo for Jake and then trek it ourselves."

The other men were grumbling amongst themselves, with some pointing to the sky and others still trying to get a signal on their cell phones. "What do you need, boss?" one asked.

"See what you can rustle up that we can use for a stretcher."

"You got it."

Tripp knelt down next to Jake's body one more time. He stared at the man and felt his own throat choking up. "Jesus, Jake. Why did that have to happen to you? This was supposed to be *your* trip, *your* deal, and now it's all over." He started to break down as he leaned over and put his hand on the man's body. "Why you? And what in God's name can I ever say to Samantha? She'll be destroyed." He gazed up at the sky again, "just like you bastards destroyed him."

Several hours later, the bedraggled crew trudged into their base camp. They had taken turns carrying the stretcher and sharing bottles of water. They had grabbed all of the water and food stashed near the rigs since they had no idea how long their supplies would last or when they could get out of the area.

They lifted Jake's body into one of the Quonset Huts, but with no motor and no air conditioning, it was already stifling inside. Jake rushed to a refrigerator that was shut down, but he grabbed water bottles that were still chilled inside and put them all around the body. *Won't help much, he thought. I've got to find a way out of here.* He shouted to the man who had been their driver. "Any old cars or trucks around here? Anything that might start?"

"Most of our cars and trucks are pretty new. But, wait, there might be one older car. One of the guys has been restoring it on his own time. Brought it out here to work on."

Tripp stood up, suddenly hopeful. "What year is it? I'd give anything for an old Chevy, an old anything, right about now."

"I don't know the exact year, but might be from the 60's. I'll go find out."

Tripp slumped down on the floor next to Jake's body. He had this weird feeling that he didn't want to leave the man. Had to protect him somehow. He hadn't done a damn thing to protect him on this trip, though. As he thought back to that dinner when Samantha came over to his condo and was so excited to see her Dad, he gave a rueful sigh. She hadn't wanted him to go. Had begged him not to go. It was as if she had some sort of premonition or something. The thing about Samantha was that her job entailed all kinds of premonitions. That's all she ever talked about. Looking ahead. Predicting what the bad guys might do next. Analyzing weapons and technology and figuring out who might use what to cause death and destruction just to make some crazy point about infidels. But this time was totally different. There were no terrorists involved here. At least none that he could fathom.

This had to be some government test. Some show of strength. It wasn't an attack. Unless some other government had set that thing off against Kazakhstan. No, that didn't make any sense. They didn't threaten anybody. If anything, other countries were trying to ingratiate themselves with the Kazakhs, trying to get hold of their oil and gas. Delegations were trooping into Almaty and Astana on a regular basis trying to bribe their way into deals all the time. No. This was a shot across somebody else's bow. Probably Russia's, and they wouldn't like it one bit.

He wondered if Russia would retaliate in some fashion. They weren't above taking on Georgia and the Ukraine. What would stop them from invading Kazakhstan on the pretense of protecting ethnic Russians living here? And God knows there are a ton of them all over the place.

As Tripp sat there on the floor, his arms around his knees and his head down, he realized he had to take action right away to get himself and Jake out of this place. All hell could break loose, and here he was stranded with a bunch of rough necks who would probably be fighting over dwindling food supplies any day now.

He heard footsteps and looked up to see the driver running his way. He stood up and called out, "Find anything?"

"Yeah. The old car that I told you about. Trouble is, the guy who owns it doesn't want to part with the thing. Says it may be his only ticket out of here."

Tripp reached for his wallet. "Tell you what. Let's try to make a deal with him. Whoever he is. Tell him I'll pay him all I've got, about a thousand, American, if he'll let us use his car and he can come with us."

"Where do you want to go? If we can't get a signal to Atyrau, they may be out of power too. So that won't do us any good."

"So we drive farther east. Must be some place, some village, somewhere we can call out. And if we can get through, I can get GeoGlobal to send a plane for us."

"That is if any planes around here are flying," the driver observed.

"We have to pray they can find one. Let's get on this right away," Tripp said. "We'll need gas. Lots of it. And water. And some food. Everyone else is going to want to get out of here too."

"Maybe the others will decide to wait it out. Maybe they'll figure it's a big power failure, and it'll come back on in a while."

"We can hope that's the case. For their sake. But right now all I can think about is getting Jake's body out of here before . . ."

"Yeah. Know what you mean. Couple of days in this heat won't be good for him or us or anybody."

Tripp pointed to the door. "Okay. Go see if you can make a deal with the guy. Keep it private. Tell him we're desperate. Well, he has to know that. And tell him about the money."

"You got it," the driver said. "But you have to realize, this is a pretty desolate country. I've got some maps in the Jeep. I'll get those and try to figure out where we can go. But, you have to understand, this could be a *very* long journey."

THIRTY

Atyrau, Kazakhstan

"Who ruined our test?" the CEO screamed? "I want a full investigation. I want a report on every system, every employee, every move that was made prior to that test, and I want it yesterday!"

How are they going to do that? Nurlan wondered as he stood in the lab along with the other workers, listening to the tirade. How could they possibly find out that he was the one who had extended the lift-off and delayed the whole detonation when none of the computers were working right now, the lights were off, and there was only a generator system that some of the workers had been sent out to check, but he hadn't heard anything kick in yet. He thought he had covered his tracks pretty carefully, and if somehow they decided that he was the culprit, he could always claim that he made a stupid mistake. If that happened, he'd be fired, but that was okay. He would have done his job to make sure that nobody was hurt by this crazy bomb. *But why are all the systems down?* He hadn't been outside. Their control room was in an enclosed, protected area, away from the nuclear plant, but everything seemed to have stopped. Then again, maybe he could blame the whole thing on some sort of massive power failure that messed up their operation. He'd have to think about that.

The investigators lined up the workers and began questioning them, taking notes, and shaking their heads. When they got to Nurlan, he showed them his original calculations which he had kept in his own private notebook, not the ones he had actually used for the test. After a grueling review, he breathed a sigh of relief when they said he could leave and moved on to the next worker.

Outside the control room, he was greeted with an eerie sight. As he started walking away from the facility, he saw people rushing along the streets, elbowing each other, and shouting questions. He saw a long line had formed at a nearby food store and another line snaked out the door and around the corner from a local bank. No cars or buses were moving. An ambulance was stopped in the middle of the road and the medical workers were trying to lift a patient out of the back. He heard someone cry out that people were trapped in elevators in a building across the street. A police car looked like it was stalled a block down and the officers were getting out, pointing to the crowds at the food store. People were pushing and shoving, and a fist fight had just broken out.

Nurlan stared at the chaos with a growing sense of dread. Had there been a huge power failure of some sort? Must have been. But why weren't the cars running? What about Zhanar and Pete? Would they still be on board the tourist boat? Would it be running while everything else seemed to be at a standstill? He ran toward the docks and after stopping several times to give his legs a rest, he finally came to the water's edge where he saw a whole flotilla of small boats hauling people out of the water. Some were flailing around, gasping for air while others were trying to swim to shore on their own. He wanted to help, but he wasn't much of a swimmer. He craned his neck and then he saw it. The tourist boat off in the distance, slowly sinking.

Oh no! Zhanar! Where is she? Was she in water? Did boats pick her up? He ran onto the main dock and watched as several older women were pulled to safety, their clothes plastered against their frail bodies, their hair askew and dripping. "Did anyone see Tour Guide?" he shouted to the dazed women? "Pretty girl gives talks on boat? Anyone see her? Anyone at all?" he pleaded.

The women looked at each other with quizzical glances. One spoke up, "I don't know. The boat stopped and was going down. We were all thrown into the water. So many people. So much trouble. The crew was throwing out the life preservers. Don't know about the Captain. I don't know about anybody else. We're just grateful for the fishermen who came out to help us."

Nurlan started to panic. Zhanar couldn't swim very well. He had told her to take lessons if she was going to work on the boat. But she never made the time. Now she might have been tossed into the water. She might have drowned. What could he do? How could he find out? Then he thought about Pete. He knew Pete was a great swimmer. He was on the swim team at college. So, sure, Pete would be okay. But what about Zhanar. He stayed on the dock and watched the fishermen bring in other survivors in. But no one seemed to know anything about his sister. When the last boat docked, he surveyed the scene, asked more questions but came away with nothing.

He had no choice now but to head back to their apartment and see if he could find Pete. He would know. He had to know. Nurlan turned and started to jog in the direction of his building, but his legs were weak. they were hurting him again, so he had to slow down. As he passed the stalled cars and buses, he saw that all the passengers had gotten off, leaving a slew of empty shells littering the roads. It was if some giant child had been playing with huge match box cars, had grown tired of the game and just left them in place.

When Nurlan got to the apartment, he shoved open the door and sagged against the edge as he heaved a sigh of relief. There was Zhanar trying to dry her hair with a towel while Pete was opening a bottle of water. Nurlan rushed over and threw his arms around his sister. "What happened? I saw boat going down? I search for you. I worried you can't swim. How you get out?"

She pointed at Pete and gave him a broad smile. Her wide-set eyes glowing. "He saved my life. I was in the water. It was awful. I went down a couple of times and all of a sudden he was there, right next to me. He held me up and got us to the dock. He had already saved some other people, and he came back for me when he saw me near the boat. He said I could have been dragged down if the boat sank. But I'm okay and Pete is my hero." She went over and gave Pete a simple kiss on his cheek.

Nurlan slumped down in one of the kitchen chairs. He looked at his friend and gave him the thumbs up. "I don't know how thank you. I knew you could swim but I so worried when I saw other people still in water. I afraid we lost Zhanar. But now we all here. This is so good news."

Pete offered Nurlan a drink from his bottle. "We're here, but we've got a lot of problems. We've got water, for now. But I don't know how long it will last. When we left the dock, we stopped at a sandwich shop and managed to grab a bunch of bottles and about half a dozen sandwiches, but people were starting to crowd in. I guess everyone realized that there was a power failure or something, and their food wouldn't last. We have a few things in the refrigerator, but it's off. Have to keep the door closed as long as we can."

"I've got some cans of soup," Zhanar volunteered. "But we can't heat it up. Microwave and ovens won't work. Nothing works. And nobody can figure out why."

"I don't know either," Nurlan said. "We did have big test this morning."

"Oh, the test," Zhanar said, putting the towel aside and brushing out her damp hair. "What happened? Do you think it had anything to do with all this trouble?"

"I not know," Nurlan said. "What I do know is my plan worked. Bomb not go off on ground. I work to make it go up higher. Want be sure nobody gets hurt or gets radiation. Bomb is bad thing. Don't know why President ordered us to set it off. But we had to do it."

"But that's great," Pete said. "You wanted to save people and you did that. The S.A.I.N.T.S. would be proud of you. Of course, we can't tell anybody. You'd get in all kinds of trouble. But at least you did it." He took a swig of water and reached for one of the sandwiches. "The question is, what do we do now? And how long will this crazy black out situation last? If it goes on for a long time, I wonder if the hospitals will be able to handle their patients? I mean, your hospital is pretty new, right?"

"Oh yes. We have all the latest equipment," Zhanar replied. "X-rays, CT scans, operating rooms. They have some generators, but those couldn't handle everything."

"So with no power," Pete asked, "what will happen now?"

Nurlan glanced at his friend and thought for a long moment. "If no power, no food, no water, no cars, things could get ugly around here." He turn turned to Zhanar. "You still have pistol I bought you long time ago?"

Her face registered surprise. "My gun? Yes, I have it in my bureau. But why? Why would I need it?"

"As I say, could get ugly, could get bad here. At least we have gun, and that may be only way we protect ourselves."

THIRTY-ONE

Washington, DC

Fast-paced, yet plaintive. That's what the music of Chopin's Etude Opus 10, Number 12 sounded like to Samantha as she drove from her Georgetown condo to the GeoGlobal office on K Street. She had her radio tuned to the local NPR station, WETA, and the familiar piece sounded as if the pianist were racing to an uncertain fate. Indeed!

She pulled into a parking lot, told the attendant she'd only be a few minutes, grabbed her shoulder bag and headed to the lobby. She took the elevator up to the third floor, walked down the corridor to the glass door emblazoned with the "GG" logo and pushed inside. "I'm Samantha Reid, here to see Godfrey Nims," she announced to the attractive woman sitting at a curved walnut desk. The reception area was the image of understated elegance, with sleek charcoal leather couches and a pair of matching chairs off to one side inviting a visitor to sit down and read a copy of today's *Wall Street Journal* or the most recent issues of *The Oil & Gas Journal* arrayed on a glass coffee table. But Samantha didn't want to sit down. She was too nervous. Too anxious to talk to Tripp's friend and colleague. As the receptionist called Godfrey's line to announce her arrival, Samantha couldn't help pacing in front of the desk.

"Mr. Nims should be out shortly, Miss Reid. Can I get you a cup of coffee or water perhaps?"

"No thanks. Already had my quota of caffeine for the morning, but thanks anyway." She continued to walk across the area, pretending to examine the collection of framed maps on the wall. She peered at one showing Europe and Asia and tried to pinpoint just where her Dad and Tripp might be right now. *That area is so vast,* she thought, *or half-vast,* she added to herself with a sense of deprecating humor.

"Samantha, there you are," a booming voice greeted her as the jovial lobbyist came through a set of swinging doors. "Come in. We have a lot to talk about"

"I only have a few minutes. Have to get to our usual morning staff meeting," Samantha said as she followed Godfrey back to his office. "But I wanted to see if you had heard anything from Tripp."

"Here, sit down a minute," he said, pointing to a dark red arm chair in front of his massive desk. "In answer to your question, I'm afraid it's a 'no.' So far anyway. All we know right now is that Tripp and Jake were out in our new test fields south of a city called Atyrau which is on the Caspian. They were scheduled to head down there to check on some wells and also take a look at a possible new field. But suddenly we lost all contact, and we figure it's a big power outage or something. Of course, there's that report in the Washington Post this morning that Kazakhstan conducted some sort of nuclear test, which was against all of the Nuclear Non-Proliferation Treaty rules, of course. But their government is trying to say it was a mistake. I don't know how you can detonate a bomb and say it was a mistake, though. What are your people saying?"

Samantha leaned forward, not certain how much she should divulge about the explosion the satellites had photographed. "We believe they did explode a nuclear device, and we're trying to figure out if that's what caused the disruption in communications. It's very likely. But the important question now is, what happened to Tripp and Jake? Are they okay? Were they anywhere near this test, or whatever it was? If they were, would they have any way to get out of there to a safer place? One where they could get a call through? Do you have any other people in the area you can reach? What about the people in Atyrau? What are they saying?"

"You see, that's just it. We can't get through to Atyrau either. And that's quite some distance from the fields. We have people in both Astana and Almaty but those cities are thousands of miles east of there, and it'll take a while for them to get to the Caspian."

"Can't they fly there?" Samantha asked, somewhat exasperated with the explanation.

"They're saying that they're trying to locate personnel along the way to see who has communications of any kind, what the state of the air field is right now, and of course if there is any radiation in the area."

Radiation? Samantha didn't think so. Not if this bomb was, in fact, exploded fifty miles up in the air. Or higher. Then again, there hadn't been any atmospheric tests in years, so what if there was some sort of fall-out that their scientists hadn't predicted? And no one knew much about the weapon either. The more she thought about it, the more upset she got. "Well, I just wanted to come by and talk to you in person because I figure you're the first person Tripp will try to contact," *after me, that is.* "But as soon as you hear anything, anything at all, you will call me, right?"

"Look, Samantha. I know how close you and Tripp are, and I know how you feel about Jake going on this trip. Tripp told me you had misgivings."

"That's putting it mildly," Samantha said. "After all, he's got a heart condition, and I was really worried about his traveling halfway around the world right now."

"I know. But I'm sure that Tripp has everything under control. He's that kind of guy. You know that."

Do I? She wondered. She glanced at her watch and got up from the chair. "I've got to run. I was just hoping that you might have heard something by now."

Godfrey got up as well and started to walk her to the door. "You can be sure that as soon as we get any word at all, you will be the very first person I call. You can count on it."

What could she count on? She thought about the GeoGlobal offices in those other cities and wondered how long it would be before they got their act together and went looking for their men? She doubted anyone would want to fly into an area where they didn't know if there was air traffic support or even a workable landing field to say nothing of the possibility of radiation of some sort. No, she couldn't count on them. She couldn't count on the lying Kazakh government. And she doubted she could count on Pentagon satellites to show any more than the images she had seen already. What now?

As she retrieved her car from the garage attendant, she felt more and more despondent. Almost by rote, she drove over to the Southwest Gate of the White House, waved her pass and watched the black iron gates slowly open to allow her access to the driveway called West Exec and park her car in one of the prize slots there between the West Wing and the EEOB. She gathered her bag, brief case, and umbrella and ducked under the awning at the door to the West Wing basement. It had been stormy the last couple of days, reflecting her mood of the moment. And she had no idea when the weather, or her outlook, would clear up. Nodding to the

Secret Service Officer seated at a desk just inside the door, she turned left and walked up the steps to her second floor office.

"Staff meeting in five minutes," her assistant, Joan, reminded her as she headed to her cubicle of a work space.

"I know, thanks," Samantha mumbled, trying to push away thoughts of Tripp and Jake trudging around in some field, cut off from civilization and stuck with no way to escape. Out of habit, she checked her iPhone, desperately hoping for an email. Something. Anything. She scrolled down through dozens of messages, saying a silent prayer that she'd see a note from Tripp. Yet she knew in her heart it wouldn't be there. Not now. Maybe not ever.

THIRTY-TWO

Southwestern Kazakhstan

"Where the hell are we?" Tripp asked, peering out the window of the old Buick as they navigated a series of intersecting tracks. "Not exactly a road, is it?"

"Hardly. Not in this part of the country," the driver remarked as he maneuvered the car over the rocky terrain. "No place to break down, that's for sure."

"But do you have any idea where we're headed?" Tripp said, "We've been roaming around for a day and a half. And all we've seen are a few foxes and a bunch of lizards. I don't want to sound like a kid asking 'Are we there yet?' but you said that there was a small city out here somewhere. Another one starting with *A*. How much longer do you think it'll be?"

Bill, the owner of the Buick had been dozing in the back seat, but he sat up and looked around. "Never been in this part of the country before. Sure is desolate," he said. "Wait a minute, up ahead, way ahead, isn't that something? Some people? A fence or something?"

The driver stopped the car and pulled out a pair of binoculars. "Oh shit!"

"What?" Tripp asked.

"Looks like it could be some of their so-called Road Police."

"Out here? Who the hell do they think they're policing?" Bill asked, leaning over the seat to get a better look.

"Let's just call it local extortion."

"Oh great," Tripp said. "So what do we do? Pay 'em off?"

"Might have to. I don't see another way around them," the driver said, pulling back onto the rudimentary path.

As they approached, they saw two bearded men dressed in what looked like cotton robes, carrying rifles. The driver pulled up, but kept the engine running. Tripp murmured, "What do you suppose they speak? Kazakh?"

"Could be Kazakh, Russian, Kurdish, Uzbek. You can't believe how many different dialects, how many tribes, how many, well, you get the idea. I'll try Kazakh and see if I can negotiate something."

He tried a friendly greeting, asking about the weather and if there had been any other cars in the area. One of the men raised his rifle and replied, "No. No cars. No people today. You have money? You have food? We want water, food. All you have."

The driver translated for Tripp and Bill.

"No way," Tripp whispered. "We need everything we've got to get us to the city you showed us on the map. Akespe or something like that? You said it was on the Aral Sea and would probably have communications. We've got to get there. Can't let these jokers take our supplies."

Bill chimed in. "Got my Glock back here. Think we can fake 'em out with that?"

"Could be pretty dicey," the driver said in a low tone. "Those guys both have guns. They could shoot out our tires and still take our stuff. Then where would we be?"

"I say we chance it," Bill said, reaching down on the floor beside a satchel where he had stashed the gun. Tell them to give us a minute to count our money or something. Then roll up your windows and floor it. What do you think, Tripp? You in for this?"

"Hey, I was in the Navy. Want me to handle the gun?"

"Nah. I was Army. Long time back, but I know what I'm doing," Bill whispered.

"You pay!" one of the Kazakhs demanded, waving his rifle.

"Give us a few minutes. We have to count our money. Then we talk."

"No talk. We want all your money. Water too," the man demanded.

"Just a minute. We don't want to cause trouble. We know you need supplies way out here, and we understand that you police the road." He paused and started to point over the Kazak's shoulder. But out there, look. It's a herd of wild boar."

As the Kazakh turned, the driver gunned the engine and blasted through a crude woven fence the men had hauled across the path.

Both Kazakhs raised their rifles, shouted, "Stop. Stop or we shoot." And then they opened fire. A bullet shattered the back window as the driver careened to the side of the path and then jerked the wheel to the right again. Tripp slammed against the door since there were no seat belts in this ancient vehicle.

Bill took aim out the broken window and took a shot at the men running after them.

"Don't try to kill them," Tripp shouted. "Just keep them distracted if you can."

"Right," Bill said, firing off another round. "Just need to teach those bastards a lesson. Wish they hadn't trashed my window. I've been working on this baby for a month now. Almost had her in shape, and they had to go and shatter the glass. Well, let's see if I can shatter their asses."

Another shot from the Kazakhs hit the back fender with a loud pinging sound. Both the driver and Tripp kept their heads down while Bill fired once more, sending the tribesmen running for cover. "We're probably out of range now, but keep going. They'll give up, and I didn't see any other cars or trucks around. They can't come after us. Probably just have some horses stashed somewhere."

The driver headed over a small ridge and spotted a couple of yurts out in a dusty field. "They must live over there."

"Yeah," Tripp said, "Got some cattle over there too. Looks like fences made out of branches or something."

"They're rushes all woven together," the driver explained.

"Well, I for one hope we can rush right out of this damn place," Tripp said, settling down in his seat. How are we fixed for fuel?"

"Got about a quarter tank left, but when we get farther away from these clowns, we'll stop and get a refill from the bottles in the trunk."

"As I was saying before we were so rudely interrupted," Tripp said with the beginnings of a wry smile, "Any idea how much longer it'll be until we get to that Askespe place?"

"At the rate we're going on these trails, it could be days."

THIRTY-THREE

The White House

Samantha slipped on her black strap heels and checked her makeup in the West Wing bathroom mirror. Since most White House staffers never had time to go home and change before attending a fancy dinner in town, they brought evening clothes to the office, and tonight she had to bring a very formal gown. It was a full length black sheath with a scoop neck and lace sleeves covering her arms. Can't wear too much décolletage in this White House. A conservative, understated look was expected. She brushed out her mane of long hair, the color of nutmeg, and pinned it back off her face with a pair of pearl barrettes. She grabbed her evening bag and headed downstairs.

She walked along the colonnade next to the Rose Garden and entered the ground floor of the public rooms. As she walked up the steps to the Cross Hall, she saw that some of the guests had already arrived by way of the North Portico, although the President, First Lady and the guests of honor, the President and First Lady of Poland had yet to make their entrance down the grand staircase from the private quarters. The Marine Band, clad in their usual bright red jackets with gold buttons, was playing a

George Gershwin tune near the entrance. As she surveyed the scene, she realized that while every single guest in the room had to be positively thrilled to be invited to a White House State Dinner, she was here only out of duty and obligation. Staff members didn't get invited to many of these affairs, but now that she was the Assistant to the President for Homeland Security, she was included from time to time. And anyone receiving a White House invitation knew it was more like a summons than an invitation. You attended unless you were in the hospital on life support.

One of the black tie clad waiters passed in front of her with offerings of wine and champagne. She took a glass of Chablis and sauntered into the Red Room. When she got her first White House job, she had been so excited, she'd read an entire book on its history. Now as she mingled with the other guests admiring the Empire furniture and the portrait of Dolly Madison hanging over the fireplace, she remembered that this was the room where Rutherford B. Hayes took the oath of office way back in the 1800's.

She didn't see anyone she wanted to talk to in that room, so she strolled next door to the oval Blue Room where they always put the White House Christmas tree because the room had 18 foot ceilings. Now that it was summer, the room served as the traditional place where the President and First Lady usually stood for photos. The staff called that the "Grip and Grin" routine. She glanced over at the Hannibal clock on the white marble mantel and saw that it was probably time for the grand entrance so she walked back out to the Cross Hall, and there they were. The President, his wife and honored guests slowly coming down the red carpeted stairs together as the White House photographer snapped a dozen shots.

"Hey, isn't it great that we both were invited to this shindig tonight?" Angela whispered, sidling up to Samantha.

"Oh, hi. Yes, although I have to admit I'm not in much of a party mood right now."

"Still haven't heard anything from Tripp, huh?" her friend asked.

"No. Nothing. Even the NSC can't get a decent report from that part of Kazakhstan. Communications are still down, so they're trying to get some of the Ambassador's people to fly over there and figure things out."

"Geez! Do you think they can find Tripp and your Dad? I mean, they'd probably go to our consulate there, I mean if there is one somewhere nearby."

"You'd think. But who knows?" She leaned in close to Angela and said in a low voice, "We think there was an EMP effect from that nuclear test, or whatever it was. And if that's really what happened, everything would be out of whack. No telling how long they could survive out there," she said dejectedly.

"That's what so amazing. I mean, you've been talking about that kind of thing here, but you said nobody was taking you seriously. Not Mike Benson and certainly not Max Federman. But now that it might have happened, has Max done any sort of mea culpa?"

"Not yet," Samantha said.

"Of course, all he's focused on is getting Jason Keller elected in November, and he probably sees this whole thing as just some sort of distraction. After all, how far away is Kazakhstan, and why would our voters give a darn about it anyway?"

Samantha sighed and took a sip of her wine. "I know. You're right. But whether something like this could ever escalate into a threat to us is one thing. Right now it's escalated into a threat to my sanity. All I can think about is Tripp and my Dad. I have no idea if they were near the test, if they were affected by it, if they're stranded somewhere, or if they're even alive."

Angela took her friend's arm. "Look. I know you're upset. Lord knows I would be too. But with all that's going on in this place, you've got to let the pros figure it out. Meanwhile, let's go get another drink and see if we can play nice with the Polish delegation. I mean, that's our job tonight, right?"

"I guess," Samantha conceded. They walked over to the third parlor, the Green Room, and saw an older gentleman sitting on the Duncan Phyfe furniture. "People don't usually sit down at these things. Maybe we should go over and see if that guy's okay."

"Actually, he looks kind of familiar," Angela said. "I know this sounds silly, but I think one of the reasons I got included on tonight's guest list is because I was fielding a bunch of requests from the Polish Meatpackers Association in Chicago. They were angling to send the head of it here to meet the President of Poland. I saw a picture of the guy. Makes sausage or something. I got the Social Office to invite him, and I think he's the one."

"Well, he should feel right at home here in Washington where everybody compares crafting legislation to making his product," Samantha said.

They chatted with the gentleman who thanked Angela profusely for getting him on the invitation list. Then they heard the chimes and meandered down the hall to the State Dining Room to find their place at one of the 17 round tables of eight, adorned with gleaming white table cloths, centerpieces of bright red roses crafted by the gang of on-site florists, name cards and menus written in calligraphy all done by the professionals housed in the East Wing Social Office. Samantha saw that the flowers matched the red rims around the china that dated back to the Reagan days.

As Samantha searched for her place, she glanced up at the portrait of Abraham Lincoln over the fireplace. He was perched on an upholstered red chair, hand under his chin, and looked like he was brooding about some pending crisis. *My mood exactly*, Samantha thought. The women found their places at different tables, and Samantha picked up the card listing tonight's menu. First Course: Spring pea soup with fernleaf lavender and chive pizzelle. She wondered what the heck fernleaf lavender was. She'd find out soon enough. It would be served with a Newton Chardonnay. She introduced herself to her tablemates, a Member of the Polish Cabinet, the Assistant Secretary of State for East European Affairs and a smattering of Polish business types and their wives.

She tried to make polite conversation but her mind kept wandering, not only to her worries about her Dad, but to her mounting In-box. She now had a ton of other projects to work on, including a new threat assessment about a possible biological attack, some intel about a large number of illegals arrested near the Texas border who only spoke Farsi, and another report about a plan to detonate a bomb inside a backpack on board a train heading to Penn Station in New York. They had found that one and arrested a guy, but who knew how many others might try the same thing?

A waiter cleared the soup dishes from the right and placed the second course of Dover Sole Almondine, roasted artichokes, and Pequillo peppers from the left. At least she recognized most of those ingredients. She wasn't very hungry and so she only took a couple of bites while continuing to sip her wine.

When the third course arrived, she stared at the saddle of spring lamb with Chanterells sauce, and a fricassee of baby vegetables and wondered how she would get through it all. And there were two more courses to go. An Arugula salad and later there would be dessert.

"Tell me, Miss Reid, is it?" the Cabinet Minister on her right inquired. "You mentioned you were on The White House staff." Samantha nodded as he continued. "Do you become involved in national security issues, by any chance?" he asked in perfect English.

"Well, yes, I do," Samantha replied. I report directly to Ken Cosgrove, our National Security Advisor."

"Excellent. Very good. I was hoping to have a chance to hear your views on the possibility of restarting the talks on the deployment of missile defense systems in our country, along with the Czech Republic. I am hoping that this issue will come up in the direct talks between our two presidents, but it is always good to elicit opinions from those doing the real work, if I may put it that way," he said with a broad smile.

"Well, as you know, there have been some low-level discussions about it. I know that this administration would like to reverse the decision to back out of our prior agreement to deploy interceptors in your country. Now that more regimes are talking about developing nuclear weapons, we feel that missile defense systems are one of our best answers. I mean, if the Iranians, North Koreans, and others who are spending their nation's treasure on nuclear weapons know that we can knock them out of the sky, it would be a great deterrent to their development in the first place."

"Precisely our view, Miss Reid," he said finishing his lamb. "Delicious dinner by the way."

"Yes, it certainly is."

They continued to discuss nuclear proliferation issues through the salad course, and then Samantha saw that their waiter had placed the dessert plate covered with a doily and a crystal finger bowl at each place. She saw the Cabinet Minister watching her. And when she picked up the bowl and the doily, setting them to the left of the plate, he followed suit. Many guests never mastered the White House dessert routine, not recognizing the little bowls of water for what they were and just staring at them with perplexed expressions. This meant that the waiters had to move the bowls to the side, along with the doilies, to make room for the dessert which was served onto the now empty plate. Fortunately, Samantha knew the drill.

Finally, the two presidents exchanged toasts, and the crowd began to move into the East Room for the entertainment. This time it was going to be a concert pianist playing the best known concertos written by Frederic Chopin, since he was born in Poland.

Samantha checked her watch, hoping she could get out of there and back to her office to check for emails before heading home. At the moment, she was seated near the fireplace where she could read the quotation from John Adams carved into the oak paneling. *"I pray to Heaven to Bestow the Best of Blessings on THIS HOUSE and All that shall hereafter inhabit it. May none but Honest and Wise Men ever rule under this roof."* As she stared at the words, she found herself wondering if there were any honest and wise men ruling in Kazakhstan, and she was afraid that the answer to that was a definite *no!*

THIRTY-FOUR

Atyrau, Kazakhstan

The banging on the door grew louder and more persistent. "It's gotta be those gangs coming round again," Pete whispered as he pulled Zhanar and Nurlan back into the bedroom and pushed a dresser up against the door.

"This is the third time this building has been raided," Zhanar murmured, crouching down behind the bed. "Do you think they can get in?"

"I put new locks last time they came," Nurlan reminded his sister. "Everyone look for food and water now. We got keep what we have."

"Remember, I've still got cans of soup and fish downstairs in my place," Zhanar said. 'I hope they don't find it. It's not much. I hid it under the bed. It should last us a few more days, but that's all."

The knocking continued, accompanied with shouts of "Open up. Police."

"It no police," Nurlan said in a low tone. Police not on streets. Must be all protecting own families from gangs." He turned to his sister, "Glad we still have your gun. Don't want use it, but we will if we have to." He reached over to the bedside table, opened the small drawer and grabbed the pistol. He checked the bullets. "We okay with this."

"I don't want to kill anybody," Zhanar said staring at the little gun.

"They probably have more powerful weapons than we do," Pete said. "But if they think no one is here, maybe they'll move on."

The trio waited with tension rising. The shouts from the hallway finally seemed to taper off. Then they heard what sounded like footsteps stomping away. "I think they gave up this time," Pete said. "They probably figure they can steal from other people so they don't have to try to knock our door down."

"It pretty strong door," Nurlan said, putting the gun back into the drawer.

Zhanar stood up and pushed the hair out of her eyes. "Maybe we got through this one, but what are we going to do now? Pete and I don't have jobs, and we're almost out of money. You have a job but you said they can't pay you yet. All banks are closed, they ran out of money the first day. Nobody can cash a check or anything. And it's dangerous for you to even go out. Everybody is scared, and nobody knows when we'll get power again. People are getting desperate. Desperate for food. Desperate for water. We'll run out pretty soon, and I don't know what to do," she moaned. "My room-mate told me that patients are dying at the hospital. They're out of food and water too, and nothing is working. They ran out of fuel for the generators. There were babies in incubators. They died, can you believe that? They couldn't even save the babies," she said in a faltering voice.

Pete put his arm around her, thought for a moment and turned to Nurlan. "What we have to do is figure out a way to get out of here. The power might not come back for a long time. Isn't that what the people at the plant said?"

"Yes. Scientists said when bomb went off, it made power fail everywhere. Even here. I no understand. They still have some generators keep things going. They say nuclear material okay. All protected. But people in city not protected. You right. We got to get out. All at plant say they want out. Nobody knows how."

"We can't just walk out of here," Zhanar said. "Where would we go? I heard that people in the villages are fighting off the gangs too because they have some cattle, and the city people are trying to steal it. It's bad everywhere. We can't go there, and we can't stay here," she said with tears welling up in her eyes.

"Hey, take it easy," Pete said. "We'll think of something. Maybe the government will send troops or something."

"They far away. All cross country. You know that," Nurlan said.

"Maybe they'll send planes or something," Zhanar said with a hopeful sigh. "Do you think they'll do that?"

"Airport's not working. Who knows?" Pete said.

Nurlan checked his watch. "Plant got some old buses. They pick us up. Take us there. I go now. See what others do." Then he scratched his head and said, "I think on this. We need way to get far off. You stay here. I go work. Come back later. But," he paused again, "I may get idea."

THIRTY-FIVE

Georgetown

"Can you believe that slime ball, Max Federaman, hit on me after the State Dinner the other night?" Angela asked, parking her Suburu in a spot near the garage elevators under Georgetown Park. Samantha got out of the car and the two women rode up to the main floor of the trendy shopping mall. They walked past a flower shop and luggage store and took another glassed in elevator up to the third floor.

Samantha faced the doors during the ride. "I wish I could get over this height thing," she mumbled. I still can't bear to look down. Next time we'll take the escalators. For some reason they seem easier to deal with."

"Sure," Angela said. "Anyway, about Max, there I was getting ready to leave the East Room, and that fatso comes over and asks if I'm game for a nightcap."

"What did you say?"

"Just to find out exactly what he had in mind, as if it weren't rather obvious, I asked him where he wanted to go. And without missing a beat, he gave me that leer of his and said, 'How about my place'?"

"What did you say then?"

"What do you think?" Angela replied. "Instead of saying what I actually wanted to, which would have been something like, 'Buzz off, you creep,' I just told him I had early morning meetings, but thank you anyway. Since we see these guys all the time, I figure I can't afford to totally piss 'em off."

Samantha shook her head and gave her friend a wry smile. "At least it wasn't like the last proposition you had from that economist. What was it he wanted to show you?"

"Oh that one," Angela laughed. "He said that if I would come by for a drink, he'd show me a drawing of his Laffer Curve. How lame is that? Of course, he thinks Art Laffer's analysis of the effects of tax cuts is positively brilliant, but I doubt if a discussion of tax policy is much of a turn-on to potential dates."

Samantha chuckled and pushed through the glass door to the back entrance of Clyde's Restaurant.

"I'm just glad to see you smiling, for once," Angela said as they worked their way past the bar, a series of small tables covered with blue and white checked table cloths and finally got up to the Hostess Station. "Reservation for Marconi. In the Omelet Room?"

The young girl checked her computer. "Yes, I have it right here. And I believe your table is ready." She handed two menus to her assistant who led the way to a booth in the front room. The popular restaurant on M Street felt almost like an old-time saloon with a long oak bar, plank flooring and oil paintings of railroads and horses. It had been a hang-out for thirty-somethings for decades and tonight was no exception. The place was jammed.

"Speaking of Max," Angela said, stowing her purse on the seat next to her, "has he said anything at all about this whole mess in Kazakhstan? I mean, has he apologized to you for your *insight* on the issue?"

"Still nothing yet," Samantha said.

Angela picked up a menu. "Well, if that whole EMP thing happens again or if we ever find out that it's some new-fangled kind of weapon, I just hope they offer a hefty portion of crow in the White House mess."

Samantha sighed and remarked, "Men like Max always act like they've been anointed rather than appointed. Infallible is probably a big part of his self-image."

"Hello. My name is Ralph, and I'll be your server this evening. Can I get you ladies a drink, some wine?" the waiter asked, setting a pitcher of spring water down on the table.

"Sure," Angela said. "How about a glass of your house Cabernet?"

"And I'll take the Pinot Noir," Samantha added.

"Very good." He turned and hustled off to the bar.

"By the way, I hear there's a great new Picasso exhibit over at the National Gallery. Want to hit that one with me this weekend?" Angela asked.

"Picasso? Sorry, but I hate all those weird paintings of chopped up women's bodies."

"Well, I'm just glad he wasn't a surgeon."

"I'll probably be working anyway," Samantha said. "More nut cases were reported casing the Statue of Liberty. Can you imagine some terrorist trying to bring that down?"

"With all the threats pouring into your office, you should ask for more staff and a bigger budget."

"I'd never get that. Not right now with all the deficit talk. But I certainly could use, say, half a million. I could add a couple more specialists with that."

"Geez. In Washington, that's not even catering money," Angela joked.

"Here you are ladies. The cabernet and the pinot. Have you decided on dinner?"

"A bowl of chili and the cobb salad," Angela said, handing her menu to Ralph.

"I'll try the turkey burger with a side of fruit, please," Samantha said. As he left, she remarked, "I'm glad this place has pretty fast service. I've still got a bunch of work to do tonight."

"And I'm just glad I was able to lure you out for a quick bite. Still no word from Tripp or your Dad, right?"

Samantha shook her head. "Seems like I check my iPhone fifty times a day, praying for some note, a word, anything. But no dice. It's getting so I can't sleep at night, and then I worry that I might fall asleep in a staff meeting."

"You wouldn't be the first. But the bigger question is whether anyone at the NSC thinks that this test over in Kazakhstan could mean anything bad for us? I mean, I don't see how it could. But I know there are an awful lot of bad guys trying to buy weapons like that."

"That's the whole point" Samantha said. "Didn't Mark Twain say something about how history doesn't repeat itself, but it sometimes rhymes? And the last thing this country needs is what some terrorist might call poetic justice."

The waiters brought their dinners, and Samantha lapsed into a kind of melancholy, thinking again about Tripp and her father, wishing there were some way she could get some news. "You know, for the first time since I can remember, there's nothing on Facebook or Twitter or YouTube coming out of Western Kazakhstan."

"You have time to check those sites?" Angela asked, spooning up some chili.

"Well, sometimes I just get so frustrated, I surf the internet looking for some item, some comment, anything from that part of the world. But all I can find is reports from Almaty and Astana."

"Almaty and Astana?" Angela asked.

"Those are the two major cities. They have tons of news stories about the test, or whatever it was. But nothing about the reaction. Nothing about the people."

"Maybe the Mossad can find them," Angela quipped.

"Get serious!"

"I *am* serious. They always know everything. At least over in that part of the world. I mean, isn't Kazakhstan near Iran?"

"Well, yes," Samantha said cautiously. "Are you saying we should be working with the Israelis on this?"

"Have you got a better idea?"

Did she have a better idea? Did she have any ideas at all? Admitting that she was bereft of them was a truly sobering moment. "Uh, not exactly."

"Don't sit there and sound like an old Hertz commercial," Angela said. "Let's try to think of something. Some way to break through this 'Silence of the Lambs'."

"I just hope that when we finally do break through, we don't find out it was a slaughter instead."

THIRTY-SIX

Naples, Florida

"Pretty warm day. Suppose we could stop for ice cream somewhere?" Jayson Keller asked his Political Director.

"Sure. There's a little place down on Fifth Avenue," Max Federman answered. "Advance guys have it on their list. Guess they stopped there when they were setting up the trip. It'll mean a USR though."

"Unexpected Stop En Route," The Vice President mumbled. "I know. But in a little town like this, I can't imagine the Secret Service is going to get upset. Just tell the driver."

They drove down the street lined with palm trees where tourists were strolling by eying summer sales of bathing suits and straw hats. Couples were clustered at little tables outside Starbucks, sipping their Frappuccinos and reading the local paper while a brilliant sun sat high in a bright blue sky. The motorcade pulled up in front of a little shop across from Pazzo's Italian Restaurant. Jay left his sport coat in the car, rolled up the sleeves of his blue and white striped shirt and put on a broad smile. Here in Florida, he wanted to project a casual, friendly style, especially since the press bus was right behind them. The bus pulled up and a gang of reporters and photographers scrambled to get off, dragging their cameras with them. Jay and Max, flanked by several members of the Secret Service, strode into the store where a hand full of customers exclaimed, "It's the Vice President!"

"Oh my gosh, isn't he handsome!"

"Will you sign my T-shirt?

"Can I get a picture?"

"Can I have your autograph?"

"Me first," a little girl in pink shorts and a white shirt with a picture of a flamingo on it cried out, pushing toward him.

Jay looked around to see if any of the photographers were in place. They were. So he motioned to the child's mother who nodded her approval. He picked up the child, patting her head. She squealed with delight as he asked, "And what kind of ice cream do you think I should get?"

"Bubble gum!"

A young boy, shouted, "Nah, rocky road is better."

"Should I get rocky road?" Jay murmured to Max.

"Uh uh. Might be a metaphor for your campaign." He scanned the list of flavors up on a board and suggested, "There's one called Smooth Sailing." Max asked the proprietor to give the VP two scoops on a sugar cone. He offered it to his boss.

"What's in it? It's blue," the Vice President asked in a whisper, gently setting the child back down and reaching for his pen to autograph a post card her mother thrust into the little girl's hand.

"Doesn't matter. Just eat it," Max said with a grin. "Press is focusing." He checked his watch, paid for the ice cream and tried to usher their entourage out of the now crowded store. "Have to get to the event," he called to the crowd. He pointed to the photographers nudging each other for a better angle. "Okay guys. Time to get back to the bus or we'll be late to the fund-raiser."

After piling back into their limousine, the driver headed down Fifth Avenue toward the Gulf, turned left on Second Street and drove south. As they approached an area called Port Royal, the houses became larger and more luxurious. Some were a Bermuda style, others had more of a Mediterranean look. One on the right way back off the road in a Japanese garden was a home of Asian design set amongst banyan trees and a series of small bridges crossing meandering ponds. They continued past a wrought iron gate with a small sign that announced *The Port Royal Club, Members Only,* and then passed a huge stone house with its own guard shack. "Looks like we'll hit the jackpot in this neighborhood," Max said, peering out the window "Place looks bigger than the West Wing."

"West Wing's not that big," Jay said. "But you're right. If this event turns out as they billed it, we should be raising a good deal of cash on this trip. Better than the take up in Tampa. And for a little beach town, that's amazing."

Max dug in his pocket for his own copy of the speech notes. "You still gonna stick to the economy on this one?"

"Yes. But I'm going to add a bit on national security. What with the tensions between Russia and Kazakhstan, this will be a good time to get a decent sound bite out there about our sanctions policy."

"Do you really think these people give a rat's ass about Kazakhstan?"

"Doesn't matter. The national press will pick up on it, and we have to look tough on the whole nuclear testing issue. Besides, the UN isn't doing diddley-squat on sanctions, at least not yet. We have to look like we're on top of things. Back in charge. Not like the previous administration that wasted years in negotiations that went nowhere."

"I guess you gotta a point there," Max said.

"I'll tell them that we're working to build a coalition and all of that. But in the meantime, we're putting plans together to possibly freeze some of their assets and see if doesn't bring them around, at least so they'll let the inspectors into their nuclear facilities."

"Yeah. I guess that'll play." Max looked through the window again and saw a guy jogging while dialing his cell phone. "Good luck with that, fella."

Jay looked over and saw the jogger staring at his phone. "Guess he doesn't realize that we jam all the cell signals when the motorcade goes by."

"Course not. We never announce that. But ever since that freak in Jersey tried to set off a bomb near the President's motorcade using a cell phone, it's been mandatory."

"Well, I know that. I'm just sorry if we have to inconvenience any potential voters," Jay said waving out the window at the guy. The jogger smiled and waved back. "He'll get his signal back in a few minutes."

"And in a few minutes, we'll be at the house. Wait till you see it. Right on the Gulf with its own beach, guest house, about 40,000 square feet. Pretty decent piece of real estate," Max said.

"By the way, anything new on that EMP thing over by the Caspian? There wasn't anything in my morning brief."

"Not that I've heard."

"Well, what about Samantha Reid?"

"What about her," Max asked cautiously.

"She's the one who raised that issue in the first place, and Ken told me that her father and some guy she's been dating might be over there. Pretty tough on her if nobody can find out anything."

"Uh, yeah. I guess you're right. Haven't had a chance to talk to her lately."

"Well, when we get back, make it a point to make nice. I know she's been a bit of a trouble maker in the past. But she's damn smart, and if we can win the election, we just might be able to use her in *my* administration."

Max held his tongue. Didn't want to differ with the boss, but having Samantha Reid around in the new White House, one where he was hoping to snag the job of Chief of Staff, just wasn't in his own master plan.

THIRTY-SEVEN

The Aral Sea, Kazakhstan

"What happened to this place? Looks like a moonscape or something." Tripp asked the driver as they followed a road along the edge of the Aral Sea.

"Talk about contamination. This used to be the fourth largest sea, lake, whatever you want to call it. But some time back the Soviets redirected the rivers that flow into it. Some sort of central planning disaster, I guess. Anyway, lots of stuff got dumped into it too, and over time it shrank about 90%. A little's coming back. But it's slow."

"Geez. What a waste. I mean there's some water, sure. But look at those old hulks." Tripp pointed out to where two rotting boats looked like they were stuck in the rocky terrain.

"Yeah. When the water went down, there were a bunch of boats that ran aground and could never get out. So they let them sit there for years."

It almost seemed like years that they had been traveling on everything from highways to goat paths. They had been careful to ration their water but they had run out of sandwiches. They had seen a lot of apple trees along the way and had stopped to pick a bunch. He had eaten so many apples he didn't want to see another fritter or a pie for a long, long time.

Tripp had been worrying that they would run out of fuel. They had filled up as many cans and bottles as they could find, siphoning it out of the stalled trucks at the camp when the other guys weren't looking. They figured the company would send some rescue teams for the workers, so they didn't feel too guilty about it. Jake's body had provided another challenge. It was wrapped up in a lot of plastic sheeting, and they had put water bottles around it. That didn't do much to keep it cool, though. So they had him hunched down in the back seat and with the air conditioning on. At least that had kept the inside a decent temperature. That is until those goons had shot out the back window.

Tripp thought Bill would complain about sitting next to a body for a few days, but he never said a word. Turned out to be a pretty decent guy considering they had commandeered his precious antique Buick. Tripp wasn't sure if a 60's Buick would be considered an antique, but he didn't care. The fact that it didn't have any new electronic systems on it, meant it was the perfect escape car.

He didn't know what they would have done without the old relic. It was the first time in his life that he envied something that Cuba had. A supply of nothing but old cars. As they drove along, he kept thinking about Jake and Samantha. He had spent the last many hours rehearsing in his mind what he would tell her about Jake's heart attack, how he would describe the bomb blast, the shock of seeing him keel over, how they had tried to revive him, how he had finally given up. Could he really describe all of that? Would she listen? Would she understand? At this point, he didn't have a clue.

The driver ran over what must have been a rock and cursed. "All we need right now is a flat tire. We're come this far. I just hope it doesn't blow."

Tripp peered out the front windshield and exclaimed, "Hey look. Is that civilization up ahead? Looks like some low buildings or something. Haven't seen anything but yurts up till now."

Bill called from the back seat. "What's the name of the city or village or whatever you said it was?"

"It's called Akespe. Some time back the World Bank built a dam, so they put in some temporary housing for the workers. Probably still around. I suppose there might be a thousand people living in the town. We can finally get some decent food. Well, it might not be so decent, but it'll be a damn sight better than apples."

"Yeah," Bill said. "Guess they don't have any 7-Elevens around here."

"In your dreams," the driver said. "But we can probably find a place to pick up some pork or mutton. And wait'll you taste the stuff they drink."

"I thought they drank a lot of green tea, that sort of thing," Tripp said.

"Out here it's fermented mare's milk."

"Horse milk?" Bill asked.

"You got it," the driver said. "Get ready, it tastes like a combination of champagne and dirty sweat sox."

"How tempting," Tripp said. "I'll stick with the tea, if we can find some"

"Looks like some mines or something over there," Bill said, pointing out the side window. "Way out there. See?"

"Yeah, it isn't just oil and gas here. They've got some gold and uranium too."

"Maybe this is where they get the uranium for their nuclear weapons," Tripp said as he pulled out his cell phone and tried to switch it on. He stared at the small screen and called out, "Still no signal. Guess they haven't got any cell towers in this part of the world."

"Not out here. There are parts of the country that are pretty up to date. Well, you were in Almaty. You know that. Got everything over there. So much oil money has been pouring in, they built all kinds of stuff in the big cities. But out on the steppe, the villages, the tribal areas, it's still like the middle ages. When we get into town, we'll have to look for a land line. And if we can find one, you said you could call the company to get us a plane or something. Right?"

"Absolutely," Tripp said. "I just hope we can find a place to stay."

"Wait a minute. If we find a place, what do we do about Jake's body?" Bill asked.

Tripp turned around to face the guy. "Big problem. Let's pull over and put it in the trunk for now. Can't exactly drag a body into a hotel. That is if they've got any hotels or inns or anything like that around here."

"If you can get through to GeoGlobal, see if they can find a casket or something," the driver suggested.

"We'll have to work that out," Tripp said. "And after I call them, the next call is going to have to be to Samantha, Jake's daughter."

"That's gonna be the tough one," the driver said, heading the Buick down what looked to be the main road of a rather large village.

"You got that one right," Tripp said, with a worrying frown.

THIRTY-EIGHT

The White House

"What do you think we'll do now that the President of Kazakhstan has stiffed the IAEA about immediate inspections?" Samantha asked, sitting in front of Hunt Daniel's desk in the EEOB. The lanky Lieutenant Colonel had a stack of classified documents in front of him along with a series of telephones, one that Samantha knew was a secure phone. She also spied a photograph in a bookcase off to the side. It was a color photo of an attractive blond woman with strawberry blond hair pushed behind some sort of headband. Samantha wondered if that was the famous Dr. Cameron Talbot. She had heard that Hunt was dating her. Must be. She didn't look much like a scientist. Then again, what was a scientist supposed to look like? Samantha refocused on what Hunt was saying about the Kazakhs.

"They are being totally obstinate on this one. They've got to realize that we'll come down hard on them, and that we'll get a bunch of our friends to join us this time."

"What about the Russians?"

"For once they'll be with us," Hunt said assuredly.

"But what I don't get is why they're behaving this way? I mean, if that test really was some sort of mistake, like their President said, you'd think they'd want to clear up the confusion and make a statement about how they're only developing nuclear power for peaceful purposes and how this was an aberration. Or something along those lines. Even if it's a bald-faced lie, at least that might placate the UN types who are always looking for a reason not to take action on something like this."

Hunt took a sip of coffee from his White House mug and asked, "You sure you don't want some coffee? We've got plenty in the ante room."

Samantha shook her head. "Had my fill for the morning, but what's your take on their nuclear situation?"

"Well, they've got several nuclear plants operating in the country. They're working out okay to provide energy. No problem there. But now with this explosion, they're obviously expanding to weapons and missiles, and I just don't see how they're going to weasel their way out of this one. The way I see it, though, is that they feel threatened by the Russians. Well, we've talked about that. And now they're just showing some muscle."

"Trouble is, the rest of the world doesn't like muscle-builders," Samantha said, "especially now with so many terrorist groups trying to buy or steal nuclear material. I mean who knows where this could go?"

"Right," Hunt said. "But back on the what-are-we-going-to-do scenario. I'm putting together a Decision Document for Ken laying out how we impose unilateral sanctions on a few specific areas and how we could include some of their top people in the mix. I've been talking to Treasury, and they're ready to roll if they get a sign-off from the President. In fact, the Veep mentioned sanctions and a possible freeze on that trip of his to Florida. You probably saw that report. So he's inoculated the news media on that one."

"Yes, I saw it in the News Summary. Now, I hope we can pull this off," Samantha said. "We can be the first in line, and then State can work on getting other countries to come on board."

"That's the plan," Hunt said.

"By the way, how is Dr. Talbot coming on her missile defense project?"

"She's been watching the development of MDA's airborne laser, but the trouble with that one is that ever since Congress cut the funding, or rather that Congresswoman from California, Betty Barton, cut the damn funding for the Missile Defense Agency, Cammy isn't sure it'll work. Not yet anyway. So she's been trying to develop a whole new approach to stop a missile. Especially one that might be detonated up in the atmosphere. It's kind of tricky though. It's classified, of course. But as soon as I learn more about it, I'll fill you in. You've got all the clearances."

"Thanks, Hunt. I really want to stay up to speed on this one." She felt her cell vibrate and said, "Oh, give me a minute. Let me just check and see if this call is worth taking." She fished her cell out of her jacket pocket and cried out, "Oh my God! It's from Tripp. He's alive!"

She jumped up and raced out of the room, calling over her shoulder. "Gotta take this. Talk to you later."

She ducked into an empty office next door as she was punching up the call. "Tripp? Is that you? Is it really you?" she exclaimed. She had been so worried, so dejected for the last several days, she had almost lost hope of ever talking to him again. "Are you okay? Where are you? How's Dad?"

"Hey, slow down and let me explain. First of all, I miss you and am so sorry I've been out of touch. But it's been absolute hell over here." He began his story slowly, just as he had rehearsed it. He started to fill her in on how they saw the blast, then how all the power was knocked out. Then he talked about trying to find transportation, finally locating a beat-up Buick and then encountering tribal marauders along the way who were trying to steal their stuff.

"My God, you went through all of that? This is amazing. And from what you're saying, it was definitely an EMP. That's been our analysis here too. But, Lord! What a mess. I'm just thankful you got out of there. Where are you now? And how's Dad? He talked about how this was going to be an adventure, but I'm sure he never figured how just how big an adventure it would turn out to be," she said.

Tripp paused. How in God's name would he tell her? How could he tell her? How could he explain that Jake had a heart attack and the pacemaker must have failed in connection with the explosion? He had been thinking about this conversation, dreading this conversation for so long, and now he had to fess up.

"Uh, Samantha, I don't know how to tell you this."

"Tell me what?" Samantha asked cautiously. "Is Dad okay? Can I talk to him?"

"Well, no, you can't?"

"Why not?" she asked, her voice rising. "Put him on. He's got to be there with you. Isn't he?"

"I've got him with me, but he can't talk to you. Oh hell, Samantha. There's no other way to say this. When that nuclear blast went off, it must have set off those microwaves you've talked about. As I said, it screwed everything up, and it must have knocked out Jake's pacemaker. He evidently had a heart attack, and nothing worked. We were out in this field . . ."

"What?" she shrieked. "He had a heart attack? Did he survive? What did you do? Was there anybody around who could help him, a doctor around or anything?"

"No. That's just the thing. We were out in a field. When the blast went off, as I said, it must have affected the pacemaker or something because I saw him grab his chest and fall down. I worked on him. Hell we all worked, giving him CPR for probably a half hour at least. I don't know, but we couldn't revive him. Samantha, Jake died right there in my arms."

"No! No! He couldn't die!" she cried out. "He said he was healthy when he left. And you promised to take care of him. You promised. But you didn't!"

"Honey, listen. I did everything I could. It was awful. Worst day of my life. You have to believe me."

Samantha started to sob into the phone, "I begged him not to go. I begged *you* not to take him on that trip. You knew he had a heart condition. But no, you and your company were going to give him this great adventure. And he died over there in some oil field." She took a gulp of air and shouted, "Tripp, you killed my father!"

"Listen, Samantha. I didn't kill him. The blast, or whatever it was, killed him. There was nothing I could do. I tried. Please believe me, I tried. We all tried. And after it all happened, we had to figure out a way to get out of there. Like I said, it was a helluva trip. But now we're in some village and GeoGlobal is sending a plane for us so I can bring Jake back and make arrangements."

Arrangements? He was thinking about arrangements? He must mean a casket, an announcement, a funeral. Oh God! How could she go through all of that? How could she go through the rest of her life knowing that her father had died early, way too early, and because of a stupid trip that could have been stopped? Could she have worked harder to stop it? Could she have used more persuasion to keep him off that plane to the crazy country on the other side of the world? She felt the guilt, the pangs of remorse wash over her.

She visualized his sparkling eyes, eyes she would never see smile at her again. She thought about the bear hug he always gave her when he walked into a room, a hug she would never feel again.

She remembered the words, "Hi Pumpkin." Words she would never hear again. She thought about the future. How he wouldn't be there to walk her down the aisle. But wait, she wouldn't be walking down an aisle toward Tripp Adams. That was for sure. She held the phone to her ear, the silence on the other end said it all. Tripp had nothing to say except to talk about *arrangements*.

"Arrangements? You mean a funeral, don't you? Well, I'll tell you something, Tripp Adams." Trying to regain her composure as the hurt and anger welled up inside of her, she spoke now in a deliberate tone. "If there are arrangements to be made, my brother and I will make them. I just want to get my father home. Back to Houston where he will be buried next to my mother. And as for you," she took a moment to wipe her eyes with the back of her hand, "as for you, I don't see how I could *ever* trust you again with anything. In fact, the way I feel right now, knowing you are responsible for killing my Dad, I don't want to see you again. Not ever!" She hit the end button, put her head down and cried.

THIRTY-NINE

Astana, Kazakhstan

"President Surleimenov Blamed for Bad Blast."

"Caspian People Stranded."

"Violence Reported in the West."

"Russia Furious."

"Baltiev Vows to win Election on Peace Plank."

"IAEA Again Demands Inspections"

"US Imposes Sanctions"

Viktor Surleimenov waved the newspapers and shouted to his aide in a voice of tightly controlled rage. "Get the Vice President in here. Now!" He studied the headlines. He was so angry and frustrated, he wanted to throw the papers against the wall. He picked up his desk phone instead. When his secretary answered, he barked, "Get the editor of Gazeta.kz over here."

"You wanted to see me Viktor?" his number two asked, rushing into the ornate office.

"You've seen the papers. This is a disaster. I order one small test. One *very* small test out in some remote area where no one would be affected. And what happens? Those idiots blow up the thing and black out the whole western part of our country. What kind of numbskulls are running our new plant out there anyway?"

"I hear you," the VP said. The tall, charismatic man with deep set gray eyes strode across the room and picked up one of the papers. "You issued that statement saying it was a mistake. Looks like nobody is buying it," he said, pointing to the headline about the opposition candidate, Sergei Baltiev. "Funny how he first campaigned on building a strong defense, in coordination with the Russians, of course. And now he does a 180 and talks about nothing but peace."

"That man practices political backflips all the time. Nobody can believe anything he says. But now, with this, he might be in position to make it a tough match."

"And what about the IAEA?" the VP asked, pointing to the story about inspections.

"They want inspections, and they want us to formally sign the Nuclear Non-Proliferation Agreement. Again. Israel hasn't signed it. Pakistan hasn't signed it. Why should we?"

"Well, what about the US sanctions? We can't afford sanctions, especially when we have so many oil and gas contracts with the Americans right now." He leaned down and read the second paragraph. "And it says here that they're not only placing sanctions on parts of our economy, they're going to be targeting the assets of some of our top people in government positions if any are held in the United States."

"I, for one, don't have any money over there. I've got it invested right here." The President raised his eyebrows and added, "Well, I might have a small account in the Seychelles, but no matter."

"I don't have funds in the states, either. But you know who does," the VP said with pointed glance.

The President thought about that for several seconds and said, "Wait. You're right. I've been so focused on the campaign ads that, for a minute, I forgot about Baltiev's investments in San Francisco. That fancy condo up on that place called Russian Hill. Considering the way he cozies up to Moscow, seems rather appropriate. Well, I used that line in a campaign speech. And I hear he's got a lot of money deposited with the Bank of America in that city. The trouble is, he's not working for the government. So the Americans won't be targeting his money. But, wait a minute, sit down. I just had a positively brilliant thought."

The other man settled down in an upholstered arm chair and gave the president his rapt attention. "What kind of thought?"

"You know the expression 'Kill two birds'?"

"Yes. Go on."

"Now think about this. Those scientists I just called numskulls might have come up with a great new weapon. And they probably don't even know it."

"What do you mean?"

"They were supposed to detonate that test at sea level, just over the Caspian. But it turns out that it malfunctioned and was fired way up in the atmosphere, which produced one of those pulse things. We talked about that in that first emergency meeting," Viktor said.

"Yes. It looked like they got it all wrong."

"Maybe yes. Maybe no. When they created that pulse, it knocked all the power out for miles around. Killed all the communications, computers, transportation. Everything. That's what our military is telling us, the ones who got through on that flight yesterday."

"Yes. It's a terrible situation. We've got to get some convoys together. Get some of our troops to the area to restore order. And we've got to get food and water to the people, especially in Atyrau. I saw the report that gangs of locals are holding up the citizens, stealing any food they can find. They're even preying on nearby farmers. We can't have such chaos."

"I know that. I already sent the order to send transport planes. But back to the subject of the mistaken test. If sending up a missile armed with a very small nuclear device and detonating it so far up can cause this kind of havoc in our country, think what it would do in a country that is much more advanced. A country that relies completely on electronic systems, the internet, all of that."

"What are saying? Surely you're not contemplating an attack on another country. That would be political suicide," the VP said, his voice rising.

"Now listen. Back to the two birds. First bird. The United States imposes economic sanctions on our economy. Second bird. Sergei Baltiev has millions of dollars hidden away in the Bank of America in San Francisco. Money I'm sure he's planning to use in his campaign against me. He's probably already drawing down that account for some of the ads he's been running. So, say we figure out a way to get one of our missiles within striking distance of San Francisco. And say we shoot it up high, way over the city. We don't kill anybody on the ground. We don't want to kill anybody. But we bring all of their communications, their equipment, their electronic records, and that means bank records, to a halt. At least for a while. This stops Baltiev. The more I think about it, if the American president is going to freeze our assets, we'll fry theirs!" he said triumphantly.

"You can't do that," the VP challenged, jumping up from his chair and pointing his finger at the President. "Are you insane? You attack the United States, you don't think they will retaliate? You are a fool."

Viktor turned on him and pointed right back. "You do not call me a fool. I know what I am doing. We can send up a weapon and cause this, what did they call it? This EMP thing and no one will know who did it. It will be a completely secret operation. We don't put our name and address on our missiles or our bombs. We'll launch it from a fishing boat or something like that. And they will never know what hit them. They'll be too busy trying to restore order to their precious city of hills."

The Vice President stared at his President with unconcealed shock. "I can't believe you are contemplating such a thing. You hear about the chaos inflicted on our own people and you want to inflict the same thing on innocent Americans?"

"Oh, don't be such a bleeding heart. So the Americans will have a set-back for a while. But in the meantime, the Americans will get distracted from all their sanctions talk, and I will have cut the legs out from under Baltiev. And that means I win the election. As for the chaos out by the Caspian, I'm sure our people will forgive me for that nuclear test once I explain that I was doing it for them, for the true Kazakhs, to keep us safe and strong from any encroachment by the Russians. See, my plan not only kills two birds, but maybe a third one – Russian designs on us. Now wouldn't that be a nice trifecta!"

FORTY

Houston, Texas

"In the words of Theodore Roosevelt," the Minister intoned, "It is not the critic who counts. The credit belongs to the man who is actually in the arena, whose face is marred by dust and sweat and blood, who strives valiantly, who knows great enthusiasms, great devotions, who at the best knows in the end the triumph of high achievement, and who at the worst, if he fails, at least fails while daring greatly, so that his place shall never be with those cold and timid souls who neither know victory nor defeat."

Samantha sat transfixed by the words, the ceremony, the casket in front of the altar. Had she simply been the critic while her Dad was the man in the arena? The man whose face was often marred by dust and sweat? When Jake worked with the wildcatters, that's how he looked. She could visualize him now in one of his checked shirts, with his wide grin and open arms. But as her mind's eye conjured up the image, the tears welled up once again. She fished in her purse for a Kleenex as the Minister announced the last hymn. Her brother took her arm when the entire congregation stood up to sing *Abide With Me, Fast Falls the Eventide*. She found her place and tried to sing along, but her voice caught in her throat. She tried to look down and decipher the words. Instead, a trio of tears fell onto the hymnal page. The words now were a blur but she heard the people behind her.

"I fear no foe, with Thee at hand to bless;

Ills have no weight, and tears no bitterness.

Where is death's sting? Where, grave, thy victory?

I triumph still, if Thou abide with me"

Triumph? Where was the triumph? For Jake? For her? For anyone seated in the little chapel just down the road from his house? Their house. The house where she grew up. The house where she raced home from school to do her homework before her Dad got in from the fields. The house where they would sit and pore over geologic reports and print-outs of various formations, making bets on where the next well could be found. The house where her Dad taught her to ride her first bicycle on the long driveway. No training wheels for her. Jake had simply held onto the seat until she first tried the brakes and pushed down to get the pedals going. Then he'd let go, and she was on her own. He was like that. Always shouting, "You can do it!" "Way to go!" and "Great job!" He wanted her to be free, independent and confident. He was never overly protective like some parents on the street.

As she thought about it, she realized that over the years, she was the one who had become overly protective. But after her mother had died of cancer and Jake was living alone, how was she supposed to react? Especially when he began to have heart trouble. Maybe she could have been even more protective. Maybe she could have talked him out of that trip. Maybe she could have saved his life. Maybe.

And what about his life or the next life. Was there a next life? She thought about the meeting they had when the Minister stopped by the house the day before. He had asked if she had any questions about the funeral. She said that it all looked well organized, thanks to her brother who had written and placed the obituary, selected the hymns and planned out the whole program. She was grateful for the help since she had been overwhelmed at the office just at the time when she should have been flying back to Texas. She had talked to her brother, sent emails, and stayed up till all hours notifying scores of Jake's friends after she finished her White House work. She had arrived in town only two days before the funeral and was relieved to see that most of the details had been handled. She thanked the minister for his time and just as he was getting ready to leave, she decided to ask him a question. One she had pondered for years. Now was the time to blurt it out. So she looked into his eyes and said, "Tell me. Do you really believe in life after death?"

He thought for a long moment and then replied, "Yes, Samantha. I truly do. Let me say this. In this life, we are like the child in the womb. Think about it. When the baby is in the womb, it only knows a certain kind of life. But then suddenly, one day, it is thrust into a new and wonderful life." Then he had taken her hand and added with a comforting smile, "And he can't go back and tell the other kids. And so it shall be in the next life."

She had thought about that. Long and hard. Was he right? Would there be some new and wonderful next life? She prayed it was so. But right now all she could think of was *this* life. And this was a life lost to her forever.

She sat and refocused on the program. At the end of the hymn, the Minister said a brief benediction and six pall bearers walked up the aisle, raised the casket and carried it outside to a waiting car. Tripp was one of them. She had tried to tell her brother to get Tripp out of the proceedings. She didn't want to see him. Didn't even want him in the church. But she couldn't stop him. At least she didn't have to talk to him. She never wanted to talk to him. Not now. Not ever. Even glimpsing him sitting in the last row when she had entered the church, made her feel that stab of pain once again. The pain of loss. Not only the loss of her Dad, but the loss of trust in a man she thought she loved.

Her brother took her arm once again and ushered her out of the church. She knew she would have to greet the other mourners at a reception at the house later on. A neighbor had planned it along with the Minister's wife. She'd just have to work to pull herself together. After all, she was usually the unflappable White House official, taking charge of staff meetings, making reports to the National Security Advisor, keeping her cool when new threats and new intel hit her In Box. Then again, all of those duties were professional. This was personal.

As she stepped outside, she shielded her eyes from the bright sun and started to walk toward the limo that would take her and a few others to the cemetery for the short burial ceremony. She felt a tap on her shoulder and turned around.

"Samantha, I'm so sorry," Tripp said, reaching out to touch her cheek.

She brushed his hand away and replied in a formal tone, "Thank you for coming. I'm sure you need to get back to Washington right away." With that she turned abruptly, got into the limo and ordered the driver to head out. She never saw the look of devastation on Tripp's face as the sleek black car moved away from the curb.

FORTY-ONE

Atyrau, Kazakhstan

"No entry without identification," the soldier barked to Nurlan who was hobbling toward the door of his apartment building. He quickly pulled his company ID out of his back pocket and waved it in front of the first officer. "You wait," the man ordered. He grabbed the ID card, peered at the photo, then up at Nurlan's face before showing it to another guard. "You live here?"

"Yes, up on fourth floor." Nurlan reached out for the card and slipped it back into his pocket. "I get inside. I have friends. Sister. Is all okay here?"

Nurlan had heard that transports filled with military personnel had landed earlier in the day and that the soldiers were fanned out all over the city, trying to contain the mobs screaming for food and water and keep looters out of the homes and apartment buildings. He had told Pete and Zhanar to stay inside and not venture out. They had been holed up in the apartment for the last several days. It was bad enough that Nurlan had to go out on the street to catch a company bus. He always waited inside until he saw it pull up, and then he raced as fast as his weak legs could carry him to make it before the doors closed.

The city was a mess. Still no lights. No power. No air conditioning. No new food supplies. No communication with the outside world. Not until today when the big government planes arrived. He heard about it at the plant where a cheer went up when their boss announced that the government had sent several plane loads of rice, bread, tea, even crates of mutton and beef. The boss said that crowds had descended on the airfield making it almost impossible to land, but the planes finally got in. He knew all of this because the government had also sent a private emissary to come to their nuclear facility with a special message.

Nurlan saw the soldier wave him inside and he scrambled up the stairs to his apartment. Pete and Zhanar were there, sharing a can of soup when he flew through the door. "I have news. Big news." He pulled a chair up to the kitchen table and told them about the transports.

"We're saved!" Zhanar practically shouted, throwing her arms around her brother. "We saw some jeeps out the window and couldn't figure out how they could be running. Nothing else is moving. But we saw them filled with soldiers. They must have brought the jeeps on the plane, right?"

Nurlan nodded and reached for a kitchen towel to wipe his forehead. It was stifling in the little apartment. Even with the windows open, there was no breeze today and the temperature was close to a hundred degrees. "Do we have any water left?"

"Only two small bottles," his sister replied.

"Okay. Don't worry. I get some at plant tomorrow. I bring home on bus. With soldiers outside, it be okay to get it home. I get more food too."

"That's great," Pete said. "I have to say this has been a helluva summer you arranged for me."

"I know it not what we planned."

"Damn right! I thought we were going to hook up with some of the protest groups over here, like the ones in Almaty. You said there would be more meetings. But then this thing hits, and everything gets totally screwed up."

"I know," Nurlan said. "It all messed up here. I sorry."

"Not your fault," Pete said. "Actually, since this whole thing happened, and I've had to hang out here, I've had a lot of time to think about my project."

"You mean your project about getting money from The White House?" Zhanar inquired. "You told me about that when you first got here. But then with all this trouble, you haven't said anything for a while."

"That doesn't mean I haven't been thinking about it."

"What you think?" Nurlan asked, again wiping beads of sweat off his face.

"I've been trying to figure out things the S.A.I.N.T.S. can do to put more pressure on those bastards."

"What kind of pressure," Zhanar asked cautiously.

"When I saw those huge demonstrations back in Almaty it got me to thinking about some of the other anti-war groups we might be able to pull together and then make certain threats. I mean, we could threaten to do a lot of damage unless they pay up. Something like that."

"I don't think violence is going to get you anywhere but a jail cell," Zhanar said, putting her hand on his arm. "I don't want you to go to jail."

"Don't worry. I'm smarter than that. I just want to get them to focus on reparations. Stuff they promised us years ago, but never delivered. After all this time and all the people who have died from their damn tests, you'd think they'd feel guilty about all of that. But no. they sometimes pass some law, but then we never get the money."

He turned to Zhanar and took her hand in his. "Look, I know your people here have suffered too. We've all seen the babies, the animals. Look at Nurlan's legs. They should be stronger. He shouldn't be in pain all the time. Okay, so he hides it. He doesn't complain. But I complain a lot. Not for me. But for my family. Well, the family I had once." He then stared into her eyes and continued in a low, dejected tone. "Do you know what it's like to listen to your own mother writhe in pain from the cancer that's eating her body? Do you know what it's like to hear her cry at night when she thinks I can't hear her? Do you have any idea what it's like to watch someone wasting away when you know, you absolutely *know* that the damn government has medicines and money that might have saved her from all of that? Do you have any idea?"

Zhanar answered softly. "Yes, Pete. Yes, I do know. I've seen it here too. I've seen horrible things. Bad things that came after the Soviets did their own tests. We've talked about all of this. And I know it still hurts you. It hurts me too. But I don't know what we can do about it. We don't have any power. Not real power to go up against big governments."

"Wait," Nurlan interrupted. "We no have time for this talk now. I said I have news. Big news. I tell you but you promise no say to anybody. Yes?"

Pete and Zhanar stared at Nurlan and said at once, "What news?"

"Now I tell. At plant today, besides food and soldiers, government sent special man with orders. Orders from President."

"From the President of Kazakhstan?" Zhanar asked.

"Yes. Right from top man."

"What orders?" Pete asked.

"President now say we made special new weapon, and he wants use it again."

"Weapon? What weapon?" Pete asked. "I don't get it. You set off a nuclear test. Does he mean he's going to nuke somebody or some country? I can't believe this. Is he nuts or something?"

"I not know why but man say we take one more like first small nuclear device and we put on one of transport planes. They leave one here while we get all ready."

"Where are you going to take it? This is crazy!" Pete said.

"I not sure yet. But I try find out."

"So they're going to put a nuclear weapon on a plane and go drop it somewhere?" Zhanar asked, her eyes wide with fear. "They can't do that. You and your people can't let them do that. It would start a war. What in the world are they thinking?"

"Man say it not kill anybody if it goes like last test. Up high. He say President no want kill anybody. He just want send message. Something like that," Nurlan tried to explain.

"Send a message?" Pete asked. "He sent a helluva message when the first one went off and set this city back to the stone ages. That is if your bomb, or whatever it was, did all of that. And from what you've said, it really was the culprit."

"I know. I know," Nurlan said. "I feel bad about first test. Now with new order, I not know where bomb goes. I try find out. We just hear today that we get second one ready."

"This is terrible," Zhanar said. "But what can we do?"

"I not know," Nurlan replied. "Maybe they send me with bomb like last time. They not know I was one who changed things on first test. They not find out. They still think I'm best computer guy."

"No! They can't send you," Zhanar cried out. "The bomb could go off. Something could go wrong. You could be killed. You have to quit. Quit now!" she begged.

"Can't quit now. Have to find out all plans. Then we see what I can do."

FORTY-TWO

Georgetown

Hunt Daniels jogged along P Street and up the few steps to his door. He had managed to cut out of his office in the EEOB with just enough time to get in a run before his guest arrived. The gray stucco house with black shutters sat back from a road paved with weathered red bricks. Gray stone urns filled with geraniums flanked the stairs leading to the black front door. He had felt pretty lucky to still have the place after his ex-wife had decided she didn't dig being married to a military type and left him for an investment banker who regularly came home for dinner. Hunt had been single since that debacle, and while he knew he had a pretty good thing going now with Cameron Talbot, they both had such busy travel schedules, he was glad when they could carve out an evening together. And tonight she had agreed to make it at his place.

It was pretty handy living in this neighborhood, about a seven minute commute to the White House. Georgetown was where JFK had lived in five different houses during his political life and where a bunch of other Senators, State Department types and Washington Post reporters now called home.

Once inside the house, he turned off the security system and raced upstairs, taking them two steps at a time. Peeling off his shorts and T-shirt, he jumped in the shower and, as usual, marveled at the powerful flow. There were a ton of things wrong with Washington, but water pressure wasn't one of them. He toweled off, ran his fingers through his short, sandy hair and caught a glimpse of himself in the mirror. Should he shave again? No time. He did look a bit scruffy, so he quickly brushed his hair into some semblance of order and hurried to his closet when the doorbell rang.

He grabbed the phone on his bedside table since it was tied to the doorbell. "That you, hon?"

"It's me," she replied. "I've got my key."

"C'mon in, I'll be right down."

Hunt reached for a pair of khakis, blue polo shirt and his old Docksiders. When he came down the stairs, there was Cammy, tossing her shoulder bag over the bannister and grinning up at him. "Hi beautiful!" He said, "Glad you could come by tonight. It's been a while." He took her in his arms and claimed her mouth. She opened to him, wound her arms around his neck and molded her body to his. When he finally broke the kiss, he looked down into her light blue eyes, eyes the color of robins' eggs, and murmured, "Been a long time. Too long."

"I know. I'm so glad to be back. The trip out to California was a total drag."

"I want to hear all about it. C'mon into the kitchen. I've got a bottle of wine I think you'll like." She followed and as he opened a Beaujolais Nouveau, she remarked, "Thanks for getting a light one tonight. You know how the cabs give me a headache."

"I have some Merlot too if this turns out to be too, well, new or whatever." He took a pair of wineglasses from the cupboard and poured them each a taste.

"Actually this is pretty good," Cammy said. "What's the dinner plan?"

"I just called in an order of Mexican from that place over on Wisconsin. You know, the one on the corner?"

"You mean the restaurant painted the color of Pepto-Bismol?"

"Yeah. Lousy ambiance, but the food's terrific and besides, I wanted to stay in and hear about your trip tonight. Okay with you?"

"More than okay. I've been in airplanes, staff meetings, strategy sessions, even test modules. I couldn't wait to get back and just be with you," she said leaning over to give him another kiss on the cheek.

"Keep that up and we'll forget about the tacos."

She laughed and pushed a few strands of strawberry blond hair back behind her headband. "No, I'm starved. For food." She paused and smiled up at him. "Well, I have to admit I'm starved for you too."

They took their wine and sat down at the kitchen table. "So tell me about California. Anything working yet on our little project?"

"Well, ever since you and Ken took me on as a consultant on this whole EMP exercise, I've been working with our people on a bunch of ideas, especially trying to check out the new Airborne Laser and see how accurate it could be. That's why I had to go out to our California facility. You know all of that." He nodded. She swirled the wine in her glass and took another sip. "So anyway, I get out there and go over the latest, but the trouble is, a lot of the work has really slowed down, Budget cuts, of course."

"Thanks to California's own Betty Barton," Hunt said with a shrug.

"Exactly. You'd think the woman would worry about jobs in her own state even if she doesn't appreciate the logic of our having decent missile defense systems. Seems like the DOD budget is always her favorite Pinata!"

"So you said they've slowed down on the laser? That's a bummer."

"Sure is. At least they're still doing some simulations. The COIL system is absolutely amazing."

"Yeah. I saw a memo on that one not too long ago. Chemical Oxygen Iodine Laser. Kind of a cool name, don't you think?"

"I guess. The one they were working on has six infrared sensors that detect the heat from the plume of a missile. Then one of the lasers swings around to the right compass bearing that they get from the sensor and locks onto it. So then they can track it. And when they figure that out, they can fire off a second laser that finds the missile. They have to add in all sorts of calculations to measure atmospheric conditions and all of that. But finally, the plan is to have the laser hit the missile with enough energy to fry its skin so hot that it just self-destructs."

"I remember that first actual test they did over the Pacific. It was pretty cool. Well, guess that wouldn't be the right description," he said, giving her a straight line grin.

"Well, now with those budget cuts, they've had to cancel the next test. Can you believe that?" Cammy groaned. "So the whole time I was out there, I was wracking my brain to see what else we could focus on to counter any sort of errant nuke that might set off an EMP. I mean, the White House knows all about the first laser, but I know you all want something better."

"So, where do we go from here?"

Cammy set her wineglass down on the table, leaned back in her chair and crossed her arms. She gazed up at the ceiling as if looking for divine guidance. "I do have some ideas. Not sure if I'm ready to go out on a limb just yet." She glanced down and went on. "Let's just say that I'm trying to wrap my arms around a concept."

"A concept?" "Hunt asked, intrigued. "Every time you come up with a new concept, it blows my mind."

"And usually blows our budget too. You should hear our CEO bitch about our bottom line."

"Your bottom line? For God's sake, you'd think he'd be overjoyed that we want to give you contracts all the time," Hunt said.

"Oh, he likes to brag about special projects for The White House. It's just that he never wants to bill you guys for actual time spent. He figures it looks better for our Pentagon contracts if word gets around that he's kind of *loaning* my services to the President, if you get the gist."

"Well, he should stop bitching. Last time the President called you in and you came up with that new missile defense system for our airplanes, you must have saved a ton of lives, to say nothing about the economic consequences."

She smiled. "Yes, but you know you're only as good as your last act. Or rather, in our business, as good as your next inspiration."

The doorbell rang. "Great timing, must be the tacos." Hunt jumped up and started for the door, calling over his shoulder, "Don't worry, I didn't forget the guacamole, and I also ordered you a salad."

Cammy got up and set the table. She had spent so much time here in Hunt's home, she knew where to find the plates, silverware and the paper napkins he had in the pantry. She was pouring more wine as Hunt came in with the bags. She watched him take the tacos, the container of black beans and all the condiments out and arrange them on a big platter. He always did things like that, trying to make things nice for her. She wouldn't have minded just eating it all out of the plastic containers, but she had to admit it was sweet to have a man want to do things right. In fact, it seemed that he waited on her almost out of habit now.

And Hunt did a whole lot more than wait on her. He confided in her. He made her laugh. And he could even make her cry. Not by making her sad. Oh no, but by making her almost cry out when they were in bed together. Just watching him now, his broad shoulders leaning over the kitchen island, his hands carefully arranging their dinner, reminded her of the first time he had ever made love to her. Those hands. Those fabulous hands of his had touched every sensitive spot on her entire body. She remembered using the phrase E-words to describe that experience. He hadn't known what she meant until she recited them. Erotic, ethereal, and ecstatic. That's how the man made her feel, not just that first time, but every time. It was almost like a drug, something she craved whenever she thought about him. And it could be darned disconcerting when she was in the middle of a staff meeting, a simulation or sober encounter with her boss, and her mind would wander to the next time when she might feel the E-words again.

"Here. Have some salsa," Hunt offered, shaking her out of her reverie. This was ridiculous. She was fantasizing about the man and he was sitting across from her. Get a grip, grab a taco and just be patient. After all, they had all night, didn't they?

Hunt had left his cell phone on the kitchen counter and when it chimed, he muttered, "Damn," and reached over to see who was calling. "Gotta take this one, Cam."

"No problem," she said, spooning some salsa and sour cream onto her taco.

"Oh Jesus," Hunt exclaimed into the phone. "Are you sure? Photos? YouTube? So we were right all along."

FORTY-THREE

The White House

"Good Morning, Samantha. Welcome back," her Admin Assistant said. "Classified papers are in your safe, your In-Box is kind of, well, over flowing. The most important summons is from Cosgrove for a meeting at eight in the Sit Room. It's on top. And the reports on that nuclear mess in Kazakhstan are all over Facebook and YouTube. The optics are really awful. Oh, and there's fresh coffee."

Samantha hung her navy blazer on the coat rack just inside the door, glanced at her desk and said, "Pictures are that bad, huh? I saw a few news reports when I got up. Can you believe all those mobs screaming for food and the soldiers trying to hold them back? My God, it looked like those student riots in Tehran some time back."

"It just means that you were right all along about the effects of a blast like that. Everybody's talking about it. Legislative Affairs says they're going to try to get some additional funding to harden the electricity grid. Guess they finally paid attention to your memos.

Anyway, glad to have you back. Nothing works right in this office when you're away. Shilling's off on some tangent about a new chemical readiness program. We've announced how we're putting our own sanctions on Kazakhstan. Well, I'm sure you saw all of that when you were in Houston. And Angela stopped by to see when you'd be getting back. We got to talking, and she told me that Max Federman has been after her again." Joan made a face like a four-year-old refusing to eat spinach. "I think that makes four White House staffers that he's hit on. So far that I know of. He thinks that just because of his *exalted* position, or whatever he calls it, every woman is going to succumb to his perceived charm."

"The old 'power being the ultimate aphrodisiac' certainly doesn't apply to that guy," Samantha said. "One of these days he's going to get sued."

"Or bounced outta here." Joan turned, "Sure you don't want some coffee?"

"Come to think of it, coffee would great. I'd get it, but it looks like I'd better get through this stuff before the Sit Room meeting." She glanced at her watch. She'd have forty-five minutes to speed through a stack that took three days to accumulate. She opened the safe, took out the folders, and began to dig in. She read through the latest intel on a series of threats discovered by an agent in Pakistan, the arrest and interrogation of a woman caught with explosives in the Short Hills Mall in New Jersey, an item about someone trying to sell a scud missile on eBay. Then she read an exchange between Ken Cosgrove and Congresswoman Betty Barton about the need for expanded missile defense systems in the face of new worldwide threats. He had told her about our picking up that the Chinese are considering developing EMP weapons to neutralize the 7th fleet in case China ever wants to attack Taiwan. That fleet is the one that would normally come to Taiwan's aid. But Barton stuck to her position that a biological attack was much more likely, and she wanted to concentrate funds in that area. As Samantha read the words, it seemed like she was watching a verbal tennis game and it was way beyond Love All.

"Here's your coffee," Joan said. "And oh, I almost forgot, you've had three calls from Tripp Adams. Said to tell you he's back in town." She lowered her voice and murmured in a sympathetic tone, "Then again, I remember you said you never wanted to see him again. Anyway, just wanted you to know he called." She turned and went back to her desk.

Did she want to see him again? Absolutely not. After those three terrible days in Houston, dealing with the funeral, the old friends of her Dad's telling her over and over again what a great guy he was and how he died "way too young," her determination to cut all ties with Tripp was reinforced. How could she spend time with the man she felt bore the brunt of the responsibility for her father's death? Sure, Jake might have had a heart attack, but if he had been here or in Houston or most anywhere in the states, she was certain he could have had immediate care. And besides, the pacemaker wouldn't have failed here. It just would not have happened. No, she couldn't face Tripp again. As she had said when he called with the awful news, she didn't want to see him. Not now. Not ever.

She finished the coffee, hoping the caffeine fix would give her some sort of a lift. She could sure use one today. She tossed the files back into the safe, picked up her leather folder and blazer and headed down the two flights of stairs to the Situation Room.

"Good morning, Samantha," the NSC Advisor said, looking up from his place at the head of the conference table. "Awfully sorry about your Dad, but we're glad to have you back." She nodded and slipped into one of the leather swivel chairs. Hunt Daniels was there along with a woman she had never met, but figured was the famous Dr. Cameron Talbot. She reached across the table to introduce herself.

"Samantha Reid."

"I'm Cammy Talbot. Good to meet you," the blond woman said.

"*The* Cameron Talbot," Samantha said with a welcoming smile. "I've heard so much about you and your work. Glad to have you on board."

"Please. It's just Cammy, but thanks."

Samantha realized she felt some sort of bond right away. She liked Cammy. There was something about her open, friendly look that made you want to forget that she was a noted Ph.D. and someone the press had called a "Savior" when she not only knocked down a missile headed for New Delhi some time ago, but also engineered a new, crazy way to protect airliners from attack that looked like something out of a SciFi film.

"Shall we get started here?" Ken Cosgrove said, nodding to a Sit Room staffer who flicked on one of the screens. Cammy saw images of hordes of people screaming at soldiers holding bayonets. They were facing off in streets where cars and buses stood still like silent sentries monitoring the action. The only moving vehicles were the jeeps filled with troops.

"These videos were evidently taken by some of Kazakhstan's soldiers flown in to restore order in Atyrau. That's the city along the Caspian that was affected by the EMP. Other villages were knocked out as well, of course, but the biggest problem is in the city where the people were more dependent on electricity, transportation, cell towers and all the rest. These pictures were uploaded to YouTube, and now they're all over the world. We're trying to assess just how far the pulse went, but as you can see, the chaos looks to be pretty widespread. There's no telling how long it will take to install new systems there. They have to start from scratch, as you all know. Could be months or even a year."

"How could the blast's result extend such a distance?" Samantha asked. "I mean, I've read the Kazakhs put out that statement about a very small device and how it was a mistake. If it really were so small, I know about line-of-sight effects, but I'm not completely sure why it goes so far."

Cammy answered. "You see, it's like this. When a nuclear weapon goes off many miles up, think about a huge phased array antennae in the sky that radiates the pulse to the ground. Then the fireball heats the field and you get a current like a geo-magnetic storm. Consider EMP as a radio frequency, a high frequency pulse that covers a wide range of frequencies. Where you have telephone lines, water pipes, they can all pick them up and project them like an antenna too. So any electronics that we turn on would be affected. And not just affected, but fried. Ruined. See what I mean."

"I've got it now," Samantha said. "When people get too technical around here I sometimes think I need sub-titles. But you've explained it. So, thanks." She turned to Ken. "Have you seen anything new from the government in Astana?"

"As you said, their President keeps saying it was all a big mistake. Human error. That sort of nonsense. He keeps stonewalling on inspections, and as the Vice President previewed the other day, we've slapped some sanctions on their top people, and we've got State trying to get Britain, Germany, Russia and China to sign on," Ken explained. "Russia's got a bit of a problem. On the one hand they're furious with Kazakhstan for developing a nuke in the first place. But there are millions of ethnic Russians living in the country, and they're hesitating about placing any major sanctions. I think they'll look at it as a menu of options though and agree to freeze some assets of individuals they don't like anyway. As for the Chinese, no cooperation at all." Another image was flashed onto the screen. It was a map of the eastern half of Kazakhstan. "China shares a huge border with the Kazakhs, have a lot of trade with them, but the biggest problem is China's thirst for oil, and they're not about to take an action against one of their major suppliers. So they'll be no help at all. In fact, they'll sabotage us when this comes before the UN next week."

"Getting down to our own worries," Hunt interjected. "It's one thing for the Kazakhs to get into a pissing match with the Russians over nuclear power. The real threat now is that since the world knows they've got this weapon and what it can do, I'm afraid it'll create a bidding war for any number of terrorist groups and other countries who will try to buy these things. If the Kazakhs have any more that is. Then it's world-wide pandemonium."

"So, not only do we have to stop the Kazakhs from developing any more weapons," Ken said, "we've got to increase our defenses on the off chance they do sell something to somebody. Not that they need the money, but corruption is so rampant in that part of the world, who knows who would sell what to whom?"

"And that brings us to Dr. Talbot," Hunt said. "Your turn, Cam."

"Well, as Hunt knows, I just got back from a trip to our California facility where they've been working on the advance Airborne Laser. And while I believe it's a great weapon to have in our arsenal, besides the budget cuts, the other problem is one of distance. The plane carrying it has to be within a range of several hundred kilometers of a launch, and who knows where an attack could be coming? Of course, we have our ground-based interceptors arrayed out at Vandenberg Air Force Base in Santa Barbara that are linked to radar and satellites in Fort Greely, Alaska. Denmark operates the radar systems in Greenland, and we're all tied together. But still. Most of these systems, even the Aegis on board our ships are designed to destroy a missile in the boost phase or, at last resort, the re-entry phase. But with this new situation, I'm trying to put together a system we could use to prevent the launch of a missile in the first place."

"How could you do that?" Samantha asked.

"We're not sure yet, but I've got several teams working on a whole host of ideas. Everything from jamming GPS systems to new radar viruses."

"How soon can you test them?" Ken asked, making several notes.

"We're on a crash course with all of it," Cammy replied. "But it could be months."

"We may not have months," Ken said.

Samantha eyed him suspiciously. "Are you saying that you think there is some sort of imminent threat here? To us or to our troops overseas or something?" she asked with growing concern.

"No actionable intelligence. Just a real sense of urgency," he said firmly.

"I wish the Hill had that same sense," Hunt said.

"In your dreams," Cammy replied. "We know all too well how hard it is to even get an earmark for a special project these days. But don't worry about the money. At this point, we're on it. And if I get my way, we'll figure out some new systems that won't break the bank."

"Speaking of breaking the bank," Samantha said, "Looking at those pictures coming out of Atyrau and then comparing what they rely on and what we rely on, I shudder to think about the chaos such an attack would inflict on one of our cities. We'd all be living like the Amish."

"Yeah," Hunt said. "But at least those people know how to survive. The question is, do we?"

FORTY-FOUR

Atyrau, Kazakhstan

"I know plan," Nurlan called out, storming into the apartment. He was hauling in bags of rice, salted beef, and several bottles of water. "Zhanar? Pete? Come here. I tell you. Plan bad. Very very bad." He set the bags on the table as Pete and Zhanar tumbled out of the bedroom looking slightly guilty. Her long dark hair was tousled, her blouse was buttoned the wrong way, and Pete was trying to zip up his khakis while simultaneously looking nonchalant. It wasn't working.

Nurlan stared first at his sister and then at his friend. "So. You are….you are…you are what?"

Zhanar would not meet his stern gaze. Pete was momentarily speechless. He reached for a bottle of water and said, "Hey this stuff is great. Thanks for getting it. We ran out last night."

Nurlan shouted at Pete. "Look you! You dishonor my sister? I bring you my country. I help you with job. We work on groups.

But you come here and you take Zhanar?" He lunged toward Pete who backed away and held up his hands in mock surrender.

"Wait. Wait. Please wait. It's not what you think."

"No? How you know what I think?" Nurlan said, inching closer to him. "She good girl. Best girl. Only sister."

"I know. Believe me, I know."

Zhanar rushed to Pete's side. "Nurlan, listen to me. It's all right. It's not his fault. I know what I'm doing."

"You not know," Nurlan bellowed.

"Yes, I do," she countered. "I've been living on my own for a long time while you've been studying in the states. I've taken care of myself. I've saved myself for…"

"For what?" Nurlan countered. "For him? Man who will leave you?"

"Who says I'll leave her?" Pete said. "I…uh…Nurlan listen to me. The first time I saw her, that first time in the airport, I thought she was the prettiest girl I had ever seen."

"Better than California girls?" Nurlan challenged.

Pete put his arm around Zhanar and proclaimed, "Much better. We've been together for weeks now. Holed up here."

"And remember, when the trouble hit, Pete saved my life," she said. "You can't forget that."

"He save other woman too, but he not take other woman," Nurlan said disparagingly.

"No," Pete said. "Of course I didn't *take* other women. I don't *want* other women. I only want Zhanar." He pulled her closer to him.

"For how long?" Nurlan asked.

"For as long as she wants me," Pete answered.

Nurlan looked at his sister and furrowed his brow. "What he mean? You think American will marry a Kazakh?"

"Why not?" she asked, gazing up at Pete with a questioning look.

Pete hesitated and took a gulp of water.

"You see?" Nurlan said. "He not take you away. He use you."

"No! You're wrong," Pete said, and then he blurted out, "I've been thinking about this, about her, about us, ever since I got here. I don't have it all worked out. I mean I still have to finish school, but that doesn't mean I don't want her with me. Look, let's all just simmer down and remain calm. I…uh…I love her," he murmured, holding a chair for Zhanar.

Nurlan let out a long sigh and reluctantly sat down at the table. "We see. We talk this later."

Zhanar sat down and said, "When you came in, I heard you say something about a plan. A bad plan. What were you talking about?"

Nurlan sat back and rubbed his eyes. "It been long day. Too long. President's man was back with final orders. I said before we told put new weapon together. We do that. Man say all is ready to load all on transport plane, and plane takes us…"

"Wait a minute," Zhanar interrupted. "Us? The Plane takes us? You mean they're making you go with the bomb?"

"Yes. They say I best on computers. All know that."

"But where arc you going?" Pete asked. "What are they going to do with the bomb?"

"It all big secret but I find out. Transport flies to base in China on coast."

"Where?" they both said in unison.

"Base outside Shanghai by East China Sea."

"Why China?" Zhanar asked. "China and Kazakhstan are friends.

"That's why China. Some China people work with us. We land there. Take bomb off plane and put on special boat. Agent there getting boat for us."

"Then what?" Pete asked.

"This is really secret part," Nurlan said. "We sail across Pacific to California."

"California?" Pete stammered. "They're going to attack California? They can't do that."

"Not all California. Man say we send up weapon from boat high again. Like before. He say no kill people. He say President wants bomb only knock out San Francisco like other bomb knock out Atyrau."

"Oh no!" Pete said, jumping up and knocking his chair back on the linoleum floor. "That would destroy the city. Nothing would work just like nothing works here. Why in God's name would they want to do that? It makes no sense. No sense at all."

"I think same. Man says he just gets order from President. He says United States punishing our country for bomb test. He says government there stopping our money, our trade, lots things. He says President wants teach Americans lesson."

Pete reached down to pick up his chair. As he sat down again, he paused for a long moment and took a deep breath. "Wait a minute. I've got an idea."

"What idea?" Zhanar asked. "What are we going to do about this? What could we possibly do?"

Pete drank some more water, and stopped to collect his thoughts. "Okay, Nurlan, you know how we've been talking for months now about how the S.A.I.N.T.S. have been trying to get reparations? And how we've been trying to figure out ways we can threaten Washington and get them to pay up?"

"Yes," Nurlan said cautiously. "What you mean?"

"Wait!" Zhanar said. "Wait both of you. I don't want to hear any more talk about threatening the Americans. I know how you feel about that money you say is owed to your people. I know all about that. But you can't go around making threats that you can't carry out. And as for this new bomb," she turned to her brother, "you said you would be there. You sabotaged the first test. Sort of.

Can't you do something to keep this one from going off? Can't you stop it?"

Nurlan shook his head. "I not know how stop it. I think about that. For days now I think it. But whole crew be there. They watch me. I changed computer before but only send higher. I can't stop it going off." Then he added with a forlorn expression, "I not know what I do."

FORTY-FIVE

Astana, Kazakhstan

"You've got to stop this madness," the number two man beseeched his President.

Viktor Surleimenov waved dismissively and relaxed in his high backed velvet chair. "Why are you so concerned about my little prank on the Americans and on Sergei Baltiev? Surely you've seen the latest ads that he's been running against me. He lies. He cozies up to the Russians by appealing to the ethnics. He promises better relations with Moscow as if that would improve the lives of our Kazakh people. He is a fool, and we must defeat him in the election. You know that, so why are you so upset?"

"Do you have any idea what will happen to people in San Francisco if you let that boat go there with a weapon? You saw the trouble in Atyrau. Our soldiers can barely keep order. We have to send more planes, more supplies, more technicians. In fact, I think that at this point, we should be asking other countries for help to rebuild that infrastructure. It could take months to replace all the computers and cell towers and cars and everything. How can you be so callous at a time like this?"

"It's not a question of being callous. It's a question of survival of my administration and of our independence."

"But you said yourself that if we explode a weapon over northern California, it won't have a return address. They won't know that we were the ones who did it. So how does that ensure our independence from Russian expansionism?"

"You're not thinking clearly. Moscow saw our little test. Moscow now knows that we have a nuclear capability and that they'd better not mess with us like they've been messing with Georgia and the Ukraine. And as for the boat to California, that is aimed not at Russia but at the Americans for their sanctions and freezes as well as at Baltiev's finances that he has stashed there."

The Vice President walked over and stood by the window overlooking the gardens. He was silent for a while, trying to conjure up arguments he might use to change the President's mind. He had to do something, had to think of some way to talk sense into the man. His President was about to embark on a fool's errand. No, not just an errand, but a journey to hell. There was no telling what the Americans would do if attacked with this new kind of weapon. Surely they would find the boat, capture the people and trace the whole scheme back to the palace. This palace. He had to stop it somehow. He turned and faced Surleimenov once more.

"Let's take a moment and think this through. First of all, the sanctions. Yes, the Americans are freezing some of our assets, but that's only because we have not allowed inspections of our nuclear facilities. We could change course on that. We could get our plants in order, sequester our remaining weapons where no one would find them, even though I never did agree with this weapons program of yours. But if we had to, we could transfer some of the scientists who had been working on them and then we could invite in the inspectors. That would take the wind out of the sails of the

Americans. They would have to back off. Besides, the UN is meeting on this next week. We could say that we are considering inspections and announce it before the UN meeting and you know that the bureaucrats would then have an excuse to do nothing, which is their usual modus operandi.

"And as for Baltiev, you can make the case to our people that he's way too close to the Russians. Keep hammering away on that point, and there's no way he can win that election."

Surleimenov pounded his desk and replied angrily, "No. You don't understand. I don't trust the Americans to back off. They fight every country that wants to develop nuclear weapons for their own protection. And as for Baltiev, I don't trust him either. I just got a report from our security chief that he believes Baltiev has paid agents who have somehow infiltrated the staff here at the palace. He hasn't found them yet. It's only rumor. But if it's true, it means Baltiev is more ruthless than we thought. I have to stop him."

The President glanced at his watch and got up from his desk. Now, it is time for us to go to the banquet. We have our Chinese guests who should be arriving soon and since they have been very cooperative with my little scheme, I wouldn't want to keep them waiting."

The door flew open and the security chief barged inside. "Mr. President. Mr. President. The banquet. The food."

"What is it? What's the problem?"

"Remember I told you about agents? Spies in our midst?"

"Yes," the President said. He motioned to his Vice President. "You see? We must stop Baltiev. If there are spies, he's the one who put them here." Then to his security man he barked, "Well, have you caught them?"

"No. But your food taster is dead."

FORTY-SIX

Atyrau, Kazakhstan

"Now that Nurlan is gone, I'm so scared," Zhanar said.

Pete held her, cradled her head and stroked her hair. "I know. I'm very worried about him. But I'm also worried about my family, what's left of it on Hawaii, that is."

"Why? Why now? Nurlan is the one in danger."

"I know. I just mean that all of this has made me think more about our campaign to get The White House to help us. But now if there is some sort of attack, all they will think about is saving the city of San Francisco. They'll have to help those people. They'll have to get them food and supplies just like your government had to help Atyrau and everyone around here. The people in Washington will be so stunned that their country was attacked that every department, the State Department, the Pentagon, everyone will be working to find out who did it and retaliate or something. I know how our government works. That's all they will do. That's what the press and the people will scream about. And I can understand that. And it will go on for a long, long time. Nobody will think about anything else, let alone our problems. No one will ever consider our pleas for money, for medical help, for anything. All of our efforts, all the things the S.A.I.N.T.S. have been doing, all we stand for will be for nothing. Nothing at all."

The daylight was dwindling now. There were no lights in the apartment. Zhanar pulled away from Pete, lit the one candle they had left and motioned for him to sit down at the table, their usual conversation spot. "I've been thinking."

Pete pulled out a chair and sat across from her. He took her hands in his and began to stroke her fingers. "I know everything is a mess. I know you're worried about your brother. I'm worried too, but I just don't know what to do next."

"As I said, I've been thinking," she replied. "What if…what if…" her voice trailed off.

"What if what?"

"I once said that people like us, we have no power."

"I remember you said that."

"But now, now I have an idea. It means we would have to get away from here, a long way away. And if we can escape this place, we just might have some power after all."

FORTY-SEVEN

The White House

"My God! Look at this!" Angela cried out, careening into Samantha's office. "You've *got* to see this." She thrust a piece of paper into Samantha's hands and exclaimed, "Could this be for real?"

Samantha quickly read the printed email. Her mouth dropped open and her eyes were wide. "This is the guy you were talking about some time ago? The kook you said was demanding money or something for tests we did ages ago?"

"The same one. Remember, I said he had sent me a bunch of crazy emails demanding reparations or whatever? I get nutty stuff all the time. But this… this…this looks real. We've got to get it to Ken."

"Absolutely. Right now!" She called to Joan. "Please call Cosgrove's office. Tell him we're on our way down. It's an emergency."

Samantha held onto the email, and the two women sprinted out of the office, down the short corridor and hit the stairs, almost slamming into another staffer on his way up. "Oh, sorry," Samantha said as they both hurried by. They stopped in front of the secretary's desk in the corner office where Samantha said, "We've got to see Ken. Is he available?"

"He's in with the President, Miss Reid. The daily brief, you know."

Samantha looked down at her watch. "Oh, sure. Of course he's in the Oval. I forgot about the time. But we've got to see him."

"You're welcome to wait."

Samantha exchanged a glance with Angela and shook her head. "No thanks." They headed out and hurried down the hall, through the reception area, past the Roosevelt Room and around the corner. They practically ran past the door to the Cabinet Room and turned left into the office of the President's secretary.

"I have an emergency," Samantha announced. "I know Ken will want to see this and bring it to the attention of the President."

"You can't go barging in there, Miss Reid. Even if it is an emergency. I'm sure it can wait a few minutes."

"Please," Samantha begged. "It's a matter of national security. And I assume the DNI is in there as well, right?"

"Yes, of course he's in there," she said politely.

"I know they're all going to want to hear this," Samantha continued. "Can't you at least get a message in to them that I'm here? Please?"

The secretary stared at Samantha, hesitated and then buzzed the military aide sitting in a small area near the door to the Oval Office. He came out and said, "Something I can do for you?"

"Yes," the secretary replied. "Go in and tell Mr. Cosgrove that Miss Reid has an issue of national security and asks to be admitted."

"Thank you. Thank you," Samantha said to her. "I truly appreciate this. Really!"

A few moments later, the military aide came out and motioned for Samantha and Angela to come inside.

"What's this?" Ken asked cautiously as the two women stepped onto the gold oval carpet. Sunshine poured through the trio of windows behind the President's desk, shining down on the collection of family photos on the credenza. The President sat at the desk while the Director of National Intelligence and the National Security Advisor stood in front holding briefing books and what appeared to be a collection of satellite photos.

"I apologize for the intrusion, Mr. President, but we have just received an email from a young man who appears to have information about a possible attack on our country."

"Attack?" the President asked, standing up and coming around the desk. "What kind of attack?"

"You see, we've been getting, well, Angela has been getting, emails from a guy for quite some time. At first we thought he was just one of the crazy types asking for money. Things like that."

"What is he asking for?" Ken asked.

"It's rather complicated," Samantha said. "But it looks like his family…"

"And a lot of his people, his grandparents, lots of people…" Angela added.

"Yes, lots of people were affected by nuclear tests that our government conducted back in the 50's ad 60's."

"Yes. We did some testing. But what could that possibly have to do with an attack now? You mean these people, whoever they are, are going to stage some sort of attack in retribution?" the President asked. "That sounds rather specious to me."

"No, it's not them," Samantha said. "He sent this email that says he knows about an attack that is planned by another country, and he will tell us all about it if we will agree to reparations for his people, money and medicine that he says was promised years ago." She handed the email to the President.

He read through it and gave it to Ken. "What do you think? Could this be legitimate?"

Ken quickly read the message and gave it to the DNI. "Can we trace this?"

"Sure," the Intelligence chief said. "Says here that he had to travel a long distance to where he could communicate. Not sure what that means, but we'll get NSA right on it. If he stays put, we'll find him."

"But are we going to respond?" Samantha asked? "I mean we have to respond to the email. It doesn't give a time frame. I mean, we don't know how soon this could happen. If it is going to happen. We have to take it seriously, right?" she asked in a pleading tone.

"Sounds rather strange to me," the President said. "We get all kinds of messages about threats, terrorists, tips. Well, you know that as well as anybody. Is this something real? Hard to say at this point. As you said, it might just be some crazy guy looking for money. Almost sounds like a blackmail scheme or something. But I'll let Ken work on the details." He turned and sat down once again, which seemed like a signal for Samantha to make her retreat.

"Yes, Mr. President. I'll work with Ken on this, sir, and I thank you for your time."

Forty-eight

East of Atyrau, Kazakhstan

"What do we do now? We're almost out of money," Zhanar whispered. She sipped the green tea she had bought in the small café hundreds of miles east of her home. A few other people were seated at small metal tables by the window and a couple of men in filthy work shirts sat at a long counter. She and Pete had driven for two days, finished most of the water they had taken along from the apartment, along with some rice and beans that Nurlan had brought from the plant. But Nurlan was gone. Gone away with the other workers. Gone on a big transport plane with a dangerous cargo. Zhanar had lain awake after he left, visualizing all the things that could go wrong. They could find out that Nurlan had sabotaged the first test. The boat could hit storm waters. The bomb could go off prematurely, although she had no idea how that could happen. She still worried.

Then Pete took over. He jumped at her idea about contacting The White House again, then he had figured out a way to get them both out of town. They had packed a few clothes, the water, what little food they had left along with what meager savings she had in the apartment. Neither one of them knew how far they would have to drive. She was scared of running out of gas out on the steppe somewhere. Some place where nobody would find them. At least Pete had figured out a way to siphon some gas from a number of cars stalled around town, and they had those containers with them. They had kept driving and finally came to this town. A town where she saw lights in the windows, and that's when she almost shouted with joy. It meant that things were working here. They had electricity. It meant that there might be a place where Pete could send an email. When they had driven down the dusty street, they had found this little café. It was where they had made a deal with the owner.

Pete studied the old computer he had borrowed from the guy running the place. He had sent his email a while ago. He thought about the time difference. It was evening here. So it would be morning in Washington. Would they answer? They had to answer. His message had been pretty clear. Deal with me, and I'll help you. Don't deal with me, and you will be facing a certain attack. But would they believe him? He figured they got lots of emails. Lots of letters. Lots of phone calls. They had never answered him before now. At least this Angela person, whose name he had found online, had never answered. Maybe he should have sent it to somebody higher up. But he didn't have an email address for anybody higher up. The only reason he found hers was probably because it looked like her job was dealing with some sort of outside groups, and his S.A.I.N.T.S. certainly fell into that category.

He looked up and saw that Zhanar was waiting for an answer. "We have to wait. We have to see if they send a reply to this."

"We can't wait here too long. That guy who runs this place keeps giving us weird looks. He probably hopes we'll give up this table so that better paying customers can take the space."

"That's the least of our worries. I tipped him to use this computer. I told him it was important, and I was going to have to use it for a while."

"What about the jeep? What if somebody official sees it and wonders why it's here? Maybe they'll figure out that we're not military and that we shouldn't have it."

"Relax. You're getting yourself all worked up. Okay, so we managed to steal the jeep. It was the only way out of the city. You know that. We were just incredibly lucky to find it down by the waterfront. The soldiers were so busy dealing with that crowd, they never saw us. At least I don't think they did."

"Actually, I was amazed that you could figure out how to start it. And then when we had to get out of town, I was really scared that they'd come after us."

"They were too tied up trying to keep order. They probably didn't miss it for hours. Anyway, we made it out. We got here."

"But what do we do now?" she asked.

"We'll just have to stick it out until we hear back."

"But what about the money?" Zhanar asked with a worried frown. "I know we can sleep in the jeep but we're going to need some more food pretty soon. I'm awfully hungry."

Pete checked his wallet. He only had thirty-seven dollars left that he hadn't converted when he arrived in Kazakhstan. He wondered how much they would buy. He wasn't about to ask the café owner. He wanted to find a local farm or someplace he could cut a deal. "Can you hang on for a little while? If we don't get some sort of an answer in another half an hour, I promise we'll go out and find some food, and then we'll tell the guy here that we'll come back later. I'll have to tip him again, but maybe we can stretch things out."

"All right," she said, drinking the last of her tea. She was watching the owner, hoping he wouldn't come over and kick them out just yet. Then she saw him turn quickly and head through a door to some sort of a back room. When he opened the door, she heard a faint ringing sound. A moment later, he rushed back into the shop, scanned the room and shouted, "Anybody here named Pete?"

Astonished, Pete stood up. "I'm Pete. How do you know my name?"

"Somebody knows you are here. I have a telephone in the back. Man wants to talk to you."

"Oh no," Zhanar whispered. "Somebody has found us. How could they? Who would it be? We only found this place ourselves a few hours ago. Do you think somebody followed us? I didn't see anybody."

"No," Pete said. "Nobody followed us. They followed this computer. This means they're taking us seriously. They must have traced the email somehow, and now we're going to have our answer."

"But what if they send somebody to arrest us?"

"Hey, you. Pete," the owner shouted. "I said get the telephone. In the back."

"C'mon," Pete said to Zhanar. "This is the moment we've been waiting for."

FORTY-NINE

The White House

"Is this Pete Kalani?"

"Yes. This is Pete Kalani. Who is this?"

"This is the White House Communications Operator. Will you take a call from Angela Marconi, Special Assistant to the President for Public Liaison?"

"Angela? Sure. But how did you find me?" Pete asked, his voice incredulous.

"I will put Miss Marconi on the line. Hold please."

Angela was nervous. She was seated next to Ken Cosgrove in the Situation Room along with Hunt Daniels, Samantha and several other NSC staffers. They were all listening as the call was being put through. They had planned this out, and now it was up to her to open the conversation.

"Okay, Angela," Ken Cosgrove said reassuringly. "We need you to do this. Gain his confidence. Take your time and be sure to keep him on the line. Tell him you got his email, that you're sorry you didn't respond to his other messages. All the things we've gone over. Keep it friendly, conversational. Check your talking points, and then turn it over to me. Are you all right with this?"

Angela took a deep breath. She had never been in a meeting in the Situation Room before. Her job didn't call for such a venue. After all, she had spent most of her time dealing with special interest groups who were trying to get on the President's schedule for one reason or another. Just yesterday she had fielded requests from the Boy Scouts, the top women's soccer team and the American Association of Professional Philosophers. Now, here she was tossed into the middle of a national security emergency. One that could mean life or death to millions of Americans. How could she be philosophical about that? She sat up straight in her chair and pulled the microphone closer. She gathered her courage.

"Yes, I'm ready. Put him on." There was a long pause, and then she heard the operator's voice again.

"I have Mr. Pete Kalani for Angela Marconi. Go ahead please."

"Pete? Angela here. First, how are you? Are you okay?"

"Yeah, I'm okay. But how did you people find me?"

"I have to admit that The White House is pretty good at finding things. Uh, people I mean. But I want to apologize to you for not keeping track of your earlier messages." She glanced down at the talking points. "You see, I did get a number of emails that had your name on them, but I have to admit that I've been swamped. What I mean is that things have been really hectic around here what with a lot of problems, the people we arrested who were trying to blow up some of our trains in New York and a lot of other issues. Well, you may have read about that. And, of course, there's the upcoming election. Now, I didn't mean to put you off. Seriously, Pete. It's just that I guess I didn't quite understand the gravity of the situation. But I'm glad, really glad, Pete, that you've contacted me again because we really need your help."

"Yeah, I figured that last message would get your attention. Like I said in the email, I know some things that I decided to warn you about."

"That's terrific, Pete. I'm so glad you are coming forward. You are truly to be commended for this. But may I ask just why you made this decision? I mean, in the other emails, I did save them by the way. In the other emails, you sounded pretty mad at us. I mean, pretty mad at our government. And yet, now you are trying to be helpful, and I can't thank you enough for that."

"Let's just say that yeah, I've spent the better part of my life hating you people. All of you people in Washington for what you did to my family. To all of our people. You made cripples out of them. You gave them diseases. You made them die young."

"He's getting agitated," Ken whispered. "See if you can calm him down and then give him to me." Angela nodded.

"Pete. Listen Pete. I hear you. I truly do. I've done a lot of research on this situation, and we've got our staff working on it right now. But first we need to talk about this threat you referred to in the email. Can I have you talk to Ken Cosgrove?"

"Who's Ken Cosgrove? Can he do anything for us?"

"Yes, Pete. He can. He is the President's National Security Advisor. And he's sitting right here next to me. May I put him on?"

"Yeah. Okay. Put him on."

Ken leaned into his own microphone and said in a soothing tone, "Hello Pete. First, let me give you my personal thanks for contacting us about this threat to our country. Can you tell me about it?"

"I might. But first I want two things."

Hunt passed a note to Ken that said *A ransom? Millions??*

"Two things. All right. Why don't you tell me what you would need."

"Okay. First, I want you to get money to the Kalani clan in Hawaii and all of the other people who were in the way of those tests. The ones in the Marshall Islands, Enowetok, Bikini Atoll. All of them."

"I can work on that. Are you saying you want money sent to you personally?"

"No. Dammit. I'm not doing this for myself. It's for all the people who suffered during your damn tests. And I don't want you to *work* on that. You people always say you'll *work* on something and then nothing happens," Pete shouted into the phone.

"I know what you mean, Pete. Believe me I know," Ken said in a calm voice. "You see getting money for reparations, or anything else for that matter, comes from the Congress."

"Yeah. And they say they'll vote money, and they write reports and they make promises and then nothing, absolutely nothing happens. Do you know how long we've been waiting for help from you guys? Decades. That's how long. I watched my mother die of cancer because of neglect. I watched other people get polio and all sorts of other things because of what you did out in the Pacific. And all we do is wait and hope. And then nothing happens."

Ken exchanged a look with Samantha who was leaning forward, listening to the exchange. "Pete. Listen to me. I've looked into this case, and you know what? You are absolutely right. I want to give you my word, my solemn word that I will do everything in my power to shepherd a bill through the appropriate committee of the Congress to get proper reparations. I give you my word on that."

There was silence on the other end.

"Pete? Pete? Are you still there?"

"Yeah. I'm here. I was just thinking, that's all."

"All right now. You said there was a second request."

"Not a request. I need another promise. An absolute promise. And if I get it, then I'll tell you everything I know."

"What else do we need to promise?" Ken asked.

"You need to promise not to hurt someone."

"Not hurt someone? We don't want to hurt anyone, Pete. We want to save people, not hurt people. Tell me what you mean."

"There's this guy, this friend of mine, this good guy. His name is Nurlan Remizov. He's from Kazakhstan, and he's an exchange student at UCLA with me."

"And this Nurlan Remizov. He's a friend of yours and you want to protect him?"

"That's right."

"Who would want to harm him?"

"You would."

Startled glances were exchanged around the table as several members of the staff were scribbling notes.

"Why would we want to harm your friend? Is he part of a plot against us? Is he planning something? Is that what you're trying to warn us about?"

"No! Yes! I mean no," Pete said in an agitated voice. "I said I would tell you, but first you have to promise, and I mean promise that Nurlan will be okay."

Hunt was scribbling again on a pad. He passed the note to Ken. It said, *Suicide bomber? Terrorist? Someone coming here? Where? When?* Ken nodded to Hunt.

"Now Pete, you say if I promise to keep Nurlan safe, you will tell me what is going on, right?"

"Right."

"Let's just go back a bit. Can you just tell me if your friend, Nurlan, wants to harm the United States. Is that it? And you want us to stop him?"

"Yes. But it's not his fault. Really, it's not his fault. He's being forced to do something, and it's not his fault," Pete sounded like he was practically crying into the telephone.

"It's all right, Pete. We're going to work together. You and me. We're going to do this together. Okay?"

There was a long pause, and then they heard Pete let out a long breath. "So here's the deal. First you say you'll protect Nurlan. You say it!"

"We will protect Nurlan," Ken said.

"Good. That's good. Now here's what I know."

Pete went on to explain how the nuclear test caused complete havoc in the city of Atyrau. How he had gone over there not just to get a summer job, but to hook up with some of the anti-war groups who had suffered under Soviet domination and testing just like his people did. Pete talked about the S.A.I.N.T.S. and how he had wanted to figure out ways to threaten the politicians in Washington. But then when the bomb went off and he saw all the people dying in the hospitals and others needing food and water, he changed his mind. He talked about the soldiers coming in big transport planes to try and restore order.

Hunt pushed another note over to Ken as Pete was describing the chaos. "EMP effects. Now what?" Ken dashed off a note that replied, "Give him time. Got to keep him on phone."

Pete then talked about his friend Nurlan, who was a computer genius and how he got a job at the nuclear facility. He described how Nurlan had tried to sabotage the original test, not knowing what the effect would be. Then he paused and said, "Nurlan came home one day and told me that the President had ordered them to load another one of the small weapons on a transport plane. I will tell you where it's going, but first you have to promise again that you'll get us the money and medicine and you'll protect Nurlan."

Ken replied. "You've got my promise on that, Pete. This is an incredible story, and I can't tell you how much we appreciate your contacting us with this important information. So please go on."

Pete took a deep breath and blurted it out. "He said they were flying to a base in China and then getting on a boat and going to California."

"California?" Ken sat up in shock as others around the conference table looked positively stricken. "Why California? Did Nurlan say why they were going to California?"

"Yes. He said that the President was upset that the United States was putting sanctions on his country and messing up trade and stuff like that. Oh, and it wasn't all of California. I know the state. I go to school at UCLA with Nurlan. I told you that. He said they were going to San Francisco."

"Is there any reason they would want to target San Francisco in particular?" Ken asked, furiously taking notes.

"I don't know."

"This is incredible news, Pete. Absolutely incredible."

"Look, I gotta go. I'm in a café and the owner is shouting at me to get off his phone. I've talked too long. I've said too much."

"No! Wait! Just one more question. Please, Pete, don't hang up. Just tell me when Nurlan left Atyrau? When did the transport leave with the weapon?"

"Four days ago."

And with that, the line went dead.

FIFTY

East of Atyrau, Kazakhstan

"That was terrific!" Zhanar said, hugging Pete. She had followed him to the back room, stood close and tried to listen in.

"Are you off my phone?" the proprietor asked in an irritated voice. "How did somebody know you were in my place?"

"We're all done," Pete replied. "And, uh, that was a friend. I told him I was coming to town, and he could call me here." It didn't sound very convincing, but he didn't know what else to say.

"We don't get a lot of calls here," the man said and then shrugged. "You want anything else to eat?"

"We probably should order something," Pete whispered. They went back to the counter, and Pete scanned a blackboard with a menu written in yellow chalk. "What does it all say?" he asked Zhanar.

"We'll take one of your lamb shish kabobs and an order of Plov. We'll split it," she said and then murmured to Pete, "I still have some of my savings. I just want it to last."

When they got back to their table, Pete leaned in toward her. "You heard most of that, right?"

"Yes. I can't believe you actually got a call from Washington. This is amazing. But do you think they can stop this? Do you really think they'll take care of Nurlan? I'm so worried about him."

"Me too. But remember, he's a pretty crafty guy. And it seems like he's the smartest guy in that whole group when it comes to programming stuff. So he'll probably be okay on the boat."

"But the Americans will try to find them. They have to find it and stop it. And if they stop it, the people on board might get into a fight or something. He could be killed," she said.

"Here's your order," the owner said, putting down their food. "Anything else? More tea?"

"No thanks, this is plenty," Zhanar said. They both dug into the mixture of rice and vegetables, and she continued in a low voice. "What do we do now?"

Pete took his time to think about a response. He had been so intent on getting out of Atyrau to a place where he could get a message to The White House, he hadn't really thought through their next move. They couldn't go back to the city. It would still be a mess. They were low on funds, and this little town didn't look like a place where they would want to stay and look for work. No, he'd have to figure out some place else to go. He had to protect Zhanar. But at the end of the summer, he had to get back to the States. Back to school. Maybe she had some relatives somewhere else. Some place where they could go for a while. They hadn't talked about that, and he didn't want to use up her savings and rely on her contacts all the time. It just wasn't right. Should he have asked that Ken person to send him some money? No, that would have made his plea for reparations sound too much like a personal ransom or blackmail or something. He didn't mean that. Besides, they knew he was here. They might have a way of trailing him. And if they caught him somewhere, he could be arrested for blackmail. At least he thought they could.

He ate some of the lamb and glanced up at Zhanar again. She was so pretty, so trusting. She had never hesitated when she outlined her idea of getting far enough away so he could send his message. And she had quickly packed up and announced that she was going with him because she knew the country, the language, and besides, she wanted to stay with him no matter where he went. She had snuck out of the apartment building with him and crept through the streets looking for some sort of car they could steal. She had been scared to steal one, but he had told her it was the only way they could get away. He had thought about the buses that took the workers to the nuclear plant, but they were parked in a lot that was too far away, so he had told her to look for the jeeps that the soldiers had brought in. They had avoided the crowds that still roamed the main streets and had finally spotted a jeep parked near the wharf. She had held a small flashlight for him as he had tried to hotwire the car, a little trick he had learned from some of the guys back at UCLA.

When they got the engine started, she had tossed their bags of food, water and clothes in the back seat and jumped in next to him. She had directed him to the back roads, winding around the most industrial parts of the city. Places that had been shut down. Places where nobody lived. It was there that they had siphoned the gas. They had driven to the outskirts and then hit the open road. It was then that Pete had gunned the engine, knowing that there wouldn't be any other cars on the road. When they got several miles out of town, he had suddenly felt free. Free of the heat. Free of the mobs, the violence, the almost claustrophobic sense of being trapped in their little apartment for days on end. He was free. They were free. But now, after their escape, after the email and the phone call. Now what? For a moment he thought back to his grammar school classes where the teacher always made the kids write reports in September with the title, "How I spent my summer vacation." There's no grade school class that would ever believe how *this* summer had turned out.

Here he was, a guy that traveled halfway around the world with a mission to find ways to get back at the United States, and he had ended up contacting the very people he had grown to hate. People in The White House who were now treating him like some kind of a hero because he tipped them off to a secret plan. It all sounded like the plot of a summer movie, not a school report. But what now? He had no money, no job and he had a woman to care for. Where should they go from here? As he thought about it, he had absolutely no idea.

FIFTY-ONE

The White House

"The Pacific Ocean covers thirty-five percent of the earth's surface," Ken Cosgrove said, pouring over a map in the Situation room. "How the hell are we going to find this damn ship?"

Hunt Daniels leaned over and pointed to an area in the East China Sea. "I know. This is going to be a bitch. 7th Fleet is out here, of course, all over the area from Russia and North Korea down to the Philippines, Australia. The whole shebang. We should be getting a report from Ignatius any minute now."

Ken called over a Sit Room staffer. "When will that teleconference be ready?"

"We're lining up all the participants right now, sir. Should only be a few moments."

Ken and Hunt watched as images of the Secretaries of Defense and Navy and the Coast Guard Commandant flickered onto one of the big screens. Each was surrounded by several staff members exchanging papers, maps and photos.

"Welcome gentlemen. We've got a helluva mess on our hands right now. That is if this crazy story is to be believed. But as we all know, we can't take a chance on its being a hoax. Since the morning briefing, the President is waiting for a report from each of you about the plans to try and track down this ship, fishing boat, whatever the hell it is that has probably already taken off from a port on the China coast. If it indeed is headed for San Francisco, as we believe, at least that cuts down our surveillance area. But since no one knows what route they might take, we have to cast a wide net here." Addressing the SecDef, Ken said, "So, Bill, bring us up to speed on your plans so far."

"As you said," Bill Ignatius began, "even though we can cut down the area from the 48 million square miles that the 7th Fleet covers, we're still talking about a gigantic challenge with not much time to deploy. Right now I've got about sixty ships, two-hundred fifty aircraft and forty-thousand Navy and Marine personnel assigned to the fleet. But it's going to take time to move even some of them to our target area. Let me bring in the Navy Secretary here for an update."

"At the President's direction, we have sent an alert out to all ships, surface and submarines in or near our target section of the Pacific" the Navy Secretary said. "We have a number already patrolling off the China coast, but as you've said, the ship we want has probably left, though we don't know that for sure. Is there any word about the President's contact with the President of Kazakhstan?"

"He put in a call this morning. Got hold of Surleimenov in the middle of some dinner and confronted him with the information we have so far. He seemed shocked at the whole story. At least that's how the President described the conversation. Surleimenov denied it all and said he'd had enough troubles in dealing with us, what with the sanctions and freezing of their assets. He almost didn't take the call, but used it as a plea for us to let up and reinstate the trade, the contracts, well everything. Evidently, the conversation went further downhill from there when our President again demanded inspections and a halt to their obvious weapons program. Our people are analyzing the whole encounter. Oh, and one other small point, Surleimenov was particularly agitated because he said that in addition to the problems we had foisted on him, that was his word by the way, foisted, he also had to deal with spies in his palace. He said that his food-taster had been murdered. At least he didn't accuse us of that. But the bottom line is that he's got a lot of problems but said nothing useful, and so the President moved on and put in a call to the President of China.

"In that call, again he got a complete denial of complicity. Beijing is saying they have no knowledge of a ship leaving one of their ports with a crew from Kazakhstan on board. He denied cooperating with President Surleimenov, but when pressed, he finally agreed to launch an investigation," Ken said.

"Fat chance of getting anything out of that," Hunt mumbled.

"We've got Mutual Defense Treaties with Japan, South Korea, the Philippines, Australia, New Zealand and Thailand, though the last three are too far away. Nothing with China, of course. But we could exercise our rights with the others under those treaties and ask for help," Ignatius said.

"The President is already taking that under consideration," Ken replied. "We're trying to keep this under wraps at the moment. I'll get to that later, but now, what about the Coast Guard?"

The four-star Admiral who currently serves as Commandant spoke up. "If that vessel is headed our way, we'll have the entire West Coast covered. I've sent word to our Pacific Area headquarters in Alameda, California, and we're bringing in our best resources, cutters, HH-65A Dolphin helicopters as well as our 14 HH-60 Jayhawks. We've also sent out a general alert to all of our maritime contacts to be on the look out, though we have no idea what flag that ship might be flying. With all of the traffic in the Pacific, it's going to be extremely difficult to find one small vessel. However, if any ship we find refuses to identify itself, you can be sure we'll take action."

"Same for the Navy, of course," the SecDef said.

"Just remember the new rules of engagement here. If we can locate the ship, you must notify the Secretary of Defense and The White House immediately for further orders. And we must ensure that there are no casualties in this operation because we have given our word that one member of that crew, a man by the name of Nurlan Remizov, a non-combatant, is not, I repeat not to be harmed in any way. You all got that order, right?"

The three nodded their assent. "This could be tough, though," the SecDef said. "If we find them, a big God-damn *if* at this point, but if we do, and if they start shooting, this could get real ugly."

"We all know that," Ken said. "We have a whole host of defensive measures we are ordering in the event the ship is not found and they try to launch a weapon. Any type of weapon, but particularly a nuclear device, which we've been told is on board."

"As we said this morning, we've got the interceptors at Vandenberg Air Force Base at Santa Barbara geared up," the Defense Secretary said. "They're tied in right now to the radar at Fort Greely, Alaska and our satellites are combing the area as well. So if these bastards do try to launch something toward San Francisco, we should be ready to knock it down."

"But with all due respect, Mr. Secretary," Hunt interjected, "I know you've been pretty successful with the latest tests against ballistic missile targets, but this thing, whatever it is, is an unknown. I mean the word we have is that they intend to launch it high over San Francisco so it detonates at least 50 to 100 miles up. At least that's what happened in Kazakhstan, and it sounded to us like they're going for a repeat performance. The trajectory would be unique, and I would hate to have us rely on a single kill vehicle to knock out this sucker. There's just too much at stake."

"Yes, I understand your concerns," Ignatius replied. "But that's not all. If, again the big if, but if we can get a location on the enemy ship, we'd also have the airborne laser deployed to the area. And, yes, I know we've only had one test of the laser since the damn Congress cut us back on that one. But I've got funding reserves that we'll re-allocate to testing and rapid development for the ABL. And I know that Dr. Talbot has been coordinating that with her people out in California. And thank God their facility is right there on the West Coast."

"Let me make one more point," Ken said. "This whole operation is to remain Top Secret. We discussed this at our meeting this morning. Since then, the President has emphasized that this must not leak out. It could cause complete panic in San Francisco and the entire surrounding area. He does not believe that an orderly evacuation could take place quickly enough and besides that, as we've also discussed, it appears that the intent of this attack is to create an EMP which would not affect the lives of people on the ground. Well, not initially."

"But it would certainly change their lives for months, if not years," Hunt said under his breath.

"So for right now, I want reports every four hours," Ken ordered. "Are we clear on this?"

"Right."

"Yes"

"Every four hours. Got it."

The screen dissolved to black, Ken gathered his maps and notes, nodded to Hunt and said, "Let's get back up to the Oval and brief the President."

"Not that we have anything good to report, though," Hunt said, pushing back from the table and heading upstairs.

FIFTY-TWO

Astana, Kazakhstan

"First we've got sanctions, then freezes, then spies murdering my staff and now a leak about my special project," President Viktor Surleimenov bellowed across the room as his Vice President came through the office door. "Find the leak. I want to know who's trying to sabotage my plan by telling The White House, *The White House* of all places, about an attack on California."

"Sorry, Viktor, I won't be your errand boy on this one. Actually, not on this one or any other one."

"What are you talking about? We have crises on our hands. We've got countries berating us for our nuclear program. We've got handcuffs on our energy contracts. We've got an election coming up where Baltiev is spending money on ads every single day. And by the way, I'm positive it's him. He's responsible for the food poisoning. I'm sure of it. And that gives me even more reasons to see that the ship gets through and knocks out communications, especially that man's bank accounts in San Francisco."

"I told you before and I'll tell you again," the Vice President said, stalking across the room to confront his President. "This is madness. You *must* recall that ship. Contact them immediately and call this off. You have absolutely no idea of the complete chaos it will cause. And now that there's a leak about the operation, don't you think the Americans will finger you with all of this? You think they'll just sit back and lick their wounds and not fight back?"

Viktor sat back and folded his arms. "We will simply say that it must have been a copy-cat attack. We'll speculate that other groups, terrorist groups, saw what happened by the Caspian and figured out they could damage the West Coast of America with just such an attack. You know they've all been trying to bring down the United States for years now. This would be their perfect solution. No, the Americans would not blame us. They would not dream that we would have the nerve to stage such an operation. And they wouldn't understand our motives. We're not a terrorist state. I'm just trying to protect this country."

"Well, you certainly have a crazy definition of protection! In fact, by your actions, all of your actions, the test, the nuclear plant, the denial of inspections and now this insane plan, you are putting this country in mortal danger. I used to think you were a leader with a vision. A vision for Kazakhstan, a vision for all of us. But now it's as if your food taster isn't the only one who's been poisoned. Something is poisoning your mind, and I no longer want to be a part of it," he said in a vehement tone. "Listen to me, Viktor. If you go forward with this lunacy, I will resign my position and run against you in the election."

The President leaped up from his chair, ran around his desk and grabbed the man by his lapels. "So now you're a traitor too? I trusted you. I brought you on board. I *made* you my Vice President, and now you think you can stand there and threaten me?" he roared. "I control the military. I control the security service. I control the election campaign. I control…"

The Vice President interrupted, "But you don't control the people!" He turned and hastily left the room, slamming the door behind him.

Surleimenov stared at the heavy door that rattled on its hinges. "We'll just see about that." He turned back to his chair and slumped down. Reaching for the phone, he muttered, "I'll see who leaked my plan too. If it's someone on that ship, I'll find him."

FIFTY-THREE

Rockville, Maryland

Traffic was light on the Beltway as Samantha moved to the left lane and veered onto I-270 toward Rockville, Maryland. On any day but Saturday, she knew this road would look like a parking lot. Whenever she drove in this part of Maryland, she thanked her lucky stars that she lived in Georgetown and not out in the burbs where a fifteen mile commute could sometimes take well over an hour on a work day. She checked her directions, drove several more miles, took a turn off and finally pulled up to a sprawling three story industrial complex. She parked in a Visitors' slot, grabbed her shoulder bag and walked between rows of poplar trees bordering the entrance to Bandaq Technologies.

When she pushed through the massive glass double doors, she saw a flurry of activity with some employees walking briskly across the reception area, others piling in and out of elevators and a quartet of military officers huddled in the corner in a deep discussion.

"May I help you?" the receptionist asked in a cheerful voice.

"Samantha Reid to see Dr. Talbot, please."

"Certainly. Just one moment." The young woman spoke into the phone, hung up and said, "She'll be out in a few minutes. There's reading material on that table over there if you want to sit down."

Samantha strolled over, took a seat and plucked a copy of the defense contractor's annual report off the table. She leafed through it and found a photo of Dr. Cameron Talbot and her "team of missile defense specialists" standing in front of what looked like two giant cigar shaped tubes that were described as Kinetic Energy Boosters, whatever those were. Here she was pairing up with an obviously brilliant woman who kept her eye on the sky when Samantha had been trained by her dad to keep her eyes on the ground and study geologic formations looking for oil and gas. Boy was she out of her league in this place. She tried to push thoughts of her father out of her mind as she read through the article about Dr. Talbot's various inventions and exploits.

Now that they were all working feverishly to locate the enemy ship, if there really was one out in the Pacific somewhere, The White House was putting a lot of its chips on Dr. Talbot's game table, praying that she'd come up with a way to win the hand. Sure, the Navy, Coast Guard and Missile Defense Agency were all being dealt in, but Cammy was seen as having the best odds of scoring in this one. Talk about pressure. And since Samantha was working with Ken Cosgrove to keep tabs on all the players, she had decided to drive out here to Cammy's lab and get an update.

"Hi Samantha, glad you could come by," Cammy said, coming across the lobby and extending her hand. In her khaki slacks and a white sweater, she looked like any other typical young woman dressed for weekend chores. But this was no typical woman. "Come on back and I'll show you around."

Samantha was glad she had brought along a blazer when she realized that the rooms were kept quite cool. *Must be because of all the computers and equipment in this place.* Cammy peered into a small box to the right of a set of doors. "Retina recognition system," she commented, as they both heard a click and pushed through to a long corridor. "There's a lot of security around here. Then again, probably nothing like what you've got at The White House, right?"

"I'm not so sure about that. Seems like the private sector is usually ahead of the government in most everything these days," Samantha said following Cammy down the hall. They passed several offices and then came to a series of doors to what looked like a command center of some sort complete with a dozen computers on tiered desks with large screens where staffers were pounding the keys, making notes and calling out various commands.

"I'm afraid it's a little crazy in here today," Cammy said, heading to her station on the far side of the huge room. "We're running a bunch of simulations."

"Is all this tied into our missile defense systems?" Samantha asked, surveying the cavernous space.

"Some of it is. We can get connections to the X-band radar, certain satellite systems and the interceptors at Vandenberg. But we have some systems here that we test on our own. The trouble is, in this particular situation, I see those systems as more of a back-up. What I'm trying to figure out is a way to stage a pre-emptive strike. That is if we can ever find the guys with the nuke. Anything new from the Navy or Coast Guard?" She pulled up an extra chair and motioned for Samantha to sit down next to her.

"Nothing yet. We're getting reports every few hours, but figuring the time line of when the transport left Atyrau and must have landed in China, if that's where it really went, then allowing time to off-load and re-assemble everything onto a ship of some sort and then sail out of there, it looks like we have two to three more days before they could possibly get anywhere near the West Coast."

"That's what we've been told too, which is why everyone here is working 24/7 on every project we could possibly employ." Cammy reached for a cup of coffee, took a sip and scrunched up her nose. "Cold, as usual. You want some? We've got fresh in the next room." Samantha nodded. "My assistant will get it," Cammy said. She reached for her phone. "I don't know what this gang would do without caffeine. How do you like it?"

"A little cream and sugar would be great," Samantha replied. As she watched Cammy place the order, she realized that the woman did have some faint circles under her eyes and the headband holding back her blond hair was slightly askew. "You've really been working hard, haven't you?" she asked sympathetically.

Cammy rubbed her eyes and focused on her guest. "You can tell, huh? Didn't leave here until after midnight, drove home, got a few hours and was back in at six this morning. Seeing you like this is the first break I've had since we got word of this thing. And now with just two days, three days, who knows how many days? Well, with this sort of a time line, it can only get worse."

A young man brought their coffee and announced, "Hey Cammy, I wanted to thank you for helping me out last night. When I figured out I had locked the keys in my car, I felt like such an idiot. But your trick really worked."

"What trick?" Samantha asked.

"Cammy swiveled around. "Well, when you're working such long hours on all these complicated simulations, it's easy to forget some of the simple stuff."

"You got that one right," her assistant said with a grin. "I told her I was stupid enough to leave the keys inside, and she told me to call my house because there's an extra set there."

"Then what? Did you have to get someone to drive you home to get them?" Samantha asked.

"No," Cammy replied. "He just needed someone at the house to get the extra key and call him here on his cell phone. Then he holds the cell phone next to the door lock and the person on the phone clicks the UNLOCK button on the extra key and voila. It opens the door."

"Amazing!" Samantha said. "How does that work?"

"Has to do with frequencies. I work a lot with frequencies," she said.

"Yeah," the assistant said, "She's the frequency genius. Well, thanks again." He took off toward his computer station.

"So it's frequencies, huh?" Samantha asked. All I know is AM and FM, and I don't even know how those work."

"AM stands for Amplitude Modulation and FM stands for Frequency Modulation."

"I call it frickin' magic," Samantha said with a grin. "I'm afraid I'm more into strategy, and I'm really glad we've got you for execution, uh, so to speak."

Cammy went on to explain her latest experiments and how there was one particular idea that was her main focus right now. She said that after she finished today's tests, she was planning to fly out to California first thing in the morning with Hunt Daniels, gather a team at their California facility and get on board a specially equipped 737 as soon as there was any word, any sighting or even a suspicion of where the enemy ship was out in the Pacific.

"I heard that Hunt is going with you," Samantha said. "He's really a neat guy."

"Better than neat," Cammy said, with the beginning of a dreamy smile on her face. "I always look forward to traveling with Hunt, even when it's on a scary mission like this one."

"I did hear you two were an item," Samantha said. "I don't mean to get too personal, but are you two? I mean, is it serious?"

"I hope so," Cammy said. "Trouble is, we both work long hours. Hunt keeps getting sent all over the world on all kinds of secret projects, negotiations, investigations. Well, you know that as well as anybody. And so we don't get to spend that much time together. But still, he's great, and I'm hoping we can put it together one of these days. But how about you? You're single, right? Anybody special on your radar scope, so to speak?"

Samantha hesitated and then said, "Well, there was once. We had some of the same travel problems. But, well, not anymore." She cleared her throat and said, "But back to our situation here. I have to say that I've been working on so many national security threats lately, biological issues, people trying to blow up commuter trains, nut cases being recruited as suicide bombers. I mean it's full time all the time. But still. I see all of those other threats and arrests and problems as the parsley on the platter. The turkey on our platter right now is the threat of an EMP attack and it's got me positively terrified."

"I'm with you there. In the past we've had warnings about things, At least for most of the ones I've heard about. Warnings from agents who have infiltrated terrorist groups, warnings from civilians who see suspicious stuff. And this time, we did get a warning. It just wasn't very specific, so we don't know where to look. I mean, I've been trying to figure out how our people can find a ship, vessel, destroyer, even a fishing boat in that incredibly huge area between the South China Sea and California, especially since we have no idea what kind of ship it might be, whether it's camouflaged, or what flag it might be flying. But if any of our folks can find it, you can be sure we'll have systems, defensive measures and redundancies ready to go." Then she added with a worried frown. "Trouble is, I really don't know if any of them will work."

"Looks like you have a ton of great ideas, though. How in the world do you come up with this stuff?" Samantha said, spreading her arms around, gesturing to the multitude of computers and screens.

"I do a lot of research," Cammy said. Then she took a sip of her coffee and added, "Okay, I did tell my boss once that I learned the Rule of the 6 P's a long time ago and try to live by that one."

"Rule of the 6 P's?" Samantha asked, cocking her head.

"Proper preparation precludes piss-poor performance," Cammy intoned.

Samantha burst out laughing. "You're amazing." She checked her watch. "Look, I know you've got a lot to do, and I don't want to get in your way here. I just wanted to get up to speed on your plans since I'm trying to coordinate all of the activities of the agencies and your company and all the rest for Ken. But, by the way, where did your company get the funny name Bandaq Technologies anyway?"

"Oh that," Cammy said. "You see, it was years ago that the founders, these two guys, were sailing down in the Caribbean. They were bare-boating it and one night, as the story goes, they got the idea for the company while they were drinking banana daiquiris. So, Bandaq!"

"And on that note, I'd better sail out of your way." Samantha got up from her chair. Cammy got up too and led her across the room toward the door.

"Thanks for coming by. Coordination is good. Especially on this one," Cammy said with a smile.

"Coordination you shall have. Now let's just pray for a conquest."

FIFTY-FOUR

The White House

"I got another email from Pete Kalani," Angela said, rushing into Samantha's office.

Samantha grabbed the note, quickly scanned it and said, "Good timing. I'm heading down to a meeting in Ken Cosgrove's office in a few minutes for an update on everything. You can come with me."

Angela plopped down on a chair in front of the desk. "Great, I've got some time now. By the way, since you were out in Rockville this morning, you missed the Senior Staff meeting. Guess you wasn't there?" she asked with a coy smile.

"Who?"

"Max Federman."

"Why? Is he out of town or something?"

"Nope. The latest word is that he's out of a job," Angela said with a slight sense of triumph in her voice.

"What happened? Did he have a falling out with the Veep?"

"From all the gossip in the EOB, sounds like the Veep got word of Max's tendency to fall all over White House staff. The young, single ones, that is."

"And he fired him just as the campaign is heating up?" Samantha asked, raising her eyebrows.

"Let's just say that the Veep wanted to get him out of here before the press found out and really put the heat on."

"Talk about a come-uppance." Samantha thought about all the run-ins she'd had with Max the last few weeks and chuckled. "You know, he never propositioned me. Guess he was too busy being ticked off every time I asked for a threat assessment. In fact, he once said I reminded him of a four-year-old in a tutu shouting, 'Look at me'."

"Oh, that's cold," Angela said. "Besides, you never do things around here for personal reasons. Your job is protecting the country, for Lord's sake."

"At least that's how I try to look at it," Samantha said. "When I first raised the issue of an EMP, I remember thinking that I didn't want my memo to be the black box you recover after our economy is shot down by that kind of attack."

"Right on. By the way, have you heard anything new about stopping the Kazakhs?

"Nothing so far. I've been checking with all the agencies, and I don't see a light at the end of the tunnel yet. Not even a shadow. But we'll see what Ken has to say."

Angela checked her watch. "So what time is your meeting?"

"Pretty soon. Let me just get my notes together here, and we'll head downstairs."

When the women arrived in Ken's office, he was seated at his corner conference table and motioned for them to join him.

"Angela got an email from Pete Kalani," Samantha said. "Is it okay for her to sit in?"

"Of course. What did he say?"

"Well, I sent a reply thanking him for his help, reiterating that we were searching for the ship and would be careful to take care of his friend, just like you asked me to," Angela said. "And then I got this return email." She held out the printed copy. "See? He says that he's traveling in Kazakhstan with Nurlan's sister, that they don't have much money left, but they're trying to get to a small city where she has some relatives. Then he has to figure out a way to get back to the states for his last year at UCLA."

Ken read the note and passed it over to Samantha. "So he's out of money. He doesn't seem to be asking for money for himself though. Looks like a brave kid to be going through all of this."

"Here at the end," Samantha said, pointing to the last few sentences, "he does talk again about the issue of reparations for the Marshall Island victims. Have we heard back from the Chairman of that committee?"

"Not yet," Ken said. "We've briefed the Intelligence Committees about the threat, the search for the ship and the agreement we made to protect that one man on board, of course. And naturally we told them about our promise to try and get a reparations bill moving quickly. They were somewhat skeptical about the whole scenario though, saying that there might not be any ship at all, and perhaps it's all just a play to get the money."

"But that's ridiculous," Angela said. "We all heard that phone call. This guy was super serious. I mean, he had all the details. Why in the world wouldn't they believe him?"

"Angela," Ken said in a calming voice. "I know you haven't been working on national security issues, up to now that is. So you haven't been privy to all the schemes, tips, threats that parade through this office. Now granted, this one is more specific than the ones we usually get. But sometimes a certain weariness sets in on the Hill when we lay out these things. A lot of them turn out to be hoaxes, of course, and others are handled quite deftly by the

FBI or CIA. This one is so broad in terms of figuring out where to look for the culprits that it's taking an entire Naval Task Force along with a good portion of our Coast Guard to hunt them down. Just imagine what that's doing to their budgets."

Angela listened intently and nodded as he went on. "Now you can figure out how well all of that is going over with the Members who complain about the Pentagon budget on a regular basis. So put that with our demand that they up the ante with money for native people who may not even be voters, well, you get the picture."

"Geez!" Angela said with a sigh. "What do we do now?"

"We keep our eye on the threat." He turned to Samantha, "What do you have for me today?"

Samantha handed over a pair of memos. "I had the FBI run background checks on Pete Kalani and his friend, Nurlan. Turns out that they're both students at UCLA. Just as Pete said. They've both been very active in anti-war groups. Well, Nurlan is a member of a group over in Kazakhstan and Pete has his group, the S.A.I.N.T.S. which has been trying to raise the reparations issue for quite some time. Haven't got much publicity though. Not much traction. He's never been arrested, and while he seems to talk a good game about hating our government, there's no record of any personal threats against the President of anything to involve the Secret Service."

Ken perused the reports and murmured, "Everything he said pretty much checks out here."

"Do we have any updates from the Navy?" Samantha asked.

"In the latest briefing, Ignatius said that the Navy was focusing their resources on a triangular area in the Pacific. But since there are major shipping lanes all through there, finding one small ship is an almost impossible task. At least we think it's probably pretty small, compared to most of the container ships and tankers out there. And now there's a big storm brewing. It'll make visibility even worse."

"When I met with Dr. Talbot this morning, she said she and Hunt were leaving first thing tomorrow to head to the West Coast," Samantha said.

"Yes, I know their schedule. There's a 737 ready for them to board at the first indication that the ship has been sighted."

Samantha glanced down at her notes again and asked a question. "Ken, I got to thinking about what kind of ship it might be. I remember Pete said he heard they were getting on a boat at a base on the China coast."

"Right," Ken said "And we're trying to figure out if it might have been Wusong. We've been in touch with their Base Commander, but he says he knows nothing about it. Same kiss off we got from the Chinese President."

"Maybe he's right. Maybe it's a private contract," Samantha said. "Maybe the Kazakhs cut some deal with a boat builder or an agent or somebody like that, and they simply arranged for a ship to be made available at some little port along the South China Sea. I mean, it could have been anywhere over there."

"Yes, I know," Ken said.

"But on the other hand, if they put this nuke, or whatever kind of weapon it is, on board along with some sort of launcher, and if their plan is to send it up and create an EMP, then by definition the pulse would knock out all of the ship's controls, so it wouldn't be able to get away, right?"

"Yes, we've thought about that," Ken said. "So that means it could be a much older vessel of some sort, or they took special pains to harden their systems to withstand the pulse."

"But if they've hardened everything on board, that might make it tougher for Cammy, uh, I mean Dr. Talbot to pull off some sort of pre-emptive strike. She said she uses frequencies, and while I couldn't begin to understand what she's been testing, it does sound like there's a chance that whatever she does just won't work on that particular ship."

"You're absolutely right," Ken said. "I'm sure she knows that. It just means that if we do find the damn thing, and if she and Hunt can get there before a launch, she'll have to use the systems they have on board the 737 and pray that they work. Otherwise, the Kazakhs launch a weapon, and then we'll have to rely on the missile defense interceptors being sent when that sucker is already flying through the air toward San Francisco. And we have to pretend we're Superman with a bullet hitting a bullet."

FIFTY-FIVE

The Pacific

Huge waves crashed over the bow of the ship. The wind howled sending the fishing trawler up and down like a giant yo-yo. Nurlan clung to a railing on the bridge as the Captain shouted orders to the crew.

"Batten down the loose gear," he bellowed over the roar. "Tie down those boxes. Rig some lines to hold on to when you're on deck. Get washed overboard in this gale, we'd never find you."

Nurlan wished he'd never found this assignment. He was sick, scared and stunned by the ferocity of the storm. He'd never seen anything like it. The dark clouds had been gathering since yesterday, but he had no idea they could unleash this kind of turmoil. He didn't know anything about sailing or ships or any of this. His world was indoors, his head was inside a computer, his experience was land-locked. And here he was in a violent storm, hanging on, afraid to let go to find a life preserver as the Captain barked the commands to everyone within ear shot.

How had it come to this? Nurlan had gone to work at the nuclear plant just so he could learn more about their plans and maybe sabotage some tests. And that's exactly what he did. Or at least, he thought he did. But now, his little experiment had morphed into an international challenge. No, not a challenge. A full-fledged attack. And they were using his idea to stage it. As he felt the guilt wash over him, he watched one crew member slide along the deck and finally grab hold of a line before being swept off in another gigantic wave.

When they had flown to the China coast, he had entertained ideas about slipping away, escaping this crazy escapade. But the men in charge had kept close watch on everybody. He couldn't find a way out. And besides, even if he could get away, where would he go? He didn't have much money, and he had no idea how he'd get to a city and find his way out of the country. And if the Chinese found him, he could be in another kind of trouble. They could accuse him of being a spy. They could throw him in jail. They didn't take kindly to having uninvited strangers around. He didn't have a visa. None of them did. Their orders were to land on that remote runway, off-load their equipment, quickly board the ship with all their gear and get moving.

So here he was, trying to control the nausea, the fear, the feeling of utter helplessness. Then he thought about a conversation he'd had with his supervisor the night before. Nurlan had asked the man how they could make their escape back across the Pacific if they launched the weapon and it set off a shock wave like what had happened back home. Wouldn't that knock out any electronics we have on board, he had inquired. So how would they make their get-away? The boss had told him that first of all, if they launched the nuke, they wouldn't need their computers anymore, so they wouldn't care if those were fried. And as for the ship, it was old, ran on diesel engines, not fancy electronics. And if they lost their GPS, the captain would just use Celestial Nav, a sextant, charts, the stars. He'd take a reading off the North Star and navigate just like Vespucci, Magellan and Columbus did. Nobody had a GPS in the 15th century, he'd said, and he told Nurlan to stop worrying about everything. But how could he stop, especially now that the ship was lurching again.

"Ship is flopping around like a cork," the Captain shouted to his First Mate. "That damn agent sold us this aging piece of junk, and they didn't put enough ballast into the keel."

Nurlan wondered how much their weapon weighed. That and the launcher they were supposed to raise at the stern when the time came. Maybe their cargo would be washed overboard. That would certainly end the mission and save them all from this insane plot. Of course, the others were counting on the huge bonuses they had been promised to carry out the President's plans. But Nurlan wanted no part of it. He had lain awake at night trying to figure out a way to stymic this launch. He thought about ways to jam the computer, though he knew they had back-up systems, so that probably wouldn't work. He thought about trying to redirect the launch so the nuke would detonate out over the open ocean, but he doubted he could pull that off either.

He stared ahead as another wave crashed over the bow. "Why we head into the storm like this?" he shouted to the Captain. The man turned and gave Nurlan a look that said he was addressing an ignorant child. "We have to head into the storm because if those waves hit us broadside, we could turtle."

"Turtle?" Nurlan called out.

"To make it simple for guys like you," he said with disdain, "we'd go over and the bottom of our ship would be up in the air and we'd look like a dead turtle, you idiot. Now for God's sake, man, get yourself a life preserver. Or, better yet, get below deck, and let us handle this."

Nurlan took one last look at the waves and headed down a ladder to the crew's bunk room. He grabbed the side of one of the bunks and sat down, hunching over to fit into the cramped space.

"Nurlan. Been looking all over for you," his supervisor said, throwing the door open and holding onto the edge of the frame as the ship lurched again. "We got a message on the satellite phone from Astana."

"From government?"

"Of course, from the government. No one else is supposed to know we're out here. But then, that's the problem."

"What problem?" Nurlan asked, with one hand holding onto the bunk and the other pressed against his forehead.

"What's the matter with you? You sick?"

"Uh huh," Nurlan moaned. "Not feel good in storm."

"Well, you better feel good pretty soon because the message we got moved up our launch date."

"What that mean? We not there yet. And we can't send up weapon in big storm."

"No. We know that. But we figure we'll get through the worst of it, and then later tonight things should calm down a bit. And even though we're still at least two hundred miles from San Francisco, they want us to launch our weapon as soon as we possibly can."

"Why rush?"

"As I said, looks like there's a problem. The message said there's been a leak about our plans."

"Leak?" Nurlan asked, jerking his head up. "Leak in Astana?"

"They don't know where it came from, but evidently the Americans are onto us. And if they are, you can be sure they've got their entire military looking for this ship. At least we're in a fishing trawler, flying a Panamanian flag. That's probably why they haven't spotted us already. So we have to launch our weapon and get the hell out of here before they do find us." He looked at Nurlan and shook his head. "Pull yourself together. We need you on those computers. And this time, we need you to do it right!"

FIFTY-SIX

California Coast

"Welcome aboard, Dr. Talbot," the pilot said, standing in the doorway of the Boeing 737. "We know you've been working on the systems we've got here on our little Electric Judy, as we call her. Sure hope you can work your magic over the Pacific."

Cammy shook hands with the man and gave him a cautious smile. "I have to admit this is one scary assignment. At last word, the Navy and Coast Guard have not had any luck spotting that ship. But when we analyzed the time we think it takes for them to come across from China, we figure we're getting down to the wire. And I'd like to be airborne and ready."

"Absolutely. Those are my orders. I know that some of the systems you've requested are on one of our F-35 fighter jets. But there's not enough space for everyone on that baby, so you've got us."

"Fine by me," Cammy said moving away from the door and stowing her gear.

Hunt came up behind her. "What do you think, hon? This platform going to work for you?"

"It's got to work," she said, tucking her white blouse into her khakis, sitting down and stretching her legs out in front of her. "Those tests we've been running are just that. Tests. There's always a degree of knowledge, anticipation, a sense of assurance that everything's going to be okay tomorrow if we screw up the test today. Even with the new airborne laser, the ballistic missile interceptors at Vandenberg, the Aegis missiles at sea, all of those tests are performed and the kill ratios may look great on paper. But this time we're not in a flight simulator. In there you can crash and still walk outside a few minutes later very much alive. Not with this. Not today."

Hunt sat down and leaned close to her. "I know. Believe me I know how you feel right now. After all those rehearsals, this is show time and you're the star. You've got to feel some jitters knowing what's at stake if those bastards slip through our net and fire that nuke. That is *if* they've really got one."

"That's the devil in this one," she said, pushing some strands of hair back behind her headband. "All we have is the word of a young student that they're out there heading toward San Francisco. And he's got his own ax to grind. I mean with the reparations issue and all of that."

"You heard the recording of his phone call though," Hunt said. "Sounded awfully convincing. At least a big enough threat that the SecDef, Navy Secretary , Coast Guard Commandant and especially Ken Cosgrove heard enough that they ordered this massive hunt. And the President is completely on board with it too."

"Well, he has to be. I mean, can you imagine what would happen in Washington if this thing, whatever it is, were actually detonated over northern California?"

"Happen in Washington? You mean the political upheaval?"

"Sure," Cammy said. "The entire administration would be painted as unable to protect the American people and Jayson Keller would lose the election."

"Quite frankly, I don't give a damn about the political fall-out. I'm thinking about the fall-out on top of the people of San Francisco and maybe millions of people living nearby."

"I know. I know. Guess I'm just trying not to think about the actual effects of an EMP, if that's the end result."

"If, and I know it's a great big if. But if they're able to launch the damn thing and it does create a pulse, it not only destroys communications, electronics, and every other thing people depend on, but think what it could do to aircraft in the area."

"Ladies and gentlemen," the voice of the pilot came through the intercom, "we're readying for takeoff. Please fasten your seat belts. When we reach cruising altitude, Dr Talbot and Colonel Daniels along with their crews will be free to roam the cabin. I'll keep you posted. Weather is beginning to clear. May have some light turbulence on our climb out, but hopefully it'll smooth out a bit as we head away from the coast."

"Away from the coast," Cammy echoed, glancing out the window. "I wonder how far we'd have to get from a detonation in order to have this plane survive."

"Actually, they've hardened some of the systems," Hunt replied. "Then again, I guess it all depends on how big the blast is. Well, you know that better than anyone on board this airplane."

She sighed. "I guess I do. Just doing a lot of what-if's in my mind right now. What if we find the ship? Will I be able to pull off a pre-emptive strike? What if they're able to launch anyway? Will Vandenberg be able to track it, launch a missile and knock it out in its boost phase? What if that doesn't work and it gains altitude? Will our airborne laser be able to nail it before it detonates? What if it does go off and all the systems on this plane aren't strong enough to withstand it, and we can't navigate or land ourselves?"

She paused and added, "Do you really think this is a good time to take God out of the Pledge of Allegiance?"

"Cammy, stop it," Hunt said, putting his arm around her and pulling her close. "You've been on the front lines of a number of attacks. In India you pulled off that incredible save when that cruise missile was heading to New Delhi. And then you figured out what that rogue Chinese general was up to and you saved Air Force Two with that new scheme you dreamed up."

"No, that was you," she said, gazing up at him with searching eyes. "You were the one who flew that little jet right underneath Keller's plane and deployed the laser to deflect the missile that was aimed at it. You were the hero in that little stunt."

"No way, Cam. You're the one who invented that laser. Look, the whole point I was trying to make is that you're a god-damned genius. You've been through some pretty hairy situations in the past. Situations where a ton of lives were at stake. And you held steady. That's what you're going to do now. And I'm right here to help in any way I can. I'm proud of you, lady. You know that, don't you?"

"MmmHmm," she murmured. "Guess I'm just getting a little nervous this time. I always get that way. I just try not to show it." She leaned her head against the soft leather headrest and thought back to those earlier days. She had invented a new technology for a defense against cruise missiles, one she'd been working on for ages. Her boss had almost pulled the plug on her budget and experiments, but he had finally stuck with her, and her new idea had actually worked.

She had been inspired to work on missile defense projects when she was just a kid. She had grown up on an Air Force Base and one night she was watching TV with her Dad. It was a long time ago, but she could still see the image on the old analogue set, the image of the President of the United States when he gave a speech about something he called his Strategic Defense Initiative.

The media later called it "Star Wars," and made fun of the whole idea. But she had been mesmerized when the President called on America's best scientists to try and figure out a way to stop a missile before it could strike American soil. He had said that if the Soviets, who were then our enemy, had fired off a missile, even by mistake, it could kill millions of innocent people. Then all we could do would be to fire one back and kill millions of their innocent people. He said he didn't like that strategy. Her Dad said he didn't like it either so they had both agreed that the president had a pretty good idea. Then the President had said, "Wouldn't it be better to save lives than avenge lives?"

And with that pronouncement, she was hooked. She said she wanted to grow up to be a scientist and figure out how to stop the big missiles. Of course, she was only nine at the time. But she was good at math and science, so why not go for it? When she had graduated from Stanford and then got her Ph.D. at MIT, she had been hired at Bandaq Technologies and started her project to try and stop all kinds of missiles.

She had tried a lot of things, but finally decided to amass a huge data base of information on all the different kinds of cruise missiles manufactured around the world. Then, since they are computer guided, she thought that just maybe she could use fast acting algorithms to figure out the frequency the enemy was using to communicate with their missile. If she could find it, she figured she could use the same frequency to go and invade the missile, take it over and, like a virus controlling a computer, redirect it back on the heads of the bad guys. She thought it was pretty clever at the time, but it took one heck of a lot of time to convince the higher-ups at Bandaq that it would ever work.

It did work, and she had used that very system when some militants over in Kashmir launched a missile toward New Delhi. She had been able to invade that one, redirect it and save the city. She remembered how Hunt had been with her on that mission and how, later that night they had ended up in a gorgeous hotel room with a view of the Taj Mahal as guests of the Indian government. What a night that had been. As she once again pictured Hunt sprawled out on that luxurious bed in a room with French doors opening to the terrace letting in warm breezes while they made love throughout the night, she longed for a repeat performance. Not in India. It could be anywhere. Any place where she could be alone with Hunt Daniels.

She paused for a long moment, looked up into his brilliant blue eyes again and said, "If we get out of this one, I mean if we can survive this whole nightmare, do you think we could . . . could we . . . maybe take a break and spend some more time together?"

"I never thought I'd hear you say that, sweetheart. But you've got yourself a deal. We nail this sucker, and I'll put in for leave, and you take all those vacation days you've built up, and we'll go away and forget all about the government, the defense industry, the politicians. It'll be just you and me."

Cammy nodded and took a deep breath. "Okay. Sounds like a plan. But first . . . first we've got to find that ship."

FIFTY-SEVEN

The White House

Samantha scanned the room and checked her notes. She had called a Deputies meeting in the SCIF in the EEOB. This particular Sensitive Compartmentalized Information Facility was just one of many such rooms within the White House complex. There were others on the Hill and in certain agencies where communication lines were scrambled and sanitized, telephones were checked at the door and computer systems were hardened. It was in these rooms where officials and lawmakers with the highest security clearances were briefed on matters of national security. And this was just such a meeting.

She saw that all of the attendees were in place, the Deputy Secretaries of Homeland Security, Treasury, Energy, Transportation, Commerce, Health and Human Services. "Welcome everyone. Thanks for coming over on short notice. As the DHS people know, we are in the midst of a national security emergency. The information you are going to receive is Top Secret. For now. If the operation is completed successfully, it will be declassified and made public. But right now, the President is afraid that if this were to leak out, it could cause panic and possibly loss of life in the San Francisco Bay Area."

With that statement she had their rapt attention. She went on to explain the threat outlined in the call from Pete Kalani, the background checks completed on both Pete and Nurlan Remizov, the demand for reparations for the Marshall Island survivors along with the promise not to harm Nurlan. She told them about the transport plane that reportedly flew from Kazakhstan to an airfield on the China coast where the crew, along with Nurlan and other technicians, were planning to load a nuclear device along with a launch mechanism aboard some sort of ship. She emphasized that no one knows the type of vessel involved, nor the flag it might be flying. She outlined the calls the President had made to the Presidents of both Kazakhstan and China and their denials of any knowledge of such an operation.

She then summarized the actions of the Naval Task Force along with the search being coordinated with the Coast Guard and told them about the flight to the West Coast of Lt. Col. Hunt Daniels and Dr. Cameron Talbot. She told them how Dr. Talbot had been working with the Missile Defense Agency and others at DOD and finally how updates were coming into Ken Cosgrove's office every four hours, or sooner as warranted.

The Deputies sat in stunned silence as they listened to the details. No one said a word or tried to interrupt as Samantha continued the terrifying details. "And if this crew of Kazakhs is able to launch a nuclear weapon and detonate it fifty to one hundred miles up in the atmosphere over San Francisco, many of you undoubtedly know that it would set off an electro-magnetic pulse that would not only disable but fry all electronics on the ground in its line of sight."

It was then that the Deputy Energy Secretary blurted out, "And that means major portions of our electricity grid would go down, not just like a temporary black-out, but perhaps for months until major replacement components could be secured. And since many of those parts are made overseas, it could be, well," he shook his head in dismay, "who knows? Years maybe."

The Deputies from Treasury and DHS spoke at once. "No banking, no internet, no telephones."

"No electronic health records, none of the machines and systems in our hospitals would work," the HHS representative chimed in. "People on life support could die."

"Think about the food supply," said the Transportation Deputy. "If our planes and trains can't get food to the cities, we're in deep deep trouble."

"Riots in the streets, or worse," Samantha said. "You all saw reports of what happened in Kazakhstan when that crazy test nuke went off at an altitude way south of that city called Atyrau by the Caspian Sea." The group nodded. "Well, it now looks like President Surleimenov is so mad about the sanctions we've placed on the country and specifically on others in high office that he's trying to retaliate by pulling the same stunt over here."

"But why San Francisco?" one Deputy asked.

"We're speculating that first, it's a place they can hit from a small ship in the Pacific. But also, the opposition candidate in the upcoming Kazakh elections, Sergei Baltiev, has a lot of his campaign money deposited in special accounts at the Bank of America."

"And if their computers are down and their records destroyed," the Treasury Deputy said, "obviously, Baltiev can't have access to the funds. If that's their plan, it's too cute by half, I'd say."

"Now, as I said," Samantha continued, "right now this is a Top Secret operation. And it could play out in the next few days.

But as soon as it does, and let's all say a prayer that the Navy can find the ship and Dr. Talbot and others can stop the attack, this will all come out. And at that time, there'll be a lot of questions about the threat of an EMP, not only from places like Kazakhstan, but from other potential enemies, terrorist groups who would love to play copy-cat and Lord knows who else. So the bottom line here is that we simply must get plans in place immediately to harden many of our own systems, especially our communications networks along with the grid, and water supplies. DOD has hardened many of their military communications facilities, of course, but our concern now is the civilian population."

"Our nuclear plants provide about twenty percent of our electricity, and those are already hardened," the Energy Deputy said. "But our gas-fired plants have electronics-based controls, so they'd be more vulnerable. Hydroelectric power is a problem. I'd have to check on coal-fired generation." He sat back and folded his arms. "This is massive. And the private sector couldn't handle the costs."

"We know that," Samantha said. "That's been the hang-up all along. And we can't ask them to do it all. We're talking national security here. But as you analyze the needs in your various areas, I would refer you to the last report filed by the former EMP Commission."

"That's right," one Deputy volunteered. "I remember we had some sort of group looking into all of this. But I haven't heard anything in a couple of years."

"That's because after they testified before the House Armed Services Committee, the Members ignored their recommendations and said they had other, more pressing needs. So they disbanded the Commission, and look where we are now." Several of the deputies squirmed in their seats. Others took notes.

"And so your job, starting now, is to put these plans together along with estimates of funding costs. There's already some work being done by our Legislative Affairs people to try and influence a few House Members about the need, in general, to harden the grid, but we also need to have replacement parts available, rescue teams ready to be called up, transportation options shifted from one part of the country to another. And since no one could ever predict where such an attack might take place, although the coastal cities seem like the best bet at this point, we should focus our initial planning efforts there."

"What about our missile defense capabilities?" the Commerce Deputy asked.

"You can be sure they're working overtime on this issue. In fact, they've been on it for a long time because they would be our first line of defense. And that means the deployment of more interceptors, more radar and satellites and more funding for the Airborne Laser among other projects. Unfortunately, Congress hasn't been on board."

"After this, you can be sure it'll get their attention," the Treasury Deputy said. "If there ever was an institution that responded almost exclusively to the latest headlines, that's it."

"Well, you can be sure our Legislative Affairs people, along with all of yours, should be on the Hill as soon as this comes out," Samantha said.

The door opened and Samantha's assistant burst in. "Sorry to interrupt," she said breathlessly, "but it looks like the Navy may have spotted the ship."

FIFTY-EIGHT

The Pacific

"We just notified the Naval Carrier Group that's out there. Told them we've spotted a ship on our radar. I tried to contact them but they didn't respond. May not be the right one. Then again, it's heading toward San Francisco, and we're going in to get a visual," the pilot said.

"How close do you think we can get without arousing suspicion? I sure hope they don't have a search radar on board," Cammy said.

"Planes fly through this area all the time," Hunt said. "It's better for us to take a look than having Navy helos all over the place."

"You're right on that score," the pilot said. "The Carrier Group is going to stay beyond the horizon. Don't want to spook these guys into launching quickly."

"Exactly," Cammy said. "But now that the storm has moved on, I'm sure that the ship can pick up speed, and since we're about a hundred miles from the coast, that means they could make their move any time now."

"So we'll head over, scope it out, contact the group again, and if it looks like it could be our target, we'll set up."

"I've been working with this AESA system, testing it out, and it looks like our best bet for a pre-emptive strike," Cammy said. But would it work? She had only done simulations. And if it didn't work and they launched, she'd have to rely on a new, untested, airborne laser. As far as she was concerned, that was just too scary a proposition to think about. No, she had to make this new AESA radar work. She was pretty proud of her company for developing it. They had named it the Active Electronic Steered Aperture, and in addition to testing it on an F-35 fighter jet, thank goodness they had also used this 737 as a test bed. As the pilot headed closer to the ship, Cammy headed to the special radar control panel.

"We can make better time now," the ship's captain said to his first mate. "Take it up to twenty knots."

"How much longer before we get close enough to launch?"

"Not sure just how many miles out we can be. I have to double check that with their supervisor. Far as I'm concerned, the sooner the better. I want to get rid of that cargo and get the hell out of here."

"I'm with you there," the first mate replied. "Wait. That plane up there. Do you think they're the ones trying to contact us? Do you think somebody is onto us?"

The captain craned his neck and shrugged. "We've seen a few planes here and there the whole time we've been crossing." He grabbed his binoculars. "Doesn't seem to have any military markings or anything. Looks like it's private. No sense in responding. We've got a job to do." He checked his watch, turned and headed down from the bridge. "Gotta go check on a launch time. By my reckoning, it could be any time now. So hold 'er steady, and I'll be back in a minute."

"Can you see that?" Hunt asked Cammy. "She's flying a Panamanian flag. Looks like an old fishing vessel of some kind. But, it's got some antennas and look at that equipment aft. That big tube could be the missile launcher, and the crew is running around like they're getting ready to set it up back at the transom. That's got to be the ship." He shouted to the captain. "Radio the carrier group. This has to be it. And it sure looks like they're preparing to launch. Jesus!"

Cammy and the other technicians on board raced to turn on the special radar. It began radiating. They worked together to position the beam, so they could aim it directly at the ship below. The pilot kept the plane on a circular course, as steady as possible. Cammy stared at the equipment, held her breath and after several tense moments, she cried out, "We've got it in range. Now we'll paint the ship" More adjustments were made, and as Hunt looked on, Cammy said, "Now comes the tricky part. Instead of such a wide beam, we've got to twist it down to a very narrow shaft". She worked the controls and began the beam shaping. It was a slow process. She had to pray that the crew on that ship wouldn't get their act together to launch the missile before she narrowed the field. Another minute, another calculation, another adjustment.

"During the tests yesterday, you said you could bring it down to a pencil beam," Hunt said, hovering over her and staring at the image on the screen. "This is amazing."

"Exactly," Cammy said, working her controls. "Now, when we get it down to the right size, we stage an AEA."

"Airborne electronic attack," Hunt said. "Kind of like what they were planning to do to San Francisco in a way right?"

"Kind of." She stared at the screen, nodded slowly and said cautiously, "Now, watch. We're going to inject a virus down the beam, aim it right at the ship. You can see it there on the radar scope. The radar itself becomes a weapon to send high powered energy down to cook the electronics on board. It's not the same kind of pulse that's in an EMP, but it has a similar result. You just have to be awfully darn accurate with this thing."

"Carrier admiral's on the radio," the pilot shouted. "He's reminding us about the promise not to harm the crew."

"An AEA won't kill the people, just their electronics," Cammy called back. "Tell him that's the only weapon we're using now. And if it works, he can send in his seals to clean up after us."

"We got the launcher ready to go," the supervisor said to Nurlan. "The erector is at the right angle. The weapon is loaded and ready. Time for you to work your magic."

Nurlan stared at the launcher. It was the deadliest, scariest sight he had ever seen. When they had set off the first test back in Kazakhstan, he wasn't right on top of it. Now here he was, watching with mounting dread as the missile was locked into place. All it needed now were his computer commands.

The supervisor started to shout to the crew. "That damn plane is up there again. What are they doing?"

Everyone on deck stared at the sky. Nurlan took his eyes off his keyboard and looked up too. "They're just up there. Circling. You think they attack us?" he shouted.

"Hurry up!" the supervisor ordered. "Get this thing launched fast. And I mean now before they... whoever the hell they are...before they can stop us." He ran to where Nurlan had set up his computer control station. "I said now!"

FIFTY-NINE

The White House

"Dr. Talbot's plane believes they've spotted the ship," the Admiral said. "We're in a holding pattern about thirty-five miles west. As soon as we find out if the AESA system is able to knock out the controls for that launch, our seals will head in." The teleconference was underway in the Situation Room where Ken Cosgrove, Samantha Reid, the Chief of Staff, and Secretary of Homeland Security were gathered around the gleaming mahogany conference table. Their eyes were glued to the screen as the Admiral from the Naval Carrier Group reported in.

Samantha had raced back to the West Wing from the meeting in the SCIF and now sat transfixed as the Admiral's image was on one side of the screen, the Navy Secretary on the other. The SecDef and Coast Guard Commandant shared a second screen.

"How will we know if it works?" Samantha whispered to Ken who was sitting on her right.

"We'll have to trust Dr. Talbot and the technicians on board the 737 on that one."

"But what if they use that new radar system and it doesn't really prevent the launch?"

"Then MDA takes over. The missile defense folks are up and running at Vandenberg. They're tracking the ship as we speak."

Samantha realized she was holding her breath as the officers continued to describe the action over the Pacific. It was happening. After weeks of searching and untold high level strategy sessions, after Presidential phone calls and FBI investigations, her nightmare of an EMP attack on America was finally being played out. She knew that Cameron Talbot was a genius at this sort of thing and that Hunt Daniels had been with her on several of her former exploits. But this one was the biggest ever. This one meant the survival or possible destruction of one of the country's most beautiful cities. And this one now depended on one kind of technology knocking out another kind. Could they do it? Samantha found herself staring at the screens again, saying a silent prayer.

Nurlan's fingers clicked over the computer keys. He first typed in the wrong password. Then he used a set of false codes. He didn't want to put in the right ones. He had been stalling as long as he could, but his supervisor and the other crew members were screaming at him to hurry. They all talked about the great victory President Surleimenov would have over the Americans. The ugly Americans who were demanding intrusive inspections. The government in Washington that was imposing sanctions on the Kazakh people along with their top officials. The President had said the Americans were to be taught a lesson, and this would indeed be a teachable moment. But Nurlan wanted no part of it. The people who lived in the city of San Francisco were innocent, just as his people who lived in the city of Atyrau were innocent. And look what happened to them.

"What's the matter with you?" his boss bellowed. "You know the right codes. Put them in. Right now!"

Nurlan began to type in the sequence and then sat stunned, staring at the screen. "Look. Something's wrong."

The supervisor leaned over the screen. It was black. "Reboot, you idiot."

Nurlan tried to reboot. But nothing was working. The screen remained as dark as the nightfall that was fast approaching. He looked up at the sky and saw the plane still circling. "It's them," he cried out, pointing to the plane. "They must have jammed the signals or something."

"How could they do that?" the supervisor demanded? He gazed up and shouted, "They're not shooting at us. They're just circling around. How in hell could they stop your computer from working? You must have done something. You're screwing up the launch and sabotaging our mission."

"I not do that," Nurlan protested. "Get others to try." He motioned to another technician.

Just then the ship's captain came running down the ladder from the bridge. "What's happening? My GPS won't work. It's dead." He looked at the men scrambling to set up additional computers. "Looks like your systems are dead too. Did you guys do something crazy with this launch system of yours?" he shouted in an accusing tone, waving his arms toward the missile that sat erect on the transom.

"No! Nothing's working. We tried the launch codes. At least Nurlan here said he tried. But the computers are dead. Look. All of them. What do we do now?"

"Must be the Americans," the captain said, peering out toward the horizon. "They must have some sort of new weapon. At least our engines are still working. We've got to get out of here before they come for us."

"What if they do come?" one technician cried out.

"The AK-47's are below."

The Navy's tank landing ship known as an LST was part of the Carrier Group. An amphibious vessel, it had been on maneuvers and now did a launch of its own. The 23-foot long Zodiac slipped into the choppy water with eight Navy Seals on board. In the darkness, their inflatable rubber boat could go over 50 MPH, but they kept their speed much lower as they made their way toward the trawler, donned their night vision goggles and pulled up alongside. They spotted two armed crewmen portside. Three seals pulled themselves up on the transom, others came over the starboard side. Two of them crept around to port, took aim and shot the crewmen with rubber bullets. The men cried out as the seals rushed over to muffle the sound. They quickly tied up their prey and moved stealthily to the bridge where they found the captain and first mate.

Seeing them unarmed, the seals shouted, "You're under arrest," and leapt forward to quickly handcuff the ship's officers. "Where are the others?" one seal asked, brandishing his weapon.

The captain was stunned. Who were these guys? How had they managed to get aboard his ship? Where were his crewmen with the AK-47's? He looked at the guns the seals were carrying. His eyes were wide with fear. "Don't shoot. I'm just the captain. I had nothing to do with anything else. I just run the ship. Others pay me to take them here."

"Where are the others?"

"Down below. Please don't kill us."

"We're not here to kill anybody. We want the others." One seal marched the two officers down the ladder while the other raced ahead. He joined the remaining seals who were about to head below to the bunk room.

When they burst in, Nurlan, the supervisor and five technicians held their hands up.

"We have no guns. Don't shoot," the supervisor said.

"You're all under arrest."

"Says who?" one technician called out.

"Says the United States Navy!"

"We're just passengers here," the supervisor said somewhat lamely.

"Passengers? Then who's in charge of that missile up there?"

No one answered as the seals swept through the room, slapping handcuffs on all seven men. "Who is Nurlan Remizov?" the team leader demanded.

Nurlan cowered in the corner. When the others looked his way, he knew he had to answer. "I Nurlan. Why you know me?"

"It's not important. You will come with us. The rest of you will stay here. Reinforcements are on the way."

A cheer echoed throughout the Situation Room complex as the Secretary of the Defense announced, "She did it." He described the AESA radar and the virus attack sent through the narrow beam, creating the airborne electronic attack. "And the seal team has secured the ship."

"What about Nurlan?" Samantha asked, posing the question through the microphone in front of her place at the table.

The SecDef turned to one of his staff who nodded and handed him a note. "He's been ID'd and sequestered from the others." He checked the note and added. "He'll be debriefed as soon as they're all moved to the carrier."

"If word gets back to the Kazakhs that he had some connection to us, his life could be in danger," Ken said.

Samantha leaned over and whispered to Ken, "Well then, we'll have to see to it that they never find out."

SIXTY

Los Angeles International Airport

The couple retrieved their baggage, stood in a long customs line, told the agent they had nothing to declare and finally were waved off toward the exit. As soon as they pushed through the double doors, they were greeted by two dozen young people wearing black S.A.I.N.T.S. T-shirts and waving newspapers.

"There he is."

"Over this way."

"Hey Pete. Welcome home.

"Did you know you were a hero?"

Pete Kalani broke into a wide grin as his friends rushed up to give him bear hugs and pats on the back. "What's going on? How did you guys know I'd be here? This is amazing."

One of the club members rushed up and said in a conspiratorial tone, "Your friend Nurlan gave us the scoop on your flight. Said he got it from a government contact. But we don't want the press or anybody to know Nurlan's name."

"What a minute," Pete said excitedly. "Nurlan is back? You've seen him?"

"Yeah. He got back yesterday. In fact, he said he'd be here to meet you. The press knows about you, just not him. You'll probably be inundated when you get back to campus."

Another member shoved a newspaper into Pete's hands. "You're all over the papers. Wait'll you see the stories. They know a lot about you. They just didn't have your arrival time. Glad that we did, though."

"What stories?" Pete asked, looking confused.

"Right here in the LA Times. Look. 'UCLA student warns US of possible attack.' And here's another one in the student newspaper, 'Congresswoman Betty Barton to visit campus and meet student hero'. Says here that she's introduced legislation to create a special reparations fund for victims of US nuclear tests in the Marshall Islands. Can you believe it?"

Pete grabbed the papers. A special fund? Help for the families? Already? Agreement that he was right all along to push for this kind of help? He quickly read the article as his friends gathered around exchanging smiles and high-fives. It said that the Congresswoman was especially pleased that a student attending college in her district was key to the dismantling of a plot to attack San Francisco, and she was looking forward to meeting this hero and telling him, in person, about the new fund. It went on to say that she had been working closely with The White House and had learned about the need for reparations from The White House Director of Homeland Security, Samantha Reid, and her colleague, Angela Marconi, Director of The White House Office of Public Liaison.

"Hey, guys, look at this. Angela Marconi is the one I've been emailing for months and now it's all coming together." He glanced down at the woman by his side. "And listen up. I want you to meet someone really special. This is Zhanar Remizov. She helped me survive over there in Kazakhstan and she's Nurlan's sister."

"Great."

"Hi there."

"Nurlan's a good guy

"Hey, he's supposed to be here."

Pete looked out over the crowd in the reception area of the terminal, and sure enough, making his way, hobbling a bit on shaky legs, there was Nurlan, waving and smiling.

"It's my brother!" Zhanar screamed as she pushed through the crowd and, as she had done so many times in the past, she threw her arms around him. "Oh my goodness! I didn't know when I would ever see you again." Tears started streaming down her face as he held her in a warm embrace. "How did you get here?"

They moved together back to where Pete was standing. He grabbed Pete and grinned broadly. "I get back yesterday."

"We just heard that. But how? When we learned that the attack was stopped and the Navy had arrested everybody on board that ship, we were so worried," Zhanar said.

"Navy people say they have orders no hurt me. They take me away. Put in special room. I tell all I knew about attack, about President's orders, about who in charge. Everything. Then they say they help me get back here so I finish college. They fly me back on special jet and say I now be like witness protection, but I not a witness any trial. I tell them you knew. They tell me you coming back too. Today. I see news stories and I figure out flights. So I tell S.A.I.N.T.S. Navy people say they not tell Kazakhs about me. Say I no go back home. So they give me political asylum. I stay here. I like America."

"So you're going to stay here for good?" Zhanar said.

"Sure. Is good place. Lots freedom here. Best place in world. When I graduate, I get job. Maybe with government. Maybe with military. Not Army. Not with legs. But they say always need good computer guy like me. Is great, right?"

"Not only great," Pete said. "This is terrific."

"Then, maybe later, I work with Semipalatinsk people. Get help for them like you got help. Never get from Russians though.

They never help. But maybe get help if we get new government in my country."

The S.A.I.N.T.S. were fanning out now, taking pictures and videos with their cell phones. "This'll be all over YouTube in a few minutes," one said.

"You're already on Facebook and Twitter," another remarked.

The group started to move toward the outside doors. "I have car here," Nurlan said. "They also give me small car and extra money for school. They good to me."

"I had a similar experience. Well, sort of," Pete said, tossing one canvas bag over his shoulder and carrying the rest.

"What happen? How you get back?" Nurlan asked.

"Well, this Angela person kept emailing me. She said that she was working with another White House woman, Samantha, who would be in contact with our embassy in Kazakhstan to get us some travel money, get us flights back to Los Angeles, and they said some other people were working to extend my scholarship funds. So here we are."

"See you back on campus," one S.A.I.N.T.S. member shouted as the gang dispersed.

"Great work!"

"Bye for now."

"Later, dude."

Pete waved, and the trio walked toward the garage. When they retrieved Nurlan's car, Pete stowed their luggage in the trunk, and they all climbed in, Nurlan drove out and headed toward UCLA.

"I forget," Nurlan said. "One more good thing."

"What's that?" Pete asked. "We're all back safely. The government types are helping us out. A member of Congress is actually flying out here to meet me, and you have a new car. What could be better?"

"When word get out about you big hero, your swim coach announce that he names you Captain of team."

SIXTY-ONE

The White House

Sunlight poured through the windows behind the Resolute Desk in the Oval Office as the President rose to greet his staff. "What can I say except job well done!" he said coming around to shake hands with Samantha Reid and Ken Cosgrove. "I'm scheduling a news conference for two this afternoon, and I'd like you both to be there. Oh, and have Angela in the room as well."

"Of course, Mr. President," Ken said. 'It's been a pretty rough couple of weeks but everyone worked together on this one."

The President sat down on a striped arm chair and motioned for Ken and Samantha to sit on one of the couches. "So much has happened in such a short period of time, I don't know if I can recall a time in my presidency when there was such an immediate threat to the American people along with so many international complications. Sure, we've had a lot of threats before, and thank God, with great work by both the CIA and FBI, we've been able to stop most of them.

"Now this one, this was something that you, Samantha, had warned us about. I mean, an attack of this kind. And I have to admit that we didn't pay enough attention to your initial memos and requests for threat assessments. I think we all agree that you had a sixth sense about just such a possibility, and I for one am going to do all I can to see that we're protected from any sort of EMP threat in the future."

Ken nodded and said, "She's already got the agencies working on contingency plans, funding requests and all the rest."

"Good. Good," the President said. He then handed them both a report. "Just got this. Came in moments ago. About events in Kazakhstan. When the details came out in Almaty, Astana and the other major cities about how President Surleimenov was responsible not only for that initial nuclear test that caused such panic over in Atyrau, but also had ordered the attack on San Francisco, he's now been brought up for a war crimes trial. Looks like he's out of the election race. Baltiev has been losing support, and now their Vice President is a shoe-in. That guy is on our side when it comes to nuclear issues. In fact, he just issued a statement saying that if he wins the election, he intends to shut down the weapons program and concentrate their nuclear resources on providing just electricity for the country."

"That's great news," Ken said. "We had our people on the ground over there making sure that all of their news outlets got the word about the attacks. We kept it rather vague, though, about how Pete Kalani was able to tip us off. We never used Nurlan Remizov's name. He's here in the states now. We gave him political asylum. So he'll probably be okay. I doubt if he should ever go back to Kazakhstan."

"Good thinking," the President said. "By the way, about the press conference, I wanted to have Dr. Talbot and Hunt Daniels available to answer any questions that might come up about that new AESA system she deployed. Pretty amazing development, I'd say. But we can't seem to get hold of them. The people at Bandaq Technologies say she took some vacation time. But do you know where Daniels is?"

Ken and Samantha exchanged a knowing look. "Uh, Col. Daniels asked for a few days off, and I gave it to him. We've been working 24/7 on all of this, so I figured he was due."

"Yes, of course. That's fine. Still, I wanted them here. Or at least I wanted to talk to them. Thank them. But it seems that for the first time in a long time, there are two people that our famous White House operators simply cannot find."

Sixty-two

Georgetown

The mail is usually late on Saturdays, Samantha thought as she left her condo and strolled toward the elevator. She rode it down to the lobby level and went over to check her box. It was jammed with fliers from Shoppers' World, Macy's, Best Buy and Walgreens Drug Store. She grabbed the stack and saw a bill from AT&T, a statement from her bank and a rather dirty, ragged looking envelope. When she looked at the handwritten address, she almost screamed.

She ran to the elevator, raced back to the condo, tossed the bills and fliers on the entry hall table and sat down in her living room. She stared at the letter and saw that the post mark had been made weeks ago. And it was from Kazakhstan. She tore it open.

> "HI PUMPKIN,
> I CAN'T TELL YOU WHAT A GREAT TIME
> WE'RE HAVING HERE IN THIS WONDERFUL

COUNTRY. THE PEOPLE ARE FRIENDLY, THE
FOOD IS PRETTY GOOD. YOU'D LIKE THE SHISH
KABOB. CAN'T ALWAYS FIND MY FAVORITE BEER
AND SOME OF THE STUFF THEY DRINK IS LOUSY
(THEY MAKE IT WITH HORSE MILK OR
SOMETHING), BUT THIS TRIP HAS BEEN
TERRIFIC.

AS I'M SURE TRIPP TOLD YOU IN HIS EMAILS,
THE CITY OF ALMATY IS MARVELOUS. THE
BUILDINGS ARE PRETTY MODERN. GUESS IT'S
ALL THAT OIL REVENUE THAT'S JACKED UP THIS
ECONOMY. WE HAD BREAKFAST ONE MORNING
IN A PLACE CALLED POSH BAR. KIND OF
UNUSUAL TO HAVE A BAR OPEN AT NINE IN THE
MORNING, BUT I GUESS THEY DO THAT TO TAKE
CARE OF CUSTOMERS WITH HANGOVERS. AND
EVEN THOUGH A LOT OF FOLKS HERE ARE
MUSLIM, THERE'S NO SHORTAGE OF NIGHT
CLUBS WITH TOPLESS DANCERS. (DON'T WORRY,
WE DIDN'T GO TO ANY OF THOSE).

THEN WHEN WE FLEW OUT HERE TOWARD
THE CASPIAN SEA, MY REAL WORK BEGAN. I
CAN'T TELL YOU HOW GREAT IT WAS WHEN ALL
THE CREWS ON THE RIGS OUT HERE
WELCOMED ME. THEY TREATED ME LIKE SOME
BIG DEAL EXPERT. WELL, I DO THINK I'LL BE
ABLE TO HELP WITH A FEW IDEAS. IT'S LIKE THE
OLD DAYS FOR ME, BEING OUT WITH THE WILD-
CATTERS.

BUT NOW THE MOST IMPORTANT THING
ABOUT THIS WHOLE ADVENTURE IS HOW I'VE
GOTTEN TO KNOW THIS GUY OF YOURS. TRIPP
ADAMS IS INDEED A FINE YOUNG MAN. I

WATCHED HIM IN NEGOTIATIONS WITH THE GOVERNMENT TYPES. HE WAS VERY PROFESSIONAL AND PUT TOGETHER AN EXCELLENT DEAL. AND WHEN WE WERE TRAVELING AROUND, I HEARD ALL ABOUT HOW HIS PARENTS GAVE HIM THE NAME HAMILTON BAINBRIDGE ADAMS, III. NO WONDER HE ONLY WANTS TO GO BY THE NAME TRIPP. HE TOLD ME ALL ABOUT HIS DAYS AT PRINCETON WHEN HE FIRST SPOTTED YOU, MY DEAR. HE SAID THAT AT THE TIME, HE DIDN'T HAVE SENSE ENOUGH TO FOLLOW UP, BUT WAS SO GRATEFUL THAT YOUR PATHS HAD CROSSED AGAIN IN WASHINGTON. I'M GLAD TOO.

HE ALSO TOLD ME ABOUT HIS DAYS IN THE NAVY AND THEN THE WORK HE DID AS AN INDEPENDENT CONTRACTOR AND HOW THAT LED TO HIS POSITION AS VICE PRESIDENT OF GEOGLOBAL OIL & GAS. PRETTY FAST RISE, I'D SAY. AND HE'S IN A GREAT POSITION TO TAKE CARE OF MY LITTLE GIRL. THAT'S WHAT HE WANTS TO DO, YOU KNOW. I DON'T THINK I'M SPILLING THE BEANS WHEN I SAY THAT HE REALLY CARES ABOUT YOU AND WANTS TO MAKE IT PERMANENT. WELL, YOU TWO HAVE MY BLESSING, THAT'S FOR SURE.

GOTTA GO NOW. I'VE KEPT YOU READING TOO LONG. JUST WANT TO ADD THAT I KNOW YOU DIDN'T WANT ME TO TAKE THIS ON. BUT WHEN I HEARD ABOUT IT, I WAS THE ONE WHO INSISTED THAT TRIPP TAKE ME ALONG. AT FIRST HE ARGUED AGAINST IT, SAYING IT WAS A LONG WAY OVER HERE AND ALL. BUT IT WAS MY

CHOICE, AND HE FINALLY AGREED. ANYWAY, I'M
HAVING THE TIME OF MY LIFE. CAN'T WAIT TO
GET BACK AND TELL YOU ALL ABOUT IT. MUCH
LOVE TO YOU….DAD

Samantha read the letter again. And then one more time as tears trickled down her cheeks. She tried to wipe them away with the back of her hand. It was no use. She got up, went into the bathroom and grabbed a tissue. She stared in the mirror and saw red eyes and a runny nose staring back. She splashed cold water on her face, dried it and went back to the living room. She picked up the letter again and thought about her dad. That wonderful man with the energy, the ideas, the drive to get things done. It was just like him to insist on flying halfway around the world to help out on a project. She had spent so much time grieving about her loss, she suddenly realized that she hadn't spent enough time celebrating his life. It was a good life. One where he had taught her and her little brother all sorts of neat things, from riding that first bike of hers to teaching her about geology, from encouraging her studies to bucking her up when the boy of her dreams asked someone else to the Junior Prom. He had taught her the value of hard work and individual responsibility, the meaning of love and forgiveness. She remembered that he had said that the three things you need in life are something to do, someone to love, and something to look forward to. She certainly had a lot to do now. But she had lost the two men she had loved. And now she had no clue what she had to look forward to.

As she pondered the advice, she glanced back down at the letter in her hands, and suddenly she knew what she had to do.

Samantha took a shower, washed her hair, took care with her makeup and poured through her closet for something casual but chic. She settled on a pair of black slacks and a jade green silk blouse. She liked that one since it matched the color of her eyes. She took one last look in the mirror, glad that the redness had disappeared. She checked her pantry, reached for a bottle of Pinot Noir, took her shoulder bag off the bed, shoved her dad's letter inside and headed out the door.

She drove across Key Bridge, went through two stoplights and turned right on North Nash Street. She pulled up to the building and gave her car to the valet. She walked through the two-story lobby, past the concierge, and up to the desk attendant. She flashed her White House ID and said she was a personal friend who wanted to surprise someone. She held up the bottle of Pinot Noir and smiled at the guard. He said he knew he'd seen her before. He nodded and pointed to the elevators.

She rode up to the 18th floor and tried to gather her thoughts. What exactly was she going to say? How could she put it? Would he even be home on a Saturday evening? And would he be alone? She was nervous. She remembered a girl she had seen yesterday walking on 17th Street across from the White House. She had been wearing a funny T-shirt that said, I USED TO HAVE A HANDLE ON LIFE, BUT IT BROKE. Samantha thought about that and about her own life and wondered, *can I repair it?*

He heard the bell and looked quizzically toward the door. The desk hadn't called. Could it be a neighbor? He glanced around his apartment and saw that various sections of *The Wall Street Journal* and *The Washington Post* were still strewn around, and a couple of plates and coffee cups from breakfast and lunch were still perched on his dining room table. He had been working at his computer much of the day, dressed only in an old pair of khakis and a polo shirt that probably should have been laundered last week. *What the hell.* Probably just a delivery or something. He walked over to the door and opened it.

"Hi Tripp," she said tentatively. "May I come in?"

He was astounded. There she stood. The woman he had fallen for so long ago. The woman who had dumped him, saying she could never trust him again. The woman who blamed him for killing her father. He stared at her and suddenly realized she was patiently waiting for a response. "Samantha! Uh, sure. C'mon in. Place is a bit of a . . ."

"I didn't come to see the place. I came to see you," she said. She thrust the wine bottle into his hands. "If you're not busy, I mean if you're alone. I mean . . ."

"You brought wine?" He glanced at the label. "This is your favorite."

"Peace offering?" she asked.

"Peace offering?" he echoed. "Uh, yes, I'm alone. Just working here. The usual. Um, c'mon in and sit down." He led the way into the spacious living room and gestured toward the black leather couch facing a wall of windows looking out over a view of Key Bridge, the lights of Georgetown and parts of downtown Washington. He lifted the bottle, "Shall I open this?"

"Sure. I think I could use a drink right about now," she replied, her voice unsteady.

He walked over to an open bar area on the side of the room, pulled out the cork, poured two glasses and handed her one. He sat down next to her and said, "Cheers? Or should I say something else? I have to admit I was pretty surprised to see you standing in the doorway. I thought . . ."

"I know. I thought so too," she said and then took a sip of the wine. She paused as if trying to decide what to say. He waited, wondering, hoping. Finally, she reached into her shoulder bag and pulled out a battered looking letter. She turned to face him directly. "I just got this today."

"What is it? Who's it from?" He couldn't see the post mark.

"It's from my dad."

"Your dad?" he exclaimed. "But when? You just got it today? When did he write it? What did he say?"

She carefully unfolded the letter and began to read. She read the first part describing the places they'd been. She skipped the paragraph where he said that Tripp wanted to make their relationship permanent. But then she fought back tears as she got to the last paragraph. "And here he says that he was the one who talked you into taking him to Kazakhstan. He says that at first you were against the idea, but he says it was his choice. And see here at the end he said he was having the time of his life."

She stopped and gazed up at him. "Oh Tripp. I was wrong. I was wrong to blame you. I was wrong to say all those awful things. It wasn't your fault. I can see that now. Yes, I was upset. In fact, when you called from over there and said that he had died, that the pacemaker had failed, I was absolutely destroyed. I wanted to lash out. I wanted to blame someone for taking him away from me. But now I realize that I was only thinking about myself. I wasn't thinking about you and all you had been through. I wasn't thinking about him, about how much this trip meant to him. About how much he enjoyed being with you."

"He said that?"

"Well, I didn't read you that part. But Tripp, really, all of this and then all these weeks, it's been so awful, so hard, so . . ."

He put his arm around her and pulled her into an embrace. "Honey, listen. I know how bad it was. I was a mess. I couldn't believe it had happened, and I dreaded making that call. All I could think about was that it really was my fault for taking him with me."

"No! Don't you see?" she protested. "It was his idea, and you know what? Ideas have consequences. Good ideas. Bad ideas. They matter. They really do. And when I got the letter, I realized that he took responsibility for his decision, and I have to accept that."

He kept his arms around her, pulled her head against his shoulder and inhaled her scent. Vanilla. *Must be her shampoo.* It felt so good to have her here. Right here in his arms. He tipped her chin up. She met his gaze and angled her head. He couldn't hold back, he lowered his mouth to hers. He was gentle, almost tentative. But she opened to him and he began to taste and touch and feel her body pressed against his.

When she finally came up for air, she realized that a tender touch can be as erotic as a wild seduction. And this one was tender, even tentative. "Does this mean you forgive me?" she whispered softly.

"Is there any question in your mind?" he asked, playing with her hair. "I've missed you Samantha."

"Really?"

"You have no idea," he replied moving his hand away and reaching for his wine glass. "I knew how you felt, and then I saw the whole threat scenario played out in the news, and it all hit me. You must have been through hell these last weeks. The warning by that kid from UCLA. Pete somebody. The planned attack. The Navy. The new radar system. Cameron Talbot." He waved his arm toward the papers on the table. "It's all there. Well, of course you know that. But I didn't know that until a few days ago. There have been follow-up reports every day now. It's unbelievable. You must have been a wreck." He touched her cheek. "Well, I don't mean a wreck. You never look like a wreck. I just mean . . ."

"I know what you mean. And you're right. It all happened so quickly, right after your call. But I don't want to rehash all of that right now. What I want to do is just tell you I'm sorry and I hope we could maybe, I mean, perhaps we could . . ."

"Get back together?" he finished her sentence. "I can't think of a better way to spend a Saturday night. For starters anyway."

He refilled both their wine glasses and stood up. He checked his watch. "We could grab dinner somewhere, if you don't have any other plans."

"Plans? Nope. No plans."

"It's still a little early for dinner so what say we take our wine into the other room for a while."

"Which room?" she asked, giving him a coy smile.

He pulled her up from the couch and said, "Bring your glass and follow me." He led her down the hallway, past a modern kitchen filled with Miele stainless steel ovens, a cooktop, microwave and Sub-Zero refrigerator. She knew he didn't cook much, but she remembered many a great evening when she had spent time in that kitchen, broiling steaks or poaching some salmon. After those dinners together, they usually had gone back to the bedroom and made love.

She hadn't brought any food with her tonight, only the wine. And she had no idea why she was thinking about cooking at a time like this. Maybe she was just hungry for him. She walked into the bedroom where she again saw the view of the bridge and the city from the sliding glass doors that led out onto a balcony. Tripp walked over and slid them open.

"Oh, maybe I shouldn't open these," he said. "I know how you feel about heights."

She looked out at the twinkling lights eighteen floors down. Then she looked back at him. "You know, now that I'm with you, it seems that those old fears are fading away."

"Well, I'll tell you one thing," Tripp said. "My feelings for you never faded away." He took their glasses and set them down on a bedside table. He yanked the navy comforter toward the foot of the king size bed, turned and pulled her into his arms once again, This time his kiss was hot, deep and urgent. She wound her arms around his neck and explored the inside of his mouth with her tongue. He stroked her hair, and when he broke the kiss, he pulled her down onto the white sheets. She kicked off her shoes, and he began unbuttoning her blouse. Carefully, one button at a time as he continued to gaze into her eyes.

"You are so beautiful, Sam. I want you. I've wanted you for weeks. Couldn't get you out of my mind. In fact, guess I should admit that when you said that you never wanted to see me again, I was . . . well . . . let's just say I was torn apart. Until . . . until the doorbell rang tonight. And when I saw you, all I wanted to do was grab you and . . ." he added with a slow grin, "haul you in here. But I want to take my time with you now"

"I'd like that, Samantha said. "And to be honest with you, all these weeks, I've been torn too. Not just about work, but about you." She touched his face and looked at him with eyes that shown with anticipation. She began undoing her belt and slipping out of her slacks. She lay back on the feather pillows as he shed his shoes, pants, pulled his Polo shirt over his head and tossed it on the floor. She tugged at his briefs and then it was his turn to get rid of hers. He unfastened her bra and took her in his arms.

He said he wanted her. She wanted him too. So much. He was running his fingers through her hair, nuzzling her neck, teasing her senses with each touch, each caress. When he kissed her, it felt like the first grace note in a symphony of sensation. He lingered. She shivered. Even as heat spread through her. She stroked his hair and captured his mouth once more. He murmured, "Relax, sweetheart. Let me make love to you."

The wet heat of his tongue moved over her body, touching, tasting. His fingers played along her thighs, gently nudging them open, gently stroking. She reveled in the feeling, the erotic build-up of need surging through her. He raised his head and kissed her again, this time deeply as his fingers continued to travel from her legs up to the center of her passion. He began a slow circling motion as he watched her face. Her eyes were closed. She was straining now, arching up for more. She wanted more.

"I need you," she murmured and reached down to touch him. He was ready.

"Not yet, baby. Another minute." Then he crushed her mouth with his but kept up the exquisite pressure. Her body tensed and the sensations radiated until she cried out, "Please now."

When he covered her body with his, she felt covered by a tapestry of emotions. As they moved together, the feeling, the friction increased. Once more and she felt her body careening, spinning and finally exploding like fireworks, sending waves of sparkling energy over every inch of her skin. She clung to him, reveled in the almost ethereal feeling of release and then the sense of floating slowly down from a great height. And he was right there, carefully carrying her down, down to a place where she could breathe once more.

"You are fantastic," she whispered, running her fingers down his back.

"Can you feel my heartbeat?" he moaned. "Trying to slow it down."

Her mouth curved into a smile, and she murmured, "Take it easy. That was quite a performance."

He let out a breath and rolled to one side, keeping his arms around her. "You are the most beautiful woman in the world. In my world! You know that?"

"No," she answered coyly. "But what I do know is that we have to make up for lost time."

"How much time have you got?"

She looked deep into his eyes. Eyes that reminded her of dark chocolate. And suddenly she was very hungry. "As much time as you'll give me. But maybe you could feed me first."

"Thought I just did."

Epilogue

A young man and woman stepped out of a taxi and walked up to the door of a white frame farm house. It was a well-kept place with neatly trimmed bushes in front and a large fenced in yard out back. A golden retriever ran up to the fence when the taxi drove away. He started to bark at the strangers. The couple stepped up onto the porch, and the young man rang the bell.

After a few minutes, an elderly gentlemen with shocks of gray hair framing a lined, friendly face opened the door. He was wearing a checkered work shirt and blue jeans along with a pair of sturdy boots. He gave the couple a questioning look and said, "May I help you?"

"Yes sir," the young man said. "My name is Pete Kalani and this is my wife, Zhanar. I believe I have something that belongs to you. May we come in?"

This is awfully strange, the old man thought. He's got something of mine? I've never seen these people before in my life. They don't look like Jehova's Witnesses or bill collectors. And how could these people have something of mine? At least they look harmless enough, especially the pretty girl. Wonder where she's from. Looks foreign. Don't get too many foreigners in this part of Iowa.

"Uh, you said you have something of mine? That sounds a bit strange. May I ask what it is?"

"Well, it's kind of a long story, and we've come a long way. Do you think we could come in and explain it to you?"

The old man hesitated for a moment and then looked at the woman who gave him a wide smile. "Uh, yes, I suppose so. Come right this way." He motioned for them to come into his living room and sit down on one of the brown leather couches. "I just came in from the garden. Weeds getting the best of me, it seems. I was making up a batch of lemonade. Would you like some?"

"That would be delightful," Zhanar said. "Can I help you?"

"No, that's okay. I'll just be a minute."

He hustled out to the small kitchen and put the pitcher and three glasses on a tray along with a handful of paper napkins. "Here you go," he said, laying the tray on a coffee table in front of the sofa.

When they all had their drinks, he settled into his own leather Barcalounger and said, "Now what's this about your having something of mine?"

Pete fished in his pocket and took out a gold class ring. He held it out. "I believe this once belonged to you."

The man grabbed the ring, a look of astonishment on his face. "Where in the world did you get this?" He adjusted his glasses and peered at the initials inside the gold band. "Yep. This was mine. Was it on eBay or something? No, wait a minute, if you bought it somewhere, how did you ever figure out it was mine?"

Pete leaned forward and pointed to the tiny initials. "Those initials, P.V.C. Those are your initials, Peter Van Cleve."

"Yes, of course they're mine. And you know my name?"

"Well, they're mine too. You see, my full name is Peter Van Cleve Kalani. My dad was Hawaiian, but my mom was from the Marshall Islands, and she named me for," he hesitated and stared at the old man and took a deep breath, "she named me for my grandfather."

"Your grandfather?" The old man could hardly believe his ears. This young man, could he be? Could he really be?

"Let me explain," Pete said. "My grandmother's name was Maelynn."

"My Maelynn?" the man almost shouted. "My Maelynn was your grandmother?" He jumped up and rushed over to the fireplace where he picked up a photo from the mantle. "Look at this. Look.

See this girl? See how gorgeous she was?" He handed over a framed black and white picture of a native girl with long black hair, sitting on a beach with palm trees in the background. That's Maelynn. My Maelynn."

Pete stood up, grabbed it and studied the photo. He handed it to Zhanar. "She's really lovely," Zhanar said. "I can certainly see why you fell in love with her."

The old man took a step toward Pete and held out his arms. "You're really. . . you're really my grandson?" he asked, tears welling up in his eyes.

Pete nodded and stepped forward, extending his hand.

The man took it, and then pulled Pete into a bear hug. When he released him, he said in a halting voice, "We have to sit down again. I have to take all this in. This is so amazing. You see, I had given Maelynn that ring when I found out she was going to have a baby. I couldn't take her with me because I was in the Navy. We had been sent out there to her island of Rongelap to set up equipment to monitor the effects of some tests, and when they were over, we had to leave. Then when I got out of the Navy, I went back. I went back to Rongelap, but I couldn't find her. I heard that many of the families had gone to other islands. I can't tell you how many islands I went to. I looked everywhere. I asked everyone, but nobody seemed to know where she was."

"She went to Hawaii," Pete said. "That's where she had my mom."

"Then what happened to her?"

"A while after that, she died. We all believe it was from the effects of one of those tests."

"Oh my God!" the old man said. He buried his face in his hands. "My Maelynn. My precious Maelynn."

"And then, you see, I heard the stories about how she had been in love with a sailor with the name Peter Van Cleve and how he had lived in a town with the funny name, Maquoketa, in Iowa.

My mom knew all about it, and that's why she gave me this name. I came to the states to study at UCLA, and then we went back to Hawaii to get married. That's when she gave me the ring. As a wedding present. So I did an internet search, hoping that you had come back to your home town." He exchanged a glance with Zhanar, and they both broke into big smiles. "And we found you," he said triumphantly.

The man looked up at Pete and Zhanar once again and sighed. "After all these years. After all these years I have a grandson. And a good looking boy to boot." He beamed at Pete, glanced at the photograph once more that Pete had set up on the table next to the lemonade pitcher. "We have so much catching up to do. So much to learn. So many stories to tell." He got up again, went over to a bookshelf and pulled down a scrapbook. He came back and sat next to Pete and Zhanar and started leafing through the book. He pointed to old, grainy photos of ships, officers and sailors.

"You see, when I was sent to Rongelap, we were all working to set up the largest hydrogen bomb test that the United States ever conducted. It was on Bikini Atoll but we had those testing stations and weather monitors on lots of other islands. It was all hush-hush at the time, of course. I took these photos later when we got back to port. But now everything we did has been declassified, and I can tell you all about it. The code name for that hydrogen bomb test was *Castle Bravo*.

True indeed.

Acknowledgments

The inspiration for this story came from an enlightening and frightening conversation I had with General "Trey" Obering, former Director of our country's Missile Defense Agency. He told me that one reason it is so imperative for us to have an excellent and widely deployed missile defense system was to protect us against an EMP attack. I knew that we had a commission preparing reports and warnings on the issue, and I want to praise Dr. William Graham and his colleagues for their great work, their warnings and their testimony before committees of the Congress. But alas, their reports were filed away, the budget ran out for their commission staffs and here we are, putting off preparing ourselves for one of the greatest threats to our national security yet. At least that's the way I see it, which is why I wrote this story.

In creating the characters, the settings and the dialogue, I do want to thank Ambassador Beth Jones who served as the US Ambassador to Kazakhstan and shared Christopher Robbins' wonderful book, *In Search of Kazakhstan*. Other valuable resources included the story of Kazakhstan's Nuclear Disarmament featuring Senators Sam Nunn and Richard Lugar, research from The Heritage Foundation, and especially diaries I found of Marshall Island survivors telling heart-breaking tales of their endurance during the nuclear testing of the 50s and 60s.

A number of friends also contributed ideas, so thanks to Jim Langdon, Richard Fairbanks, John Kubricky, Gene Lawson, Kirt Anderson, and Andy Weber among others. Thanks to you all for your thoughts and support as I endeavored to tell the story of *Castle Bravo*.

The **Honorable Karna Small Bodman** served in The White House, first as Deputy Press Secretary and later as Senior Director of the National Security Council.

She began her career in San Francisco as a TV news reporter and anchor first for KRON-TV and then KGO-TV. She later moved to Washington, DC to anchor the Ten O'clock news on Channel 5, host a nationally syndicated program on business and economic issues as well as a three-hour news/talk radio show.

When Ronald Reagan was elected President, he stood in front of Blair House and named Jim Brady as his Press Secretary with Karna as Jim's Deputy. She had almost daily meetings with the President and traveled on Air Force One. She was also sent to South America and the Far East to give speeches to government, business and student groups on the President's economic priorities.

Bodman was named Senior Director and spokesman for the National Security Council. She attended arms control talks with the Soviets and traveled with the team that briefed the leaders of Great Britain, France and Italy as well as Pope John Paul II. Those were 'evil empire' days, so it was a unique experience to chat with the Soviet Union's General Secretary Gorbachev at that first Summit meeting in Geneva. When she left The White House to become Senior Vice President of a Public Affairs firm, she was the highest ranking woman on The White House staff.

By then, she had written TV news scripts, briefing papers for the President, newspaper columns and magazine articles, but she had always wanted to write novels. She hopes you will enjoy her new thriller, *Castle Bravo* as well as *Checkmate, Gambit, Final Finesse,* and her short story, *The Agent*. She is currently working on #5, *Affairs of State.*

Visit www.KarnaBodman.com for more information.